DOWN
AMONG
THE
DEAD

C.S. Green is a bestselling author of psychological thrillers and an award-winning writer of fiction for young people under the name Caroline Green. Written under the name Cass Green, her first novel for adults, *The Woman Next Door*, was a No.1 ebook bestseller, while the follow-up, *In a Cottage in a Wood*, was a *USA Today* bestseller and a *Sunday Times* top ten bestseller. She is the writer in residence at East Barnet School and teaches courses for City University and Writers and Artists. She lives in London with her family. *Down Among the Dead* is the third volume in a new series featuring the UCIT.

𝕏 @carolinesgreen

Also by C.S. Green

Sleep Tight
The Whisper House

WRITING AS CASS GREEN

The Woman Next Door
In a Cottage in a Wood
Don't You Cry
The Killer Inside

C S GREEN

DOWN
AMONG
THE
DEAD

HarperCollins*Publishers*

HarperCollins*Publishers*
1 London Bridge Street,
London SE1 9GF

www.harpercollins.co.uk

HarperCollins*Publishers*
Macken House, 39/40 Mayor Street Upper,
Dublin 1, D01 C9W8, Ireland

Published by HarperCollins*Publishers* Ltd 2024
1

A catalogue copy of this book is available from the British Library.

ISBN: 9780008390907 (PBO)

This novel is entirely a work of fiction. The names, characters
and incidents portrayed in it are the work of the author's
imagination. Any resemblance to actual persons, living
or dead, events or localities is entirely coincidental.

Typeset in Sabon LT Std by
Palimpsest Book Production Ltd, Falkirk, Stirlingshire

Printed and Bound in the UK using 100% Renewable Electricity
at CPI Group (UK) Ltd

MIX
Paper | Supporting
responsible forestry
FSC™ C007454

This book contains FSC™ certified paper and other controlled sources
to ensure responsible forest management.

For more information visit: www.harpercollins.co.uk/green

To the students and staff of East Barnet School. I have loved being your Writer in Residence for all these years.

Alice Goode's a-weeping
Soil upon her head
Come and find her sleeping
Down among the dead

Prologue

'Let me out! Let me out!'

Her throat is raw from screaming and panic rolls through her body, but no one comes. The last thing she remembers is running through the woods, then tripping and crashing down, slicing her knee open and grazing her hands. Confusing voices, coaxing her, and now she is in this dark, rank space with the sweet-rotten stench of death all around.

The girl tries to calculate how many breaths she has left until all the air has gone. A hundred? Fifty? Even fewer? She tries to breathe more slowly but thinking about the air running out makes her pant in terror even harder.

She wants to move but she's too scared to feel what is around her, those stinking bodies, already being gnawed by maggots. She'll be next. She can almost feel them crawling over her skin and nibbling at her flesh. Her stomach heaves but she doesn't want to let the foulness out so she swallows it down, acid burning her throat.

'Help me! Please.' Weaker now.

It's no use. Even though she can hear them talking and laughing out there, no one cares.

No one is coming.

1

They slow to a stop for yet another temporary traffic light. It feels like the whole of north London is one knot of cars this morning. DC Rose Gifford and her colleague DC Adam Lacey have been crawling along congested roads for twenty minutes and barely made progress.

Privately, though, Rose doesn't mind the delay. She needs time to mentally prepare herself for where they are headed.

'Bloody hell, this is taking forever,' says Adam, drumming his fingers on his thigh. He looks at Rose. 'Any idea what Silverton Street want?'

'Not a clue,' says Rose. 'All I was told was they need our input on a case.'

'Hmm,' says Adam thoughtfully. 'Maybe it's about what I heard on the radio this morning. It's been a "record breaking" weekend of gang violence in north London.'

Rose grimaces. 'Could be we're just extra hands on deck, then.'

The light finally changes to green.

'More importantly,' says Adam, as they pull away, 'how d'you feel about going back to your old gaff?'

Rose contemplates how to answer this. It's a very good question. How does she feel? She has been trying to work this out since the call came in.

For the first few months in her new role at UCIT, the Uncharted Crimes Investigation Team, Rose longed to go back to her previous job. Working on the murder squad at Silverton Street had its challenges, not least the tricky relationship she had with her old boss, DCI Stella Rowland. But at least there, she was only dealing with the real, tangible world of flesh and blood crime. She didn't have to think outside the realms of what seemed possible. Rose had enough of 'all that' growing up and wasn't wholly ready to accept that there was a part of the Met that investigated supernatural crimes taking place in the capital city.

No, it's fair to say it has taken time for her to settle in at UCIT.

'I'm not sure,' she says finally. 'Bit weird. It'll be good to see everyone. Well, almost everyone.'

'Intriguing,' says Adam with a laugh. 'Anything – or anyone – you need to warn me about?'

'Nah,' says Rose, turning to give him a quick grin. 'I'll let you make your own judgements.'

The call came in right after they had arrived at the UCIT building on Reservoir Road that morning, asking if they could be at Silverton Street station for 10 a.m..

It had been clear there was no time for small talk from Mack's brisk tone. For a moment she'd experienced a prickle of worry that it was because she hadn't been in touch since that weird time months ago, but then she realised he was merely busy. She had been meaning to call for ages but it was all a bit . . . awkward.

Turning up at someone's house practically incoherent with tears and caked in mud would do that.

Her cheeks prickle with shame when she thinks about that night.

The case she had been working on involving a missing boy, which ended up unearthing a fifty-year-old murder, had taken her on a very dark track about her own complex childhood.

She had taken some facts about the birth mother she didn't remember and spun them into a tale that had her digging the back garden at 2 a.m. and looking for her body.

She cringes every time she thinks of this.

Mack was not only her old colleague but like a father figure and had told her only the day before that she mustn't hesitate to ask for help. So, without fully explaining what had happened, she ended up in his spare room where she slept for fourteen hours straight. He hadn't asked questions, knowing her long enough to know that she would tell him about it in her own good time, if at all. She'd given him a garbled version of events about losing a ring in the garden and he hadn't really pressed.

After two days she moved into a depressing house share in Highgate that was only meant to be temporary. But it hadn't quite panned out that way.

Rose sighs, thinking about her miserable living situation.

But there's no time for worrying about that now. They pull into the car park at the back of the old red brick building just off the High Road in Harringay.

She's back. But does she belong here anymore?

2

Memories come flooding back as she locks the car and looks up at her old station.

There was the woman she once questioned over the suspicious death of her eighteen-month-old daughter, who finally, and calmly, admitted drowning her in the bath because, 'she wouldn't stop going on'. Or the teenager who stabbed a rival gang member six times but looked like the little kid he still was as he sat hunched in the interview room, swinging his feet with oversized trainers back and forth. But most of all, there was the serial killer, James Oakley, who snatched Rose from her own bed, turning an already poor sleeper into someone who was grateful if she got four hours a night.

But there are good memories here too, like the nights in the pub when they had closed a case, basking in the sense that she had finally found a family. And laughing until her stomach hurt with Sam, in the kitchen over late-night snacks.

At the thought of seeing *him* again, Rose's insides do an unhelpful flip.

It's been ages, she tells herself, getting out of the car and locking it. All that is water under the bridge, isn't it?

When they walk into the station, Rose's face splits into a grin at the sight of Omar, the giant of a desk sergeant with a penchant for musicals.

'Why, what do my eyes behold?' he says in his booming baritone, somewhat startling the ratty-faced man in his twenties he appears to be in the middle of processing. 'Not you, sunshine,' he says. 'You're not quite as pleasant to look at. And that's you done, so get yourself out of here now and I'll no doubt be seeing you again very soon.'

The man doesn't need telling twice and slips past Rose and Adam almost at a run.

'Hiya, Omar,' she says as he comes around from the other side of the desk and envelops her in a bone-crusher of a hug, while smiling a greeting at Adam, who grins back and introduces himself.

When he finally lets her go, Omar extends a meaty paw. 'Any friend of DC Gifford's is a friend of mine,' he says.

Then he turns to Rose again and regards her carefully as though checking something out, finishing with a little grunt that signifies who-knows-what.

Rose laughs, suddenly self-conscious. 'What does that mean?' she says.

'Nothing,' says Omar. 'Just looking to see if there was some obvious reason why you have neglected us for so long. Like, I don't know, a missing limb or something.'

Rose's cheeks warm. Fierce blushing is a curse she has had all her life. She has no control over it and it often happens at the most inopportune times.

'I don't know,' she says awkwardly, 'time flies, I guess?'

Omar makes a harumphing sound. 'I would have thought time positively crawled working on that dull paperwork all day. I don't know how you stand it.'

There's a beat before realisation hits. To most, her department is a dry place that focuses on compliance and training. The real purpose of UCIT is restricted as much as possible. She manages to recover quickly.

'It has its moments,' she says with a smile.

'I'll have to take your word for that,' says Omar. 'Now let's get you both checked in.'

A few minutes later, Rose and Adam walk together down the corridor to the main office.

'Feel strange being back?' says Adam quietly.

'Bit,' says Rose.

They push through the double doors and Rose is hit with the familiar waft of mushroom Cup-a-Soup and body odour coming from the nearest desk, which is occupied by DC Kev Wallis. He frowns and his gaze swivels between Rose and Adam.

'Alright, Rose,' he says. 'Thought we'd got rid of you.'

'Charming as ever, Kev,' says Rose and he guffaws, revealing yellow tombstone teeth.

'Only joshing with you,' he says, then, loudly, 'look who's here, everyone! Like a bad penny!'

Lots of heads shoot up and Rose is instantly warmed by the smiles wreathing faces, from DS George Bello, to DC Julie Fenton, to DC Tom Skinner; all of whom she spent many hours working with.

'Rose!' DC Ewa Duggan gets up to hug her. 'It's so good to see you! What are you doing here? Are you coming back to us?' It's flattering how hopefully she says this and Rose hugs her back hard.

'I'm afraid not!' she says. 'Mack wanted to see us, so here we are.'

'Ah, okay, that's a shame,' says Ewa. 'It's not been the same without you.'

'Thanks Ewa! This is my colleague Adam Lacey.'

Adam shakes a few hands and introductions are made. He must be clocking the exchange of glances too. Everyone is evidently in the dark about why they are here.

'Where is Mack anyway?' says Rose, looking around.

'He popped out for a bit with Stella but hey, look, there they are now.'

Rose turns to see Mack, whose face lights up and DCI Stella Rowland, whose face does not.

Rose had a difficult relationship with her old boss. Sure,

some of this is because Rose cocked up a few times, such as when she went too far in an interview with a suspect and massaged the facts of some important forensic evidence. But others made errors and didn't get quite the same treatment. Rose knew she had never really had a chance after something that had happened on a night off duty. She'd been out with a friend in a pub in central London when she saw her boss in a tearful conversation with a very senior – and married – police officer. It was immediately evident they were having an affair and after that night, Stella Rowland's cool exterior became positively arctic towards her junior colleague.

'Hey,' says Mack with a big grin. 'Good to see you!' He gives her a quick hug.

'Ma'am,' she says then to Rowland, who is staring at her, unsmiling.

'Good to see you, Rose,' says the other woman, her expression telling an entirely different story. She turns her eyes to Adam and extends a hand, which he takes.

'DCI Stella Rowland,' she says.

'DC Adam Lacey.'

'Okay then,' says Rowland. She looks tired; the skin around her eyes drawn. 'Let's go to the briefing room and we'll fill you in on why we asked you in.'

It's strange going back into this room that was once so familiar; its whiteboards plastered with the faces of victims, villains and those in between. So many stories; so many destroyed lives.

Rose feels the contrast between this space that was never quite big enough for everyone, with its unreliable old radiators and vague smell of human breath, to the open plan area in the UCIT building, where it's all comfortable sofas and state-of-the-art equipment. Even if, once you step out of the main office, you're back in another era. It's one of the many curiosities of the UCIT building; the new plastered on top of the very old, like thick make-up on a heavily lined face.

Mack stands at the front and Rowland leans against the

desk at the back of the room, arms folded across her chest. Adam sits next to Rose.

Today he's wearing a soft, black, V-necked jumper and jeans and smells incredibly good. Something citrusy but warm and spicy. Like Christmas. Rose knows she shouldn't be noticing these things about her colleague but can't seem to help herself.

'So we need your help,' says Rowland, bringing her back to earth. 'We currently have fourteen open cases in this team and we had a very bad weekend with gang violence. Frankly, we're overwhelmed.' She turns to fiddle with the technology and then a picture fills the screen.

It shows a close up of a woman's upper body. She's in outdoor clothes and lying on bark chippings, her head at an angle, mud all over her evidently lifeless face.

'Mack, you can summarise,' says Rowland. Mack gets up.

'This is the body of Suzette Armstrong,' he says. 'She was a thirty-seven-year-old PR executive who was found dead at the bottom of a twenty-metre-high platform that is part of a climbing centre known as Crazy Climbz in Elford Country Park. She died last Saturday during the hours of 7 and 11 p.m..'

He pauses. 'We know this because the manager of Crazy Climbz, one . . . ' he looks down at his notes, 'Joshua Simmons, had eyes on the location between those times. There was a bad storm, you might remember. He wasn't able to close the site in the usual way. When he finally was able to go round, he discovered Armstrong's body. The post-mortem shows that death occurred from an upper spinal break that transected her aorta and cut off blood to her heart, causing almost instant death. She broke her neck, basically. Marks on her knees and arms are consistent with climbing the rope ladder too.'

'We're not thinking suicide?' says Adam.

Rowland gives a tight, grim smile. 'Be a lot easier if we were, but there are a lot of questions around this. For a start, why would you do it there? In the middle of a filthy storm? It feels more likely she was somehow forced up that ladder and then pushed off. There are too many questions.'

'Can I ask one?' says Adam.

'Of course,' says Rowland.

'I'm wondering what this has to do with UCIT.'

She looks at Mack. 'Show them.'

Mack changes the image on the screen.

'What the hell is that?' says Adam peering more closely. Rose does the same.

It looks at first glance like a bundle of sticks but on closer inspection it's apparent that it is some kind of doll. There's a head made from cloth with string tied around it, and crosses are stitched on for eyes. The lack of a mouth somehow makes it even more creepy.

'We have no idea,' says Mack. 'It was found right next to her body, so neatly it was as though it had been placed there post-mortem. Now it *may* have been something a customer dropped earlier in the day, but they have all been questioned and no one appears to have any knowledge of it. And staff frequently check the landing areas for the zip wires to make sure there's nothing that shouldn't be there. Everyone who has seen the picture has had the same reaction.'

'Which was?' says Rose.

'Exactly what Adam said. "What the hell is that?"'

'Look,' says Rowland, leaning forwards a little bit and looking hard at both Rose and Adam. 'We think this is a murder case. It seems incredibly unlikely that someone made a special trip to those woods in the middle of a storm, specifically to chuck themselves off. I mean, there are multi-storey car parks and bridges aplenty in North London. It would be a darn sight more convenient than going here. So, no. Not buying that. But the truth is we are well past the golden hour now and we have absolutely nothing to show for it.'

'Any suspects?' says Rose.

'We're interested in the husband, Rufus Armstrong,' says Rowland. 'Because we're told the relationship was rocky but there is no sign of his car moving that evening and we don't have enough to formally question him. We're relying on his goodwill for now.'

Mack points at the screen. 'But this doll is partly why we called you in. It looks to us like it has some sort of folklore or esoteric meaning? Although we can find nothing similar on HOLMES, we thought it might stir something in terms of other cases you've worked on?'

Rose looks at Adam, who has worked for UCIT a lot longer than she has, but he is shaking his head.

'Nothing is coming to mind,' he says. 'But Moony may have some thoughts, and anyway, we have our own database for this sort of stuff. We'll run it through that.'

'Thank you,' says Rowland then looks at her watch. 'Damn,' she says, under her breath.

Rose has never heard her properly swear, which is only one of the ways in which her former boss makes her feel like a naughty Year Nine pupil.

'I'm sorry but I am going to leave you now. I want you to go over this case from scratch. You will report directly to me as the SIO but you can work from your own building. Everything clear?'

'Yes,' says Adam and Rose mumbles her own response.

'In that case, I'll look forward to hearing from you soon. Now, if you'll excuse me . . . ' She swishes out of the room in her immaculate skirt and silk blouse, already keying a number into her mobile as she goes.

'I'm getting the entire document pack sent over to you,' says Mack. He hesitates for a moment but clearly has something else to say. 'At first, I met a little opposition from the boss when I suggested getting you guys in . . . ' He runs a hand over his head; a tic Rose knows very well. He's trying to find the right words for something awkward. 'It wasn't only because we needed extra hands and, well, because of the weird doll.'

'No?' Rose prompts gently.

'No,' says Mack. 'The truth is something about this feels

11

. . . off to me? I don't know, I guess the whole experience of working on the Oakley case shifted how I see things. I've thought about a few cases we've worked on and wondered whether there's . . . more. Stuff I've missed. Stuff that was too strange for me to be able to accept that it could be the explanation.'

'Welcome to our world,' says Rose with a smile. Adam nods and murmurs, 'We'll do what we can.'

Mack gives a rueful laugh. 'You know what they say: when police hear hoofbeats, we expect horses, not zebras. Well maybe I'm starting to think that sometimes it actually is a bloody zebra.'

3

The wind whispers through the trees and unseen things scurry in the undergrowth. The only light is from his phone and he looks nervously at how much battery life he has left. Fifteen per cent. Not enough to be hanging out in the middle of these sodding woods. He doesn't much fancy being in the pitch dark here.

Where the hell is Mikey? He looks around and pulls the collar of his jacket a little higher.

He's always hated this creepy place. Mum was always wanting to come for picnics when he was small but Mikey would wind him up with stories about headless horsemen and one time he wet himself because he was so scared. His cousin thought it was hilarious even though he got a stinging telling off from Aunt Jenny.

Ever the comedian, Mikey.

Such a surprise to hear from him after all these years. Less so that he is dealing now but that could be good news. As he said, blood is thicker than water and it was kind of nice to be thought of . . . maybe given a bit of preferential treatment when it comes to price.

'BOO.'

The breathy voice is right next to his ear, making him yelp and whirl around, 100 volts of pure shock zipping up his spine and flooding his body with adrenaline.

13

There's no one there.

'Who's that? Mikey? What are you playing at? This isn't fucking funny, mate. What's going on?'

His heart feels like it's going to rip its way out of his chest like the alien in that film. It throbs so hard it almost hurts and he hates himself for the small whimper that escapes his lips.

Who said that? Who the hell spoke, when there is no one here? When he finds out who is behind this he is going to—

But what's that? There's a movement in the trees – a flash of something white in the moonlight – and then it's gone again.

'Hello?' he calls, feebly. He clears his throat. 'Is someone there?'

There's that thing again, and now it's sort of flitting around between the trees. He tries to point his phone at it to see but the light just bleeds away into nothing. How are they doing that? Some sort of special effect? He looks around, half expecting to see equipment that's making this happen but there is nothing like that.

'Mikey, what the fuck man?' he says and he's furious now, furious that he has been lured here and that someone is taking the piss out of him but now the thing in the trees is closer, spinning around him, so fast it makes his legs buckle at the knees. There's a roaring in his ears and it seems to be everywhere at once. He cries out in terror and with everything going on it takes a moment to understand the bright pain in his chest until he looks down and sees the handle of the knife sticking straight out.

4

She nips to the ladies' toilets on her way out, agreeing to meet Adam at the car, and is coming out of the door, shaking her hands dry to avoid the manky roller towel in there, when she sees Sam approaching from the other end of the corridor.

She so nearly made it out, too.

When Sam sees her, the look of delight on his face warms Rose though, despite her misgivings.

Sam Malik had been Rose's best friend since they trained together at Hendon Police College. He was the person she spoke to most about her life. Well, some aspects of her life, anyway. No one knew about the strange haunting she experienced at home, when Adele Gifford, the woman who had raised her and was now dead, would randomly appear in the house, sometimes dressed in a ratty old fur coat as if she was going somewhere, sometimes moving around doing domestic chores, just as if she were still alive.

As to Rose and Sam, everything had been good until the burgeoning attraction between the two spilled over into them getting drunk one night after a case finished and ending up in Rose's bed. It had been wonderful, and terrible, all in the space of a few hours. Wonderful because, well, it was Sam and it couldn't have felt more right, but terrible because of how Rose reacted when she woke to find the ghost of Adele sitting on the bed. This was something new, something more intrusive and horrible. She practically ejected Sam from the house after that and he had never really been given an explanation. Not long after, he got back together with his ex-girlfriend, Lucy. Last Rose had heard, they were getting engaged.

'Hey stranger!' he says. He appears to hesitate and Rose spares him the awkwardness by going in for a hug anyway. His familiar soapy smell makes her close her eyes for a brief second before she releases him and plasters a big smile onto her face.

'How's it going?' she says. 'How's Lucy?' In her haste to mention his fiancé, she has already made it weird; she can tell by his expression.

'She's good,' he says, and pauses. 'Actually feeling a bit rough, to be honest.' His eyes search Rose's face. 'First trimester of pregnancy so she's suffering a bit with sickness.'

Rose works hard to keep the smile fixed there.

'That's wonderful!' she says, then, hurriedly, 'not about being ill, obviously! But you know, about the baby.'

'Thanks,' he says but looks uncomfortable. He clearly can't wait to get away, so what he says next comes as a surprise.

'Look,' he says, 'I've really missed you, Rose. Will it be weird for us to just hang out again? I'd love you to meet Lucy properly.'

Rose has met Lucy briefly and has no intention of making it 'proper'. She found her to be snooty and has no idea how she could possibly get on with Sam's hilarious, earthy sister Zainab. But it's so flattering that he missed her, she has to be willing to try. It's one of the things she promised herself that night, after she washed the mud from her arms and under her nails after digging in the back garden for a body that wasn't there; to do normal things. See people. Stop hiding from ghosts.

'I'd really like that, Sam,' she says softly. Then, feeling her cheeks tingle with heat, 'I've missed you too.'

He beams at her. 'Brilliant!' he says. 'Ah, that's so great.

Look, we're actually having a bit of a do on Friday. House-warming at the new flat. Can you come? You can bring someone?' Was this last line said too eagerly? Maybe she's being paranoid.

An excuse is forming in Rose's mind when she reminds herself: *Be more normal.* It's her new mantra.

'Okay,' she says. 'I'll be there.'

'Fantastic!' he says. 'I'll see you then!'

Rose tries to put the thought of this out of her mind as they start the drive across North London towards Reservoir Road, the old Water Board building that is UCIT's home.

'So?' says Adam almost the minute they have left the car park. 'What's the dealio with Rowland?'

'What do you mean?' says Rose.

Adam is rummaging in her glove compartment for the mints he knows Rose keeps there. He offers her one, which she takes, then pops one into his own mouth. 'She doesn't seem like your biggest fan, is all I'm saying.'

Rose laughs. 'Is it that obvious?'

Adam does a pretend motion of shivering. 'The atmosphere between you two was about ten degrees colder than an Icelandic winter.'

'Yeah,' says Rose with a sigh. 'I'm actually glad you could see it. I wondered if I was being paranoid.'

'Not being paranoid,' says Adam. 'She clearly hates your guts.'

'Wow, cheers mate! Way to make me feel better!'

He grins, then loudly crunches the mint. 'Sorry,' he says. 'Just felt it was a bit strange, I mean, you have your quirks, but you're not actively offensive. You don't smell *too* bad.'

Rose barks a loud laugh. 'Best compliment I've had in, ooh, ages.' She loves their banter. They are capable of sniggering like a pair of ten year olds sometimes.

'Seriously though,' he says. 'What happened?'

She ponders this for a moment. Rose doesn't owe Rowland

anything. She has been the very picture of discretion since she saw her in that pub. And has she had any thanks for it? No, quite the opposite.

'Okay,' she says. 'So, part of it was that I messed up a couple of times.'

'Who doesn't mess up?' murmurs Adam and she feels a squeeze of affection for him.

'That's what I thought,' says Rose, 'but there's something else. Something you have to keep to yourself.'

She tells him the story of what happened that night in the pub and he lets out a low whistle at the end.

'That's quite something,' he says. 'I know DAC Thomlinson, of course. Always found him to have a stick up his arse. Got a distinctly superior air about him. They're quite well suited. But it's really not fair to take it out on you.'

Rose mumbles her gratitude. The sense of solidarity from her colleague feels good.

The UCIT office on the outskirts of London has its quirks, it's fair to say. There's the unsettling sensation that all the angles of the refit are not quite as they should be. Then there's the ghostly 1940s tea lady who can sometimes be seen pushing her squeaking trolley down the corridors. At least Rose and Scarlett, their civilian admin assistant, can see her. The other two members of the team are oblivious.

Rose rather envies them this.

People talk about 'gifts' but her occasional ability to sense the dead feels quite the opposite. It's not that useful, for a start. She can't wander into a crime scene and see murder victims lurking in the background like the most useful eyewitness you could ask for. It's not even consistent. Perhaps it's because she spent a good deal of her life in denial, so this dubious skill never properly developed. She hasn't 'worked at it' as they say. The fact is, if Rose never sensed another ghoulish presence as long as she lived, it would be a very welcome thing indeed.

While Scarlett is 'very much into the woo' as Adam put it

recently, Rose has no desire to signpost an ability to see things that shouldn't be there, not least dead Adele.

Moony says 'we're not here to do exorcisms, we're here to solve crimes' and that is fine by Rose.

They're sitting in UCIT's briefing area, bringing Rose's boss, DS Sheila Moony up to date. Even the drinks are better here, than at Silverton Street. Moony, an inveterate coffee snob, insists on the good stuff, made with an expensive coffee machine.

They all hold steaming mugs now as they look at the image of Suzette Armstrong's broken body, blown up on the white-board. Scarlett is there too, dressed in a cream, short-sleeved blouse with a dark green pencil skirt that wouldn't look out of place on one of the women working at Bletchley Park in the 1940s.

'Right then,' says Moony, running a beringed finger along her jaw in contemplation. Her small chubby hands are never without her knuckle dusters of silver rings. 'This doesn't feel like a UCIT case to me but if the Queen Bee asks, then I suppose we have no choice.'

Rose and Adam exchange amused glances. When she first met Sheila Moony, at Silverton Street, it was evident there was no love lost with Stella Rowland. Chalk and cheese doesn't even begin to cover it with those two. On the one hand you have Rowland, all immaculate blonde hair, pale silk blouses that never get creased and self-control, on the other, Sheila Moony, who rides motorbikes, smokes, drinks and swears like breathing. Beneath the very different exteriors, though, both women have a backbone of pure steel. This, Rose has thought before, might be why they don't get on. They have more in common than they care to admit.

'Better get on with it,' says Moony getting to her feet. 'If she says you're to check in directly then that is what you must do, but keep me in the picture. I want you both to get totally up to speed on this while I focus on watching the crazies. I'm here for batting it all around when needed.'

UCIT's most recent task has been helping other departments with online surveillance on a group of occultists who are a splinter group of some of the conspiracy theory crazies who have been in the news for several years. In the last six months they have carried out a series of attacks on churches, mosques and synagogues. The Met are taking a similar approach to Operation Trident, where gang violence is monitored via watching social media and chatrooms. It's important, but repetitive work and Rose can't help feeling a lift at having something new to get her teeth into. Moony, as the senior officer at UCIT, can't be spared.

Her feelings on this are revealed quite clearly on her face as she heads outside for a cigarette.

Rose goes back to her desk and opens the document pack on her screen. Clicking on the photos, she brings up the first image of Suzette Armstrong's broken body and lifeless face. Rose stares at it, as if she can find an explanation for why a woman would go to the woods in the middle of a severe storm, climb a rope ladder twenty metres up, then throw herself off to her death just by looking.

Someone is behind this. And she is going to find out who.

5

It takes more than two hours to read through the entire document pack. The team congregate at the briefing area to discuss their findings.

'Let's do a quick overview of what we have,' says Rose, sitting down on one of the sofas next to Moony. Adam takes the one opposite her by Scarlett, which is a good thing because Rose can find Adam's physical proximity distracting.

Rose wishes dearly she didn't have such a crush on her work colleague. Aside from wanting to rip his clothes off, she really does like him as a friend. Nothing could ever happen anyway, she tells herself all the time. It's pointless to even think about it. Aside from the professional implications, Adam – a few years older than Rose – has a difficult ex-wife and two daughters he adores. His personal life is complicated. He simply isn't an option. And anyway, wasn't it only this morning that she had to cope with the strangeness of seeing Sam, her last disastrous workplace liaison?

She forces her mind back to the new case.

'So here's where we're at, as far as I can see,' she says. 'According to Rufus Armstrong – the victim's husband – Suzette went out in a hurry on that Saturday evening, apparently to buy cigarettes. She didn't come back and he was contacted at 1 a.m. by the police. Her body was found at 11 p.m. by the manager of the Crazy Climbz centre, Joshua Simmons. There's no CCTV in any of the country park at all, unfortunately, but her car was seen on ANPR driving the most obvious route from her home in Alexandra Palace and a CCTV camera on Mercer Road caught an image that seems to show she was alone in the car.'

'Anything on her phone?' says Moony.

'Nothing that seems relevant,' says Adam. 'But we haven't yet received the entire extraction report that would include deleted messages. There's a backlog on that at the moment so will take a few days.'

'If she was meeting someone there illicitly, it's possible there was a burner phone in play,' says Moony thoughtfully. 'Anything found?'

'Not that I can see here,' says Adam.

'What about the husband's alibi?' says Moony.

'He claims they were in watching telly,' says Rose, looking down at her notes. 'And then Suzette said she was going out to get cigarettes. He says he stayed in all evening. He was logged into Netflix during that period, but that doesn't really mean anything.'

'Any CCTV showing him leaving the house or movement from his car?'

'Not directly,' says Adam, shaking his head. 'But I think the team have only had time so far to look at the nearest roads. He lives in a pretty busy part of the suburbs so widening that net would take time and maybe more bodies than we have.'

Moony sighs. 'Me and Scarlett can help with that. I need to be around today because I have a couple of meetings later on another case. I want you two to go and see this Rufus Armstrong straight away, then get over to the park and interview the guy who found the body.' She pauses. 'But first we need to talk about that bloody creepy doll. Scarlett? What have you got? Anything?'

'Not sure,' says Scarlett. 'But I think it's a poppet.'

'A poppet?' says Moony. 'What the bloody hell is that?'

'It's a sort of homemade doll that tends to be associated with spells and magic.'

'A voodoo doll then?' says Moony, then frowns, adding thoughtfully, 'can't believe we've never had one of *them* before, now I think about it.'

'I'm not sure they were only used for bad stuff, is the thing,' says Scarlett. She taps quickly at the laptop screen on her knees. 'Look, this is what I found. "In folk magic and witchcraft, a poppet (also known as poppit, moppet, mommet or pippy) is a doll made to represent a person, for casting spells on that person or to aid that person through magic. They are occasionally found lodged in chimneys. These dolls may be fashioned from such materials as a carved root, grain or corn shafts, a fruit, paper, wax, a potato, clay, branches, or cloth stuffed with herbs with the intent that any actions performed upon the effigy will be transferred to the subject based on sympathetic magic."'

'As I said, a voodoo doll,' says Moony.

Scarlett shrugs. 'Well, it can be but may also be used for healing spells.'

They are all silent for a moment as that sinks in.

'So it's not beyond the bounds of possibility that some-one put the doll there after, with a . . . good intention?' says Rose.

Moony huffs a quick laugh.

'This is UCIT, Rose,' says Adam. 'Nothing is beyond the bounds of possibility.'

Rose gives a weak laugh in turn. It's both the blessing and the curse of working here. You are able to look further than ever before into the depths of criminal intent. But where on earth do you stop looking?

'Hang on,' says Moony. 'If someone is lying in front of you with a broken neck, you call an ambulance. You don't stick a homemade doll next to them and scarper. No . . . there's some-thing decidedly odd about this case.' She gives a quick grin, revealing the snaggle tooth at the front of her mouth. 'Luckily "odd" is our bread and butter.'

The Armstrongs' home is in Alexandra Park, a leafy, affluent part of the city with views right across London from certain vantage points. Rose parks on the hilly road lined with tall Edwardian houses, a few streets away from Alexandra Palace itself.

The three-storey house the dead woman lived in is immaculately maintained. A path made from neat black and white tiles leads to a pale green front door with original stained glass.

Rose presses the digital doorbell and hears it chime inside.

After a few moments a man's voice comes through sleepily. 'Yes?'

'Hi, we're looking for Rufus Armstrong?'

'That's me.'

'I'm Detective Constable Rose Gifford and I'm here with my colleague DC Adam Lacey. Can we have a word?'

A few moments later the door is opened by a tall, slim man in his early forties with a bald head, dressed in a faded red hoodie and saggy black jogging bottoms. His jaw is stippled with grey stubble; his eyes puffy and reddened.

'Has there been a development?' he says, stifling a big yawn that releases stale breath. 'Sorry, I was having a nap.'

'We'd just like to go over everything again with you, if that's okay?' says Adam.

Armstrong hesitates and then, with a sigh, opens the door wider.

'Come through.'

They follow him into a large sitting room painted in tasteful dark grey. A vast mirror hangs over a wood burning fireplace and reflects the golden floorboards and mustard sofas. On the longest sofa, a thick cashmere blanket in pale blue is bunched up and a pillow rests there.

'I can only seem to sleep down here,' he says. 'Since . . . you know. Since.'

There's a clicking of claws on wood and a little brown dog enters the room, tail wagging so hard its rear end swings from side to side like its back is hinged. Rose fusses the dog's head for a few moments and then the man clicks his fingers.

'Hup,' he says, and the dog neatly bounds up next to where he sits by the blankets before promptly curling up close to him. 'Good boy.' He places his long bony hand, knuckles shaded with fine hairs on the dog's back and very gently strokes it. Something about this whole movement snags in Rose's mind and she makes a mental note to come back to it.

'Thanks for seeing us,' Adam begins. 'First of all, we are very sorry for your loss.'

Armstrong doesn't reply. The dog gets up and turns a circle on the sofa before coming in even closer; curly head on its owner's lap.

'Can you tell us exactly what happened on Saturday evening?' says Rose.

The dog gives a big huff and closes its eyes. Armstrong looks down at it with affection.

'I have done this several times now,' he says, meeting Rose's eye again. 'Is it really necessary?'

'I'm afraid so,' she says. 'Sometimes important details only come back to you later. And we're only joining the case now so would really appreciate hearing it all in your own words.'

Armstrong sighs and runs a hand over his bald head.

He tells them that he and Suzette had dinner together around seven, then he watched television while she caught up on some work upstairs.

'Then,' he says, 'at about nine, she says she is going out to buy some cigarettes.'

'And how long would you estimate that would have taken her?' says Adam. 'To go to the nearest shop?'

Armstrong shifts in his chair and removes his arm from under the dog with a small wince. Rose watches this carefully.

'Not long, I guess,' says Armstrong. 'But I was very tired from work and dropped off on the sofa. The next thing I knew, it was late and the police were knocking on my door with the terrible news.'

'And you didn't wake up at all and wonder where she was in that time?' says Rose.

'No,' says Armstrong, frowning. 'Look, before you ask, I don't know why she went up to those woods. I'm wracking my brains.'

Rose waits a beat before speaking again.

'How did you hurt your arm?' She says it so casually that Armstrong is caught off guard and his other hand immediately flies to his upper arm, making the little dog look up worriedly at him.

Rose waits and the silence seems to thicken around them into an uncomfortable pressure.

Then Armstrong leans forward and places his head in his hands.

'Look,' he says, his voice slightly muffled until he looks up at them. 'You may as well know because it's not exactly a secret that Suzette and I had a bit of a fiery relationship some-times. We had a row on the Friday night before she died and, well, she threw a radio at me. Hit me on the arm. Look.' He takes off the hoodie to reveal a crumpled white T-shirt under-neath. Holding out his arm, it's easy to see a large bruise on his bicep. He puts the hoodie back on. 'It's not the first time I've been in the firing line and it wouldn't have been the last. But I never raised a finger to her in return, before you start wondering. It's all a bit humiliating, obviously, so I don't talk about it.' He is breathing heavily now. 'I have no way of making you believe this but it's the total truth. I would never, ever have hurt her.' His voice cracks and he blinks several times.

Rose and Adam exchange a glance.

'Can you tell us what you fought about?' says Adam.

Armstrong grimaces. 'She blew up over a casual comment I made about the credit card bill.'

'Did you argue about money often?' says Rose. Looking

around this room with its classy furniture and giant Apple television, it strikes her they don't seem like a couple who ever goes short.

'It wasn't that,' says Armstrong, rubbing his stubbled jaw. 'It was the fact that she seemed almost compulsive about it. Like,' his eyes roam around at the memory, 'she bought two crates of a Barolo that cost almost fifty quid a bottle! We already had plenty of wine!'

'Was she drinking a lot?' says Rose carefully.

Armstrong sags a little. 'It was certainly increasing.' He pauses for a moment. 'Look,' he says, searching for Rose and then Adam's eyes with his own, 'I've obviously been thinking about all this a lot. I don't believe this was suicide. There's just no way. She was actually quite unsympathetic about people doing that. But I do have to tell you that my wife was very stressed before she died.'

'In what way, stressed?' says Rose.

'She had run of bad luck,' he replies. 'She kept losing things, for a start. Her keys, then her phone. Then there were all sorts of tech problems that caused her enormous stress, like a virus on the laptop that wiped a load of work files. Some old friends didn't seem to have time for her anymore. Then there was, like I say, doing stuff like ordering too much wine or expensive clothes she really didn't need. I mean, we're not short of money but it felt like it was getting out of hand a bit.'

There's a pause.

'I hope you can appreciate my honesty here,' he says. 'I don't know why she went to those woods and I don't know why she climbed that platform.' His voice, quiet and staccato at first, has been gradually rising and now he roughly swipes at his eyes. 'But I certainly didn't have anything to do with her death. She drove me to bloody distraction and we probably weren't the best mix but I still . . . ' his voice breaks and he continues with difficulty, eyes glistening with unshed tears. 'I still loved her. Suzette was my everything. If someone did this to her . . . please . . . I beg you. Please find them.'

They stay for another five minutes after that but everything is a repeat of what they have already read.

'What do you think?' says Adam, as they get back into Rose's car.

Rose doesn't turn the engine on immediately but looks out of the windscreen, thinking.

'We have a suspicious death of a woman who was in a physically abusive relationship with her husband and he has a crap alibi,' she says. 'In any other circumstances, I would be liking him very much for having done it. But in the majority of cases of spousal murder, you know as well as I do that it's a heat of the moment, I-couldn't-take-it-anymore sort of deal. Chasing someone up a climbing platform and then pushing them off in a raging storm is all a bit weird. I can't get my head around it at all.'

'I know what you mean,' says Adam. 'But he bothered me a bit.' He turns to look at her. 'Nice spot with the arm,' he says. 'I didn't even notice that.'

'It was the way he was holding it around the dog,' says Rose. 'I could tell it was uncomfortable. I'd like to know if any of that stuff about physical fights would have come out if I hadn't asked him.'

'Presuming no domestic violence was flagged up initially,' says Adam. 'I'll double check when we get back but I didn't see anything.'

'Me neither.'

Rose yawns.

'Sorry,' she says. 'Feels like it's been a long day. Let's go off and meet this manager bloke.'

'To the woods it is,' says Adam.

Rose's eyes prickle as they join the long queue to cross the North Circular Road. It's only 4 p.m. but it feels so much later. It's that time of year when everything is gearing down and she can feel her own energy levels respond. But maybe it is also the prospect of going back to that depressing house later.

Rose would never have believed she'd miss her old home with its bad memories and frequent visits from the dead woman she called mother, but at least it was familiar. She had lived her whole life in the scruffy house in East Barnet, watching a series of dupes traipsing into the house who believed Adele was a professional medium who could connect them with loved ones on 'the other side'. In reality, Adele was laundering money for an organised crime network, whose contact was a man called Terrence Bigham, now currently serving a long sentence at His Majesty's pleasure.

Rose never liked the house, particularly since the ghostly visitations from Adele, who died some years previously. Rose had almost got used to this, but in the last few weeks before she moved out, it had all got more sinister. Rose had been convinced that Adele was trying to tell her something before she left, something that may or may not have involved the murder of a woman who was in the house one night with Adele and Bigham, a man known to her then only as Mr Big. Something had happened that night; Rose is certain of this. Adele changed afterwards and became even more unpleasant to live with.

But a combination of stress from her case and possible PTSD from the one before had, Rose now thinks, sent her down a rabbit hole that finally had her up to her elbows in muck in the back garden.

She was in her last weeks at that house anyway, because her long-term rental agreement had ended. But what happened that awful night pushed her to leave even sooner. She realised quickly how lucky she had actually been when she started looking for somewhere to rent. Wanting to stay in North London, she ended up in a nice area but in a grim little house called The Squirrels, in Highgate. Her first night there was spent trying to locate the source of a mystery smell and if you were in any doubt about the owner's enthusiasm for the squirrel species, a little walk around inside will soon put you right. Ceramic squirrels cover every surface, and Rose feels the little painted eyes on her almost as much as those of her creep of a landlord, Jimmy.

It's only temporary, she tells herself. She'll find somewhere else better very soon. The fact that she has been saying that for several months now doesn't make it any less heartfelt.

It's not as if she hasn't been looking. Rose has seen plenty of places on Rightmove and other websites that seemed suitable online. But so far, she has experienced the sharp end of property hunting in the capital city. There was the wideboy creep who peppered his sales talk with thinly-veiled double entendres and then bluntly propositioned her as she was viewing the place. Then there was the landlord who insisted she put down a £4,000 deposit. Not to mention the old lady who haughtily told her, 'I don't like renting to young women,' which was baffling and probably illegal.

So, for now, Rose keeps on looking. She has managed to make her bedroom more homely anyway with some fairy lights and new bedding. But there is still the matter of the mystery. It's like something has died in there. When she mentioned it to Jimmy, he launched into a lengthy description of an issue with his sinuses that causes 'excess mucus' and difficulty in smelling.

Still, she sometimes wonders whether the sweet-rotten scent of death is inside her own head.

'Ever been to these woods?' says Adam, breaking into her thoughts as they pass through the streets of Southgate towards the far reaches of the capital, where Elford Country Park is located. He's reading something on his phone.

'Not that I'm aware of,' says Rose. 'You?'

'Yeah,' says Adam. 'The woods are massive and really ancient, from what I remember. Scarlett's doing a bit more research on it all for us back at the office.' He pauses. 'We had a few picnics and walks here as a kid.'

This kind of family activity wasn't really on the agenda in Rose's childhood but she says nothing.

There are several ways into the park, but they head for the main entrance. It's at the end of a long, narrow road, thickly wooded on each side. The trees seem to reach towards each other overhead giving a secretive, gloomy air that feels surprising when they aren't that far from the M25 motorway.

'Proper old-fashioned spooky woods,' says Adam. 'Not exactly somewhere you'd want to be running around at night by choice.'

'Especially in a howling gale,' Rose murmurs.

They turn into a large car park and get out of the car. There's a café with a partially covered outdoor seating area over to the right, plus a building called The Visitor Centre. Various signs point off in different directions into the woods.

Adam is staring at the café, whose light is warm and appealing in the growing gloom of the autumn afternoon. It looks like staff inside are getting ready for closing but the door is still open.

'I don't know about you,' he says, 'but I'm bloody starving.'

'Extremely good idea,' says Rose. 'C'mon.'

A thin, slight woman with an Eastern European accent serves them. They both choose posh caramelised onion and thyme 'hog rolls', which they take outside to one of the benches. They munch the sausage rolls in happy silence, flakes of buttery pastry falling like confetti on both laps. Rose's unhelpful imagination pictures having a picnic on a summer's day. With Adam. She tries to brush the image away with the crumbs in her lap.

'C'mon,' he says, when they have both finished. 'Let's go look at where it happened. We haven't got much of the light left today.'

They walk through the trees along a path towards the Crazy Climbz course. The aerial sections must be obscured by the trees, which still bear the last vestiges of their faded leaves. The first sign they've arrived is the adventure playground near the entrance, plus a number of carved animals: deer, squirrels and various birds that Rose presumes are inhabitants of the country park. Each one looks like it has been carved from a single piece of wood and is surprisingly realistic.

A large jaunty sign marks the entrance to an area marked YOUR CRAZY CLIMB STARTZ HERE! but there's a chain across

31

it and on the main building, a large hut in a log cabin style, there's a CLOSED sign in the window. But someone is there because the lights are on and movement can be made out inside.

Rose knocks on the door.

A man in his late twenties with a doughy, round face, glasses and thinning blonde hair opens the door and regards them.

'Police, right?' he says. 'I got a call to expect you. Come in.'

Inside the cabin there is a single desk cluttered with paperwork and a chair. A filing cabinet is on one side, and a surface covered with a kettle and tea and coffee making paraphernalia on the other. A pile of certificates saying, 'I survived Crazy Climbz!' has to be removed from a small bench seat before Rose and Adam can sit down.

The irony of this wording must be lost on no one.

Introductions are made and Joshua – 'Call me Josh, please' – sits at the desk with his hands on his thighs.

'You're finished for the day?' says Adam.

'It was very quiet, so I sent everyone else home,' says Josh. 'Hasn't exactly been the best advert, what happened.'

'Must have been a terrible shock,' says Rose. 'Didn't you want some time off?'

'I was actively encouraged to take a holiday,' says Josh, pulling a face. 'But I felt like I may never come back if I didn't get back on the horse straight away.' He pauses. 'If that makes sense. Meyer, our parent company, are actually a really good employer about stuff like this. Not that "this" is like anything that has ever happened before.'

'I know you've been through it all already,' says Adam, 'but sometimes little details can make all the difference. Can you talk us through what happened that evening?'

Josh nods, looking down, a little muscle working at the side of his mouth. 'I keep thinking about the fact that if it hadn't been for the storm, it couldn't have happened at that time of night.'

'How so?' says Adam.

'Normally all the ladders would be too high to reach.' He

pauses. 'So we are pretty much open all year round apart from the major holidays,' he says. 'And the only thing that closes us down is thunderstorms. I mean, you can't have people swinging through trees if there is any prospect of lightning. And that means our staff too, who usually go round at the end of the day to tie everything out of the way. There was still a party on site five when we saw from the weather app that the storm was coming in earlier than first thought.'

'Site five?' says Adam. 'That's where it happened?'

'Yeah,' Josh nods. 'There are five different sections to the course, each one getting progressively higher and more challenging. Five is the final one and has the longest zip wire at the end. We have a final sign-in time for customers but because we can never quite predict how long people will take going round, we can't be certain what time everyone will finish. This lot had been slow because one of the party was especially nervous. It was already getting dark when I heard the first rumble of thunder and had to go and tell them we were closing.'

'So what time was this?' says Rose.

'It was about 6.30,' says Josh. 'The site was clear within fifteen minutes and so I followed our procedures for storms and headed back to the cabin to wait it out.'

'What are those procedures exactly?' asks Adam.

'Normally, as I said, the team will go round and tie up all the rope ladders on each of the towers so no one could get up when we're closed,' Josh explains. 'But in a thunderstorm the rope ladders are left partially hanging because it's too dangerous for staff to climb up and fix them properly to the top of the platform. For that reason we're not allowed to formally close up and the manager, i.e. me, has to stay all night if needs be, or until the storm has totally passed.' He pauses for a moment and rubs his cheek with the heel of his hand. 'I'm meant to patrol now and then and keep an eye out but I didn't do it as often as might have been ideal because the storm was so vicious. I mean,' he looks at them both individually, 'did you hear it?'

'Sure did,' says Adam. 'Thought the roof was coming off at one point. But surely it had calmed down by about nine? Unless that was just over my way.'

Josh shifts in his seat and avoids looking at the two police officers.

'What is it, Josh?' says Rose. 'It's really important you tell us everything.'

'I fell asleep.' His tone is flat. 'I'd had a really late night and was knackered. I should have gone and locked up earlier but I didn't. I keep thinking that if I hadn't dropped off, I might have been able to stop it.'

Silence stretches for a few moments.

Rose waits a beat before speaking again. 'Tell us what happened next.' Her tone is gentle.

'When I woke up,' says Josh, 'I went round to close up all the sites and it took a little while. I got to site five last. Because it was dark, I didn't realise at first what I was looking at. My first thought was someone had left a coat on the ground. Then I saw her.' His voice shakes a bit. 'I realised she was dead quickly because, well, her head was at a horrible angle.'

'Okay, thanks, this is all really helpful,' says Adam. 'I just want to double check there's no CCTV at all here?'

Josh shakes his head ruefully. 'No, but the ironic thing is that we were talking about getting it installed for other reasons.'

'Oh yes?' says Rose.

Josh sighs. 'Yeah, we've had a bit of aggro,' he says. 'Not everyone approved of the adventure trail being laid in these woods,' he says. 'Ancient space and all that. Yadda yadda. The fact is, we have a good idea who's behind it but can't prove anything.'

'Who's that?' says Adam, sitting forward a little.

'The main objector is a bloke called Malcolm Reece,' says Josh. 'He fancies himself a bit of an expert on the country park. He walks his dog along the course and has been known to shout at our customers from the ground. We can't prove the

34

other stuff is down to him, but there has to be a good chance he's behind it.'

Rose and Adam look at each other. She wonders if he is thinking the same thing. There has been no mention of this man until now, nor of the fact that the activity centre had previously experienced local hostility.

'Was that the extent of the "aggro"?' says Rose.

'It was more annoying than anything,' says Josh. 'Like a homemade "keep out" sign that was left at the entrance when we first opened. And we're always finding dog poo on the landing spots. I mean, that could be general idiots. But sometimes it seems almost deliberate.'

'Do you have any contact details for this Malcolm Reece?' says Adam.

'No,' says Simmons. 'But he lives in the distinctive pink cottage right inside the Harley Road entrance. You can't really miss it.'

Rose makes a note to follow this up.

'Can you show us now where it all happened?' says Adam.

'Of course.'

They get up.

The final site is close to the main building so they don't have to walk far to get there. They're standing underneath a long zip wire on a landing site made of wood chips. No fences surround it apart from an open enclosure around the far end of the landing site. Anyone in the park could access this spot, even if, according to Josh, they wouldn't normally be able to reach the ladder. The platform itself would be impossible to climb without equipment.

A week on, the crime scene has been cleared away. This is, after all, a business that will have been keen to resume, especially when it has been hit by publicity like this.

Josh walks over to the tower and points at the ground.

'She was lying just there,' he says.

'And that's how we think she got up, right?' says Adam,

walking over to the tower and pointing up at a rope ladder secured at the top of the platform, just underneath where people would stand.

'Yes,' says Josh, 'unless she came in from the beginning of the course, but customers are given a key code to access that bit.'

'You mentioned the ladder being partially tied up,' says Rose. 'Can you show us how high that was?'

'Sure, to about here.' He holds his hand up and it's clear anyone of average height could have accessed it, easily.

But why did Suzette Armstrong climb up there? Rose thinks. *Who or what was she trying to get away from?*

'Josh, did you see anything else lying near her body?' she asks.

The young man looks blank. It's clear he hasn't been told about the poppet.

'Well, I mean it was dark and muddy and . . . but no, not really. I was very shaken as you can imagine.'

'I bet,' says Adam kindly. 'Look . . . .' There's a pause. 'You've done really well, thank you. I think we're done.'

'Thanks.' Josh looks almost weak with relief at this.

They walk back to the entrance to Crazy Climbz with him. Darkness is seeping in now and it's getting trickier to see their way.

When they reach the building Rose and Adam make their goodbyes and leave Josh with a business card to get in touch if he thinks of anything at all he's forgotten to say.

Rose and Adam are turning to head back towards the car park when something makes Rose stop.

She scans the darkness of the trees behind the climbing course. The smell of rot and mulch is strong here. Of things dying and turning to muck. From this spot it looks as though these woods go on forever. Looking up, she gets a sudden, disorientating feeling and then the back of her neck prickles with an unmistakeable sensation. She stops abruptly and Adam follows suit, watching her.

'Hey,' he says. 'What's up?'

'I don't know,' says Rose quietly. 'Nothing probably. Just felt a bit funny. Almost like someone is watching us.'

They both stand still for a moment, senses on high alert. Adam turns a slow circle, scanning the trees. Then there's a loud crackling sound and Rose flinches as a small West Highland Terrier comes charging towards them like a furry white missile.

'Maurice!' calls a panicked voice. 'Come back here now! Maurice!'

An elderly woman appears through the trees. Her cheeks are pink, and she is breathing heavily.

Maurice the dog sniffs around their feet with excitement, then jumps up on Adam's legs, painting the bottom of his trousers with thick, tarry mud.

'Maurice!' shouts the woman. 'You naughty, naughty dog! Come here right now!'

Rose grabs the dog's collar as the woman gets to them, her face scarlet now.

'He's a very bad boy,' she says. 'I'm so sorry.' She clips the lead to the collar of the dog, who registers protest by planting its behind on the ground and not moving.

'Don't worry about it,' says Adam, not very convincingly, attempting to dust the mud off his clothes but only making it worse.

The dog's owner drags her recalcitrant animal away, continuing to admonish him as she goes.

'Oh dear,' says Rose, stifling a giggle at Adam's outraged expression. 'Let's get out of here before your clothes get completely defiled.'

'Hmph,' is all Adam manages in reply.

They start to walk away. The humour at Adam's situation seems to cool inside Rose fast. She looks back briefly to where they stood, still having that odd feeling at the back of her neck.

Somehow, she has the weirdest sense it wasn't the disobedient Maurice or his harassed owner who had been watching them.

6

She won't tell anyone about this. She'll say he came back of his own accord.

It would be too embarrassing to admit that she, a professional woman, has driven (over the speed limit, too) to this gloomy place without telling anyone where she was going. She'd thought about calling a friend or even her brother, but it's such a cold evening and it might be a wild goose chase anyway.

Plus, they just don't get it.

'It's only a cat.' The number of people who have said that! She's had to clench her fists in her pockets to stop herself from saying something she might regret.

Tiggy is so much more than 'just a cat'. He's her comfort, her confidante, and he represents home. Being without him this last week has been one of the worst times in her whole life. She'd come in from a long day at work and change into casual clothes before walking the streets, calling his name. Then she'd spend all night picturing him lying broken in some alleyway or at the side of a road, unable to understand what had happened. It was literally unbearable.

She never gave up though so when her phone rang tonight with that unfamiliar number, she'd felt hope surging in her chest in a way that was almost painful.

They'd been out walking their dog, they said, and were

surprised to see such a well-looked after, 'handsome' cat in the middle of these woods. They'd seen her posters and made a note of the number, they said, because, 'well, you never know, do you?'

The trouble was they had their dog with them and couldn't actually pick up the cat. But they'd seen where it went, into the old outhouse by the big lake. The Enderfield Road entrance. Did she know it? She did and was in the car before five minutes had passed.

She should have waited until the daylight, she knows this. But the temperature has dropped again and there's talk that there might even be more snow tonight. Tiggy could die in that sort of temperature. Pulling her woolly hat down over her ears she tentatively walks past the sign that says LAKE AND WATER GARDEN and heads through the trees. The remnants of hard snow lacing the ground make it eerily light and it's like walking through a strange monochrome world as she crunches onwards. She's grateful for her voluminous ski jacket, even though she had hated the trip she'd bought it for. It feels like being enveloped in a big comforting marshmallow. She's not even that cold, despite the sub-zero temperatures.

She quickly reaches the lake and can see what looks like a ramshackle stone building on the other side. That must be it; the outhouse. Her heart starts to speed at the thought of holding that little warm body again. She'll kiss him all over his fluffy head and never, ever let him go.

A sound stops in her tracks, breath curling in wisps before her. What was it? High pitched and distressed. Tiggy?

She calls his name, then again, louder. 'Here puss!' She makes the ch-ch-ch sound that usually draws him but can't tell where the mewling is coming from because it seems to be all around, all at once.

That's when she sees the wooden platform going out into the lake. There's a shape on there. A person, bending over something.

'Hello? Is someone there?'

The cat's distressed howls get louder and more distraught and she hurries over. It looks like someone – she can't tell if it's male or female – is hunched over something on the ground. Are they helping Tiggy? Or . . . hurting him?

She runs now and within a couple of moments she is on the jetty.

'What are you doing?' she says but the end of her sentence gets lost in her gasp as the figure turns to her.

'What?' There's a moment of confusion at what she is seeing. There's no Tiggy. Just . . .

And then the ground splinters and gives way beneath her feet.

The shock of the icy water takes her breath away and she flails but the big heavy coat just sucks in more water and pulls her down, down, down.

7

It's easy enough to find Malcolm Reece's cottage, as Josh Simmons said, even though it's now almost fully dark.

He lives inside the park near an entrance slightly hidden from the main road. The chocolate-box cottage has wooden beams and a thatched roof that hangs like a frowning brow over small, mullioned windows. Thick ivy climbs up one side of the building.

'Cute place,' says Adam.

As Rose knocks on the heavy old wooden door, it strikes her that it looks like the sort of house you might see in a fairytale. When the door opens, she's almost surprised to see a man in his sixties with mustard cords and a checked shirt under a fleece bodywarmer, and not a witch or one of the three bears.

Malcolm Reece is fit-looking for someone of his age, apart from the slightly hunched bearing common to very tall, older men. He has thick grey hair swept back from his forehead and tortoiseshell glasses resting slightly low on a hawkish nose. By his side is a small white terrier, who gazes up with rheumy eyes and gives an unconvincing little bark of protest at the guests.

'Quiet, boy,' says Reece. 'Can I help you?'

'Mr Reece?' says Adam and introduces them both. 'We're

41

sorry to bother you at this hour but we just wanted a little of your time if that's okay?'

Reece appraises them both for a moment, frowning. 'I suppose you'd better come in,' he says and opens the door wider.

Reece moves quickly, light on his feet despite his size, and guides them through to a low-ceilinged living room, dog close to his side. The small room is dominated by a huge arched fireplace set into the far wall. Horse brasses hang along the top and there's a sort of carved circle design in the middle. The walls are hung with pictures of horses and watercolours of flowers. Small windows and the very low ceiling give the room a claustrophobic feel, not helped by a strong doggy smell.

'Please,' says Reece. 'Sit. Now what is this about?'

He gestures towards an elderly beige sofa covered in a patchwork blanket, then sits in a large, wing-backed chair across from them; both hands on his corded legs, as though preparing himself for whatever is coming. The dog curls at his feet, occasionally glancing up anxiously under tufty eyebrows.

'Did you hear about what happened recently, Mr Reece?' Rose begins. 'The death at Crazy Climbz?'

'I did,' he says. 'And I was very sorry to hear about it.' There's an arrogant tilt to his chin. 'But why people feel the need to swing from trees rather than enjoying their natural beauty from the ground is beyond me.'

Good, thinks Rose. Straight to the point.

'You object to the climbing centre?' says Adam.

'I do, yes,' says Reece. 'As an active member of the Friends of Elford Park committee, that's on public record.'

'Why are you against it?' says Adam.

Reece makes a frustrated little noise in his throat, as though this is the stupidest question he has ever heard. 'Because that place is a scar upon the landscape,' he says. 'It's all about corporate greed. And it was only a matter of time before something like this happened.'

'It was?' says Rose.

'Yes,' says Reece with a smug smile. 'You'll think this eccentric, of course, but I believe that truly ancient places are living entities, if you will. They ultimately repel foreign agents, like a body with a splinter. That aberration of an activity centre, or whatever you want to call it, shouldn't have been built. Don't even get me started on the stupid, ungrammatical name.' He seems to visibly shudder at this.

Rose looks over at Adam, wondering if he is thinking what she is thinking. Malcolm Reece is clearly on the box-of-frogs end of nature loving. But does that make him mad enough to kill?

'Have you ever left dog excrement at the centre, Mr Reece? Or put up a sign dissuading people from visiting?' says Adam.

Reece's cheeks flood pink. 'I would never vandalise or cause damage to these woods,' he says. 'That is the very opposite of the conservation I believe in with all my heart.'

Rose regards the man, who is clearly trying to control his outrage at this suggestion. It does seem unlikely he would in any way harm this park, even the climbing centre. But that doesn't mean he couldn't harm a person. Maybe, Rose thinks, he's like one of those extreme animal rights activists who put a human life below that of a mouse.

'Okay,' says Rose. 'Can I ask where you were on that Saturday night, the eighth?'

'You can,' he says. 'Like everyone else, I was inside staying out of that storm. My wife Mary was here too.' He pauses. 'She's at a doctor's appointment now and not here.'

'That's fine for now,' says Adam. 'But one more thing: can I get you to have a look at this, please?'

Reece takes the phone from his hand and peers at it, his eyebrows shooting up.

'Oh, very interesting,' he says. 'Looks like a modern version of a poppet doll.' He looks up. 'Why are you showing me this?'

'One of these dolls was found near the woman who died,' says Rose, watching his expression carefully. It's very hard to tell what he is thinking.

'Really?' he says eventually. 'How odd.'

'We think so too,' says Rose. 'But you don't know anything about it?'

'Not a thing,' says Reece, frowning, and then looking at the photo again. 'I'm very interested in that sort of folklore but frankly, this is quite a poor representation.'

'How so?' says Adam.

'It looks sort of thrown together,' he says with a sniff. 'It's a bit of a special interest of mine; this sort of thing. I've made studying the folklore of the woods a personal mission.'

'That sounds interesting,' says Rose. 'Can you tell us a bit more?'

'Happy to.' He looks slightly puffed up now, reminding Rose of a pigeon. 'Everyone goes on about Epping, but these woods are even older. My knowledge of the place is one of the reasons I was asked by the council back in the nineties to help develop the visitor centre. I was in charge of the section on the history of the park. They have replaced it now with stuff about cycle lanes and so on.' He grimaces and then brightens again. 'But this house itself is a testament to the history of these woods.'

He goes to stand at the fireplace. 'Do you see these markings here?'

'Yes, I noticed them on the way in,' says Rose. 'What are they?'

The markings are a series of concentric circles that have been carved into the stone. Reece smiles pompously.

'Witch marks,' he says.

Rose and Adam exchange quick glances.

'Witch marks?' says Adam.

'I mentioned this cottage is very old,' says Reece. 'This was one of the ways people protected themselves against perceived threats. Carvings like these were designed to ward off evil and can be found by doorways or chimneys in many buildings of this era.'

'Fascinating,' says Adam and clearly means it by the way

his eyes have lit up. This has not gone unnoticed by Reece, whose tone becomes positively ebullient now.

'Oh yes,' he says, 'we have found all sorts of things here. Look, let me show you this.' He goes over to a shelf and comes back holding a small, green glass bottle that looks very old. The contents are murky but something shrivelled is in there like knotted string. He hands it to Rose, an almost greedy expression on his face.

'What is it?' says Rose, holding the little bottle up to the light to try and make out what's inside.

'It's a witch's bottle,' says Reece. 'It's filled with hair, nails and urine.'

Rose is proud of herself for barely flinching, but she hurriedly hands back the bottle all the same. 'Right, okay.'

'We also found the remains of a cat up the chimney,' Reece continues. 'These things all share the same purpose. To protect the house and its occupants.'

'No dolls up the chimney?' says Adam.

Reece gives a patronising little shake of his head. 'No dolls,' he says. 'Whoever did that has been watching too many films, methinks.'

'"Methinks"?' says Rose, sniggering as they get back into the car. 'I mean, who says that?'

Adam laughs. 'He's quite the character, isn't he?'

'Certainly is,' says Rose, then lets out a yawn. 'Do you believe him? About the dolls? Seems a bit of a coincidence that he's a folklore and witchcraft expert, doesn't it?'

'Hmm,' says Adam. 'Maybe. And I don't like those. Maybe it's a bit too much of a coincidence.'

'As in, someone else wanting him to come to our attention?'

'I don't know,' says Adam. 'Perhaps. I don't think Josh Simmons has anything to do with this but let's run some further background checks on him, just in case.' He then yawns too. 'God, you've got me at it now. Let's call it quits for the evening?'

'Yep,' says Rose. 'Rather than going all the way back to

Reservoir Road for your car, I'll drop you home and then pick you up in the morning.'

'Great!' says Adam. 'Got my girls over tonight so getting home earlier helps me out.'

'It's no problem.'

Rose isn't only doing this to be kind. As much as more time with Adam is always welcome, the thought of an evening in that house drags at her mood.

She has just dropped Adam off when her phone rings.

It's Rowland.

'Hi,' Rose says tentatively. 'Has something else come up on the case?'

'No,' says Rowland. 'I've had a strange request land on my desk. In relation to you. I think they believe you still work here.'

Rose feels a tiny flutter inside; moth wings in her chest. 'Oh yes?'

'It's come from Brixton Prison, from an inmate.' Rowland's next words turn the moths into something much more substantial. 'Does the name Terrence Bigham mean anything to you?'

'I'm not sure,' she manages to say. 'Why?'

'Well, he's certainly heard of you,' she says. 'He's put in an official request to speak to you.'

46

8

Rose microwaves a ready meal and then takes it to her bedroom, but she can't face eating it. Her thoughts are swirling and her chest feels tight.

What the hell does Bigham want? Keeping the grubby fingers of her past from her career is one of the most important things in Rose's life. Joining the police was an attempt to put it behind her as far as she could. Yet it seems those fingers will never stop reaching out and grabbing at her however hard she resists them.

For years, something held Rose back from looking properly at Mr Terrence John Bigham. She doesn't know for certain that he is the 'Mr Big' who frequented her childhood home for all those years, but it seems likely.

But on her last case she had worked with a DCI who had given her some details about how Adele – without knowing Rose's close connection – had worked for Terrence Bigham as part of a larger crime network run by a man called Michael Cassavettes. Bigham had been one of the many scalps offered up by Cassavettes in return for immunity.

Bigham is now serving a life sentence of thirty-five years after being found guilty of conspiracy to murder three people – two of whom were the elderly parents of the main focus – in a revenge killing after a member of Cassavettes' crew was gunned down in a McDonalds in East London. When Rose learned about all this, she had pressed Moony to tell her what she knew about her mother; Moony was one of the officers called out to Rose's childhood home and, in a strange wobble of fate, been one of the reasons she had become a police officer.

Moony told her that it had been an altercation between Rose's absent mother, Kelly, and Adele Gifford that had brought her, as a young policewoman, to the house. Kelly had thrown accusations around about Bigham, which sparked interest because he was the focus of several ongoing cases. Then, according to Moony, Kelly had simply disappeared, apart from a brief sighting six years later. This would have coincided with the evening seared into Rose's memory, when something happened at the house involving Adele and Bigham that left Adele in a bad psychological state for some time afterwards.

But it was over-thinking this that had her digging up the back garden of her childhood home, which makes her literally shudder with shame every time she thinks about it.

She can't open that door wider. She won't see Bigham.

Rose sleeps badly. The next morning she is blearily looking at her reflection in the age-stippled bathroom mirror when there are two sharp knocks on the door.

'Are you going to be much longer?'

The high-pitched, nasal whine has its usual effect on her; invisible hackles rise on the damp skin of her back, like she's more feline than human. She's only just out of the shower, if you could call a rubber, hand-held hose attached to the taps, a shower. This place makes the avocado-coloured, hot water lottery of her old bathroom seem like a luxury spa.

Tempting though it is to ignore her landlord, Rose forces herself to reply.

'Nearly done,' she calls through gritted teeth, then repacks her soap bag with her toiletries. As she is doing it, she's thinking that nothing says 'this isn't your home' like carting your tooth-brush back and forth to a bathroom. But there's no way she's leaving it in here and that's not only about hygiene. It's more that leaving items would suggest she's here to stay. Also, she has visions of Jimmy fingering her belongings. The very thought makes her shudder.

Slipping her long hoodie over her shoulders, Rose zips it all the way up to the neck and opens the door.

Jimmy practically falls into the room and she gives a little shriek she immediately regrets.

'Excuse me,' he says, imperiously. As usual his eyes rest well below her face. 'It's just that I have an important appointment and am in a hurry.'

The man in front of her has an oversized bald head, giving him the look of a giant pink baby, emphasised by the pot belly on his small, hunched frame. His expression, she realises quickly, is brimming with hope that she'll ask him about the appointment, but she's fallen into that trap before and doesn't intend to do it again.

Rose grunts in response, trying to ignore the almost physical sensation of his little beady eyes skittering over her body. She scrunches her bare toes inside her slippers in an involuntary spasm of disgust.

'Me too!' she says. 'Those arrests won't make themselves, will they?'

Unease washes over his face and Rose smirks as she hurries back to her bedroom. She enjoys reminding him that she is an officer of the law. He has the look of a man dying to stand a bit too close, or try a little feel, but he wouldn't dare. She almost wishes he would so she could arrest him.

Jimmy is the forty-something landlord of the house, owned by his mother, who Rose has never met. The other occupant of this tatty, terraced house in Highgate is a young Polish nurse called Zofia. She is silent and shadow-like, barely giving Rose eye contact when they cross paths.

Yes, overall, it's fair to say this is an extremely depressing place to live but at the moment, it's all Rose has. Beggars can't be choosers, and all that.

Inside her bedroom, she turns the key in the lock and starts to get dressed, hurriedly. The sooner she can get out of here, the better.

It is raining heavily this morning and Rose calls Adam from outside his house, rather than getting out of the car.

He comes running out a few moments later, a rain jacket held over his head, and gets in.

'Bloody hell!' he says with a grin. 'Hope we don't have to do any more poking about in woods today, not in this.'

'Hmm,' says Rose. 'You'd really need good reason to go there in bad weather, wouldn't you?'

'Yeah. What are you thinking?' He turns to look at her. There's a tiny bit of fluff stuck to his chin and she fights the urge to lean over and wipe it away with a gentle swipe.

'I was just thinking on the way here,' she says. 'Maybe she went there to meet someone she didn't want her husband knowing about.'

'I've been thinking the same,' says Adam. 'Hoping the deleted stuff from her phone will be coming through soon because I'm guessing that's where we'd find out.' He gives a quick laugh then. 'You're looking at me weirdly. What is it?'

'Oh!' Rose flushes. 'You have a little something here.' She points to her own chin.

'Shit.' Adam rubs at his skin. 'Gone?'

'No!' Rose laughs.

Adam pulls down the passenger side mirror and then studies his face. It gives Rose a moment to look at him too, in profile; those thick eyelashes and his soft lips, which she has admired in snatched glances so often. Clearing her throat, she starts the engine.

Inside the UCIT building, the large, panelled windows with their old glass bring a murkiness that almost feels subterranean.

'Come on then,' says Moony. 'Let's hear everything.'

They pour coffees and head over to the briefing area. Scarlett lays a plate of peanut cookies made by her wife, Maz, and they all pounce on them.

Rose munches the buttery, nutty biscuit and sips her coffee, before launching into an update of the interviews with Simmons and Reece.

'So if Armstrong was forced up that ladder,' says Rose, 'it was either sheer luck that it hadn't been put away because of the storm, or they somehow knew it wouldn't be, which doesn't seem all that likely.'

'I don't know,' says Adam. 'There are loads of storm tracking apps these days. It's a bit far fetched, but in theory someone could have planned this.'

They all think about this for a moment.

'What was your impression of this Malcolm Reece bloke?' says Moony.

'He seemed like a pompous knob, to be honest,' says Adam. 'He was almost a bit snobbish about the doll not being "authentic".'

'Hmm,' says Moony, tapping her biro against her bottom lip thoughtfully. 'It seems like a bit of a coincidence that he is into all that folklore and this unfortunate victim has a weird doll near her. But even if he left it there, it doesn't mean he murdered her.' She pauses. 'We don't even know this *is* murder at the moment.'

'I took a look at the history of Elford Country Park,' says Scarlett, looking down at her notebook. 'There was something that may or may not be relevant but might be worth mentioning.'

'Go on,' says Rose, sitting forward on the sofa.

'Well, first of all,' says Scarlett, 'those woods were a favourite spot for gangland murder victims for a time in the seventies and eighties. A few bodies were found there with connections to organised crime. But nothing seems – on the surface at least – to relate to this case. Going back much further was interesting though.'

She pauses and changes the image on the whiteboard to what looks like a very old woodcut picture. It depicts a pile of bodies with agonised faces, hands reaching up to the heavens.

'Wow,' says Adam. 'What the hell is that?'

51

'These are seriously old woods,' Scarlett continues. 'And it seems they were planted over what was once a plague pit.' She looks down at her notes. 'This was during the Black Death.' She grins. 'Which I'm sure you know wiped out more of the world's population than any other event in history: about fifty million people. The first plague pits were in central places like Charterhouse Square and the area around the Tower of London. But there were too many bodies so they had to go further afield. And this is where the legend of Alice Goode comes in.'

She changes the slide to one that simply shows a rhyme.

> *Alice Goode's a-weeping*
> *Soil upon her head*
> *Come and find her sleeping*
> *Down among the dead*

'Creepy,' says Moony. 'But how is this relevant?'

'It may not be,' says Scarlett. 'But I'll tell you the rest. So it seems that Alice Goode was a twelve-year-old girl living in the Elford area of what was then Middlesex in the mid-1300s. All of her family died of the plague within two days of each other. Alice stayed in the house with their corpses because she was so overcome with grief. Legend has it that when the body collectors came to take them away, she got taken to the pit, still alive.'

'Nice,' says Rose with a grimace.

'Hey!' says Adam, animatedly. 'I used to like a punk band in the nineties called Bury Me Alice. Wonder if that's where the name came from?'

No one responds to this.

'And so this all spawned a legend,' Scarlett continues, 'which is that Alice still haunts the woods, full of malice and wanting revenge. She wanders about clutching her doll. If you see her, you'll die soon after.'

'Ooh,' says Moony, looking around at the rest of the team. 'A doll!'

Scarlett's cherry-red lips part in a grin. 'A doll,' she says.

Rose looks from Moony to Scarlett and back to Moony again. Although she has now been involved in three major investigations in this team, she still isn't completely clear on where their parameters lie.

'You're not suggesting this Alice Goode character did it, are you?'

Moony looks at Rose, unsmiling, and there's an awkward beat where no one says a word.

Then Moony guffaws loudly. 'Got you then,' she says. 'I mean, what we do here is batshit but there are limits.'

'Are there though?' says Adam thoughtfully rubbing his chin and looking at the rhyme. 'I mean, really? Because it seems to me we are pushing them on almost every case we investigate.'

Moony regards him, still smiling.

'He's right,' says Rose. 'I'm still relatively new to this department but it seems to be that we should rule nothing out. It feels like this is somehow relevant to me, even if we don't know how.'

'Okay,' says Moony, getting to her feet. 'I'm not quite prepared to accept a 700-year-old ghost is to blame here but I've been wrong before.'

Rose sends an update to Rowland and receives a curt response about staying in touch. But there is a PS to the email.

What do you want me to do about this Brixton request?
Bin it?

Rose's heart races and she taps out her reply.

Yes please.

The day passes with endless conversations with friends and family of Suzette Armstrong. Her closest friend, one May Carmichael, confirms that Suzette was 'super stressed' before she died but doesn't accept that it was a suicide attempt.

'Not Suzette,' she'd said and echoed what Rufus Armstrong said about Suzette not being especially sympathetic about suicide. When pressed on the question of an affair, Carmichael had gone quiet and then vehemently ruled it out.

'There is simply no way she wouldn't have told me,' she said. But she did confirm Suzette's temper and said that Rufus was always on the receiving end. As far as she knew, he had never been violent to his wife and loved her with what she referred to as 'puppy dog loyalty, whatever she did'.

It's after six when they reach the bottom of the list and the little daylight there was on this gloomy day has leached away.

Rose stretches her stiff body and gives a wide yawn. The bed in her new place is lumpy and unforgiving. She has a constant low-level backache for the first time in her life. Going back there tonight is a depressing prospect.

Scarlett's head pops up from her computer. Her desk has lots of personal items that make it more cheerful than anyone else's in the office. There's a photo of her and Maz in a bright purple padded frame, both smiling into the camera and holding oversized ice creams. There's also a little wooden elephant that came from her travels in India, plus a small row of fairy lights pinned to the top of the divider unit.

'Shit!' she says. 'I have to go! I'm meant to be meeting Maz and a pal. I totally forgot!'

'Yeah, I'm off too,' says Adam. 'Got a football match with the lads tonight.'

Rose shifts in her seat. Moony has already gone off for a meeting. She doesn't particularly want to be the only person in the building, which she has managed to avoid for the most part. But likewise, she isn't relishing the thought of an evening in that Highgate house either, with its mystery smell, and Jimmy lurking about outside her door. Plus, she wants to do a bit more research and the Wi-Fi is patchy in her room.

'I'll stay for a bit longer,' she says. 'Have fun, you two.'

A few minutes later, Rose is alone. She gets up to make a

cup of herbal tea; any more caffeine today and she'll be awake for a week. While she waits for the kettle to boil, she thinks about her living arrangements again.

The reason she had clung onto her childhood home for so long was, apart from the low rent, the fear that Adele's spirit, or whatever the old ghoul was, would simply follow her. This felt like a life sentence. So far, nothing like that has happened, which is a huge relief. But she can't keep living in that house. It's like she's letting her youth simply ebb away with nothing but her rather strange job to fill her days. Living somewhere decent feels like the first proper step to having a life independent of her past. But then . . .

Terrence Bigham wants to see you . . .

Rose emits a growl of pure frustration before taking her cup of chamomile tea back to her desk. There's a radio on Scarlett's desk, which she turns on low to Capital. The background poppy hum is a comfort as she settles in and tries to think about the case in hand.

It was most definitely a living, breathing person who planted that doll near Armstrong's body. That horrible poppet . . . Rose is glad it isn't physically in this room with her anymore, having been sent off for DNA testing.

Rose looks through the information sent by Scarlett again from her research into Elford Park. The few bodies that were found there had clear gangland links, as Scarlett said. Rose decides to take a look at any and all deaths that may have taken place in the park, whatever the cause and logs in to the Integrated Intelligence Platform. This searches a whole bunch of databases, including CAD, the computer-aided despatch system, which records all the incident calls coming into the emergency services.

She gets some hits within seconds.

Aside from the cases she is aware of, there are a few more. A toddler fell into the lake and drowned in the late nineties. Next is an unsolved murder and an accidental death, both of which happened in the last ten years.

The murder was of a man called Alex Weston, stabbed to death in the middle of the woods in December 2013. He was an estate agent, found with drugs in his pockets and, judging from the notes, his death was believed to be connected to that fact. But despite a host of interviews no one was ever arrested.

The accidental death was a woman called Haniya Shah, a twenty-eight-year-old pharmacist registrar who drowned in one of the lakes in the park. It was late one evening in January 2018. An odd sort of "accident", Rose thinks.

She makes notes as she reads on. This is definitely an odd one. Other reports suggest that Shah had recently seen her own GP for stress-related ailments, which the coroner took into account but ultimately gave a verdict of accidental death, rather than suicide. Unless a suicide is very clear cut, it isn't uncommon for the families to be given the consideration of this more open-ended verdict. The coroner needs to be satisfied on the balance of probabilities, but evidence is required for a verdict of suicide. If someone's death is merely suggestive of suicide, then that alone is often not enough.

Rose makes a note of all the details she can, in case anything is relevant. There is no strong connection to Suzette Armstrong's death. But Rose knows that meaningful connections can sometimes be elusive.

She is so engrossed she has lost track of the time. It's getting late and her neck is aching. Plus, she needs something to eat. She saves all the information she has into one document and plans to write it up later, or first thing, to share with the team. It's as she is doing this that something occurs to her, and she hurriedly scans her notes again.

She finds the three names and three dates.

Haniya Shah (DOB 12/04/84)

Alex Weston (DOB 12/09/83)

Suzette Armstrong (DOB 05/07/84)

All three were born within ten months of each other. Does that mean anything?

She ponders this as she gathers her things. Turning out the

lights in the office, she takes a trip to the cavernous ladies toilets down the hallway. The refurbishment for the UCIT office evidently didn't stretch beyond the main offices because this room hasn't changed much since the 1950s. There is a vending machine on the wall that once sold sanitary pads that came with an actual belt. The mirrors are spotted and ancient, albeit clean, thanks to an early morning cleaner called Hannah, a Senegalese woman who always smiles tiredly at Rose's 'good mornings' but rarely speaks. Only Scarlett has ever got more from her, including the fact that she once said she always had to listen to loud music on her earbuds when here because the building unsettled her.

She's not the only one.

Going to wash her hands, Rose looks down at the sink and something catches her eye. What looks like a few long, curly red hairs are lying stark against the off-white enamel. A little repelled, Rose turns the tap on and they swirl for a moment before disappearing down the plug hole.

Who left them there, though? No one in the office has red hair. Scarlett changes hers a lot because she's married to a hairdresser but Rose feels she'd remember if Scarlett had been wearing some sort of red extensions today. But maybe she didn't notice a few streaks in Scarlett's hair, with everything going on?

She comes out of the ladies and starts to walk down the corridor, which is lined in old bricks painted in thick yellowish-white paint. Her footsteps echo on the stone floor and she tries not to hurry but she is grateful there is no sign of the ghostly presence Scarlett calls Hilda. She is the only other person who has seen her, this round little woman with her pinny and scarf, pushing a squeaking trolley of tea and biscuits for all eternity. Rose isn't scared of her as such. It's more a feeling that when it becomes completely normal and not even noteworthy to see the ghost of a 1940s tea lady, her life has maybe gone too far in this new direction.

But before she gets to the end of the corridor, she stops abruptly as a deep banging starts reverberating from somewhere inside the building. It's a rhythmic, metallic sound, as if someone is rapping on a pipe; too regular to be the plumbing and anyway, she has never heard this before. Bang-bang-bang . . . like one-two-three.

She wants more than anything to simply leave. She hasn't fully explored the UCIT building and has never had any desire to do so, beyond a quick look around on her first visit.

But it is literally her job to investigate. She has to at least take a look. What if it was the plumbing and there was some sort of catastrophic leak she ignored because she was too chicken to check it out? Moony would not be happy in the morning. She is always going on about how they need this building, despite all its strange flaws.

Swearing under her breath, Rose resolves to have a quick look and then leave.

She goes back down the corridor and goes past the UCIT office, taking a turn to the left, trying to follow the source of the sound.

There it is again.

Bang, bang, BANG.

Darkness spreads before her. She fumbles for a light switch until her fingers find the nubs of an old-fashioned set. Snapping them all upwards, there's a loud buzzing and then three strip lights above her head, murky with fly corpses and general dirt, stutter on slowly, lighting a long corridor that ends in blackness. The final strip light is faulty and fades in and out for several moments like someone is snapping the switch on and off. In one brief moment of illumination, Rose sees a movement at the end of the corridor. Hilda? It didn't seem like her; much too quick and nimble.

'Hey!' she calls. 'Is anyone there?' Her own voice seems to mock her, echoing back. The banging starts up again, violent now, like the very walls are shaking with it around her.

Rose's heart thuds almost in rhythm as she creeps along the corridor towards the source of the sound. There is a door marked ROOM 65. It's coming from inside.

She touches the handle. It's so icy cold it burns and she draws her hand back sharply. She doesn't want to go into that room. Not at all. But she pulls her sleeve over her trembling fingers and tries again.

The room inside is massive, with long windows on the other side and a pile of old office furniture at one end. The floor is stone and there are piles of stained builders' cloths in one corner with some ancient, rusting tins of paint.

One of the windows is banging open and closed. Surely that's not the source of the sound? Perhaps the acoustics in this old place are a bit confusing. But what about that movement before? Just her imagination playing tricks?

Rose hurries over to the window, which is a long rectangle of pure darkness. She sees her own reflection reach up to close the top panel.

Then she lets out a scream of surprise. A woman with long curly hair is standing directly behind her, eyes large in a pale face. One hand reaches towards Rose's back.

Rose spins, shock hurtling through her as she raises her hands defensively.

But there is no one there.

Gulping air as though she has been drowning, Rose looks around wildly. No sign of any woman.

She is out of that room in seconds, hurtling along the corridors to the office to get her things, then to the entrance as fast as her legs will carry her.

Outside, the rain chills Rose's face and hair as she hurries to the car and climbs in before locking the doors.

She sits there for a moment, eyes scanning the front of the building and waiting for her heart rate to calm down.

That was horrible but more than scared, Rose is suddenly quite furious. It's clear that woman wasn't a living, breathing human being. Not anymore. But why does Rose have to see these things? She has no desire to and she doesn't understand the point of them.

What does the woman want?

9

THE DARK HISTORY OF ELFORD PARK
Chapter One

The woods and environs of what is today known as Elford Park have a rich and turbulent history. First described in the fourteenth century, the area was part of the Thorne Chase, one of Henry IV's favourite hunting grounds.

At this time, the city of London, some twelve miles away from the area of Middlesex known as Elford, had grown from a mere 15,000 people in 1100 to 80,000 but it was soon to be decimated by what remains the most devastating disease to affect Western civilisation.

In 1348, the Black Death came to these shores for the first time and it ended up halving the population of the country. The disease was caused by a bacteria carried by fleas on rats that spread from Asia to Europe along trade routes. The symptoms were quite horrific; large swellings known as 'buboes', hence the name 'bubonic plague', which oozed pus and blood. Vomiting and fever followed, with death days behind.

By the time of the second biggest epidemic, popularly known as The Great Plague, London had in fact endured up to eighteen outbreaks of the disease. From 1665 to 1666, records show that some 68,596 people died during the epidemic though the actual number was believed to be more than 100,000.

Finding places to bury the dead was a huge public health problem and space was at a premium. Once the mass burial grounds – the so-called 'plague pits' – in central London were full, people looked to the outer environs of the city, where the population was much less dense. And so it was, early in 1666 that the decision was made to create a plague pit in the woods now known as Elford Country Park. An interesting fact that has come to light in recent times is that, contrary to popular opinion, unlike in the first major outbreak in the fourteenth century, bodies were buried in coffins with the proper Christian habit of facing the head west and feet east.

From the mid-1800s onwards, stories emerged of the woods being a cursed place. One can surmise that, with so much death buried beneath these ancient trees, it is perhaps not surprising that dark deeds are associated with this part of the world.

10

The next morning, Rose shares what she has learned about the deaths in Elford Park with the whole team.

Moony grimaces when she's finished speaking.

'Who knew a scenic country park could be so dangerous?' she says. 'Taking your life in your hands there.'

'I wonder if there is any connection between them,' says Adam. Then, to Rose, 'Where did the other two people live?'

Rose looks down at her notes. 'Haniya Shah lived in Clapham, and Alex Weston didn't live in London at all. He lived in Kent. His girlfriend lives in Stratford though.'

Photos of the deceased are put on the large whiteboard with their ages and the date they died.

Rose and Adam spend a moment looking at the three faces. Suzette Armstrong looks confident and in charge in her photo. Scarlett has managed to find a photo of Alex Weston from a Facebook memorial page, looking tanned and relaxed with a beer in his hand in some sunny foreign place. He was a good-looking man, with floppy sandy hair that hung over blue eyes creased with gentle laughter lines. Haniya Shah's picture comes from a piece she wrote for a professional pharmacy journal. She peers out, expression cool and professional, her large dark eyes framed by glasses, and her hair covered in a hijab.

'So Haniya Shah was twenty-eight when she died,' says

Adam. 'Alex Weston was thirty-four and Suzette Armstrong was thirty-seven.' He frowns. 'All quite young.'

They stare at the three faces for a moment longer.

'I meant to say,' says Rose. 'I noticed that they were all born within ten months of each other. Could that be significant?'

'Hey!' says Adam. 'They would have been in the same school year in that case. What if they went to school together? What if they knew each other?'

Rose feels a thrum of excitement at the feeling of something sliding into place. It could be significant.

'Worth checking,' says Moony. 'Good work, you two.'

Rose gets straight on the phone to Rufus Armstrong.

'I don't have any news at this stage,' she says quickly, in case his hopes have surged at the phone call, 'But I do have a question, well, two.'

'Okay.'

'Do either of these names mean anything to you?' She tells him the names of the two other people who have died in Elford Park in the last ten years.

'Nope,' he says. 'Absolutely nothing.'

A Pause

'Why do you ask?'

She hesitates for a second, unsure whether the information about their deaths will send him in a wild direction, but quickly decides he needs to know.

'They both died in Elford Park,' she says. 'One was murdered in what may have been a drug-related event and one was an accidental death. This may have absolutely no relevance, but you don't remember her ever talking about an old friend dying or anything?'

There's a silence at the other end of the line.

'Hmm, no,' he says after another moment. 'I'm pretty certain that the only folk Suzette ever knew who died were her parents. Never any of her friends or contemporaries. Why? Did these people die in the same way?'

'No, not at all,' says Rose.

'What have they got to do with anything then?' says Rufus. 'I can't see a connection.'

'Probably nothing,' says Rose. 'We're simply looking at all avenues right now and we noticed that these were also sudden deaths of people who were all very close in age. Which leads me to the last question,' she continues. 'Can you tell me everywhere Suzette went to school, plus any further education?'

'Well, she went to Cambridge,' says Rufus, 'because that's where we met. I don't remember the name of her primary school, but I know where she went to secondary. It's called Woodfields. It wasn't that far from where . . . well, where she died. She said it was one of the reasons she didn't particularly like that area.'

The initial call in to the secondary school is met with some confusion by the person on reception but Rose finally manages to get across the seriousness of the matter.

Half an hour later, the school rings her back. After listening for a few moments, she thanks the person on the other end and hangs up.

'Hey,' she says to the room and three heads pop up from behind desks.

'That was Suzette Armstrong's school calling back. They confirmed it. All three of them were pupils there in the nineties.'

'Hmm,' says Moony. 'If they all grew up in that area, then the park would be well known to them and possibly still somewhere they liked to go. But how many kids are there in a secondary school?'

'The one my girls go to has about 2,000, I think,' says Adam.

'That's a lot of kids . . . '

'Yes, it might be nothing,' says Rose. 'But it's worth investigating.'

'Agreed,' says Moony. 'Get more on Alex Weston's murder and do what you can in finding next of kin details for both him and the one who drowned. We want a solid connection to continue with this line of investigation so make sure you're thorough.'

An unsolved murder and two unusual, though probably accidental, deaths of people who may have once crossed paths. It's not much to go on, thinks Rose. But if it's another odd coincidence, they seem to be stacking up fast.

It doesn't take long to find the next of kin for Haniya Shah, her brother in Clapham. He is home and sounds very open to speaking to them.

While Adam uses the gents, Rose goes over to Scarlett's desk and leans down to speak quietly to the other woman.

'So I was here last night,' she says, then goes on to tell Scarlett about the person standing behind her.

Rather than dismissing her – or even looking spooked – Scarlett perks up.

'Ooh, I wonder who that was?' she says. 'I've only ever seen Hilda here. What did she look like?'

'I only saw her for a second. About my age, or younger. Lots of long curly hair. It was bloody scary.'

Scarlett grins. 'I'm sure she didn't mean you any harm,' she says. 'I mean, imagine if that was all you had to communicate?'

'What do you mean, communicate?' says Rose. 'What could she have to communicate?' This conversation isn't exactly helping much.

Scarlett shrugs. 'Got me there,' she says and her attention is pulled back towards her screen.

Rami Shah, brother of the young woman who drowned in Elford Park, lives in a neat, semi-detached house in a leafy street not far from Clapham Common.

A tall man with dark, tired eyes and a neat beard answers the door. He's dressed in tracksuit bottoms and a soft purple jumper, with sheepskin slippers on his feet.

'Mr Shah?' says Rose and he nods and holds out a hand to shake.

'Call me Rami, please.'

Introductions over, he leads them into a dining room where a slim MacBook is balanced on a table that's otherwise covered with piles of folded washing. Most of it seems to be tiny baby onesies and white muslin cloths. There's a smell of warm laundry and a tumble dryer rumbles in the background.

'Sorry about the mess,' he says, pulling his fingers through his beard distractedly. 'We've got a two-month-old baby. She's out with my wife right now, and I was trying to quickly get some work done but not getting very far as it happens. Not just because of you coming,' he adds hurriedly. 'It turns out that having broken nights and trying to focus on spreadsheets aren't compatible. Who knew?'

They both smile at him.

'Remember it well,' says Adam. 'And we're really sorry to disturb you but we did want to have a chat.'

Rami waves a hand in the air. 'No problem,' he says, 'if there is anything new about my sister's death then I'm all ears. We haven't got ages because they'll be back soon and if Haniya is hungry there will be hell to pay, so let's hear what you've got.'

There's a moment while that settles.

'You named your little girl for your sister?' says Adam, his tone gentle.

Shah nods and sadness clouds his eyes. He rubs his beard again. 'Yeah, you know . . . ' He seems to run out of words.

'Okay,' says Rose, 'I have to say straight away that we don't have any new information about what happened to her. But we are working on a death that occurred in the same country park, which has some question marks over it.'

'Right,' says Shah, frowning, then in a rush, 'I mean, we were given a verdict of accidental death at the inquest, but it never sat right with any of us, especially me. If there is anything at all that can shed light on that night then I need to hear it. It's taken me years to be able to accept what happened to my sister. I still haven't, if I'm honest.'

They all sit down.

'You were close then?' says Adam. 'You and your sister?'

Shah sits back in his chair and looks down at the table. 'Yeah, we were,' he says. 'Although now I wish we had been closer. She was very serious and quiet, Haniya. While other students were out partying, she pretty much put a social life on hold until she was qualified as a chemist. She really worked to get where she was, you know? Made sacrifices. And it seemed like things were really starting to come together.' He pauses and taps his index finger on the table. 'The thing is, she was such a careful person. I used to tease her about being so sensible. That's why what happened was so unbelievably unexpected. She was the last person to go stumbling around at night like that.'

'We've read the coroner's description of what happened,' says Rose. 'She fell into the lake in Elford Park?'

'In January, yeah, at night!' his eyes are bright; his voice is raised. 'Have you ever heard anything so mad? What a way for a person to die.' He stops, visibly swallowing. Then, in a quieter voice again. 'It simply makes no sense.'

'Do you think she was meeting anyone there?' says Adam. 'Were any messages found on her phone afterwards?'

Rami shakes his head. 'You lot, I mean the police, didn't find anything obvious. There didn't seem to be any suggestion in their minds that there was foul play involved.'

'Can I ask if these two names mean anything to you?' Adam says the names of Armstrong and Weston. Shah thinks for a moment then shakes his head.

'Not at all, sorry,' he says. 'Why?'

'We can't say too much,' says Rose, 'but they also had unusual accidents in the park and there may be nothing at all in this, but we're examining every possibility right now.'

'Right, right,' says Rami, real gratitude in his expression. It's always hard to witness, the hope in the eyes of people who have lost loved ones through crime or misadventure. They want answers written in black and white, when sometimes they come, if at all, in shades of grey.

'Do you happen to know who she was friends with at secondary school?' says Adam. 'Any names come to mind?'

The other man frowns, evidently confused.

'School?'

'Yes,' says Adam.

'Not really,' says Shah. 'I mean, her best friend for a while was a quiet little thing called Leah, I think? But Haniya left school to go to Woodhouse College for her A levels, so she made new friends then. Why are you asking about that?'

'We're just exploring all avenues in this other case at the moment,' says Adam. 'I'm sure you'll understand.'

He evidently doesn't but nods anyway.

'Why do you think your sister went to Elford Park that night, Rami?' says Rose.

'Believe me,' he says tiredly, 'I have asked myself that question over and over again over the course of these years. The only thing I can think of is that she had lost her cat and was really upset about it. Maybe she was looking for it there? Although it was a bit of a long way.'

'Did the cat turn up?' says Adam.

'Yeah. Strolled up like nothing had happened a few days after she'd gone. We ended up having it for the rest of its life.' Rami manages a laugh. 'I don't even like cats but it felt like a connection to my sister so I was pretty broken up when it died.'

'Okay,' says Rose carefully. 'I have to ask you a difficult question. Was there any reason to think that Haniya would take her own life?'

Rami shakes his head and looks down at the table. 'No way,' he says. 'For a start it's forbidden in our faith, but much more than that, she had no reason to do that. And she was a really cautious person who was a trained chemist to boot. I mean,' he gives a short and bitter laugh, 'if my sister had wanted to die, she could have done it peacefully and painlessly. She wouldn't have thrown herself into freezing water when she couldn't even swim.'

'You mentioned pharmaceuticals,' says Rose, glancing down at the notes. 'She did have diazepam in her blood, which is generally taken for anxiety.'

'Yeah, I know,' says Rami, frowning. 'That was really out of character. I even wondered if she had taken it accidentally. All I can say is that I didn't know, and none of us knew, that she was on anything like that.'

'I know this is a long shot,' says Adam, 'but I don't suppose you have her computer or phone still?'

Rami shakes his head. 'Both wiped and given away. Why?'

'As I said, just looking into different avenues,' says Adam, which is a non-answer but Rami seems to accept it.

'This is going to seem like an odd question but bear with us,' says Rose.

'Okay,' he says, a little suspiciously.

'Did Haniya have anything odd in her car or on her person? Something you wouldn't expect her to have?'

Rami looks thrown by this question. 'Nothing that I can remember,' he says.

'Sure?' says Rose.

'Oh, wait!' His eyes widen. 'Unless you mean the bundle of sticks in her car?'

Rose feels a cool tingle at the base of her neck.

'Sticks?' says Adam, leaning forward.

'Well,' says Rami. 'They'd been sort of tied together but you couldn't really make out why.'

'Was it possible it was a doll?' says Rose, heart rate gently increasing.

'I guess it could have been,' says Rami. 'But we just threw them away. I never could work out why she had dirty old sticks under the seat. She was always meticulous about her car.'

Rose and Adam look at each other.

'Inside the car?' says Rose.

'Yes, as I said, under the seat.' Rami leans forward, 'Are you saying there are similarities with this other case?' he says, leaning forward, excitement in his voice now.

'We really can't discuss details of an active case at this time,' says Adam, hurriedly. 'Sorry.'

Rami sits back. 'I understand,' he says, shoulders slumping. 'But if there is any way you could find an explanation for what happened to Haniya, I would be so grateful. It pretty much killed our parents. They never got over it.' His voice cracks. 'And neither have I.'

'We can't make any promises,' says Rose. 'These cases may be totally unconnected, but we are making sure we cover everything, and you have been extremely helpful.'

They get up from the table.

'But you will tell me,' he says, 'If new information comes to light about my sister? Anything at all?'

'We'll do our very best,' says Rose.

'I mean it,' he says. 'You have no idea what agony it is, not really knowing or understanding something like this. It stays with you every day of your life. It's impossible to move on. I think it's going to haunt me for the rest of my life.'

11

Everyone is assembled in the briefing area looking at the white-board. There is now an image of the twig doll blown up, with arrows going to both Suzette Armstrong's picture and Haniya Shah's.

'This does give us some information,' says Adam, crossing his arms. 'If there has been some sort of attempt at intimidation here, or murder, then we are clearly dealing with someone who is into things like witchcraft. It would take a certain mindset to go to the trouble of planting this stuff.'

Scarlett is looking down at her phone. 'Hey,' she says, 'I just got a hit on Sarah Bramwell, Alex Weston's girlfriend. I found her via Facebook and she's replied to me. Seems she works as a tour guide in the Canary Islands but can speak on the phone.'

'Great,' says Moony, rubbing her hands together. 'Let's see what we get from her. Then we need to find the connection between these three.' She looks at the rest of the team, her expression grave. 'If there isn't one, fine.' She pauses. 'But I'm sure you're aware of the implications if there is.'

'Yes,' says Rose quietly.

They're all thinking the same thing. If these deaths are all murders, and all linked, they might have a serial killer on their hands.

They get back to work. Adam makes the call to Sarah

Bramwell. His head is lowered over his desk as he writes notes for what seems a long time before he hangs up.

When he finally does, he looks up.

'What've you got?' says Rose.

Moony's head pops up from behind her screen, as does Scarlett's.

Adam stands up and comes round to the front of his desk. He leans back against it and crosses his long legs at the ankle.

'I'm not sure,' he says. 'Sarah Bramwell says Alex may have been a recreational drug user, but the way it was presented – as a drug deal gone wrong – never felt right. She says Alex would never have gone to meet someone in a park at night like that. She has a very poor view of us, the police, and the original investigation. But one thing she said stood out. Before he died, he too seemed unhappy and distracted. Like he had things on his mind. And he was forgetful, which could, of course, have been his lifestyle choices.'

'Any weird dolls?' says Rose and Adam shakes his head. 'Not that she knew of.'

Moony taps her hands on the table, her silver rings clacking loudly on the wood.

'Okay people,' she says. 'I feel like we're getting something here but it's still about as substantial as smoke. There's only one actual murder. At this stage, we'd have a heck of a job getting these cases back in front of the CPS. And as to whether they're connected . . . well, my feeling is . . . they are. What about you two?'

Rose and Adam exchange glances.

'I think so too,' says Rose. 'I haven't a clue why though.'

'Same,' says Adam.

'Okay,' says Moony. 'Well, first thing Monday I want you to find the connection between these three people. Speak to their teachers if anyone is still around. Find out who their school friends were. I'm going to call in the general registry docket for the Alex Weston murder and we'll go through everything there with fresh eyes.'

She sits back in her chair and yawns widely. 'But I want to save overtime costs until we can really justify them. We'll come at this fresh on Monday morning. Not much more you can do this evening so fuck off home now and do something fun.'

There's a general shuffling of movement as people start gathering their things.

It's only now that Rose remembers Sam's party this evening. She received a text from him earlier reminding her and had conveniently managed to park the idea because she was involved in other things. The prospect does not fill her with anything good right now, but an evening staring at ceramic squirrels with psychotic eyes and dodging Jimmy is even worse.

Moony and Scarlett leave quickly in a flurry of goodbyes. Adam doesn't seem to be in quite such a rush to go. His expression is serious as he takes his mug over to the sink and washes it at a leisurely pace.

'Plans this evening?' she says as she joins him at the sink.

He sighs. 'Well, I did,' he says. 'I was having dinner with an old friend I haven't seen since university. But his little boy has come down with chickenpox and he has to stay in.'

'Oh, that's a shame,' says Rose.

'Yeah, I was really looking forward to it,' he says. 'I don't have the girls this weekend.' He looks fed up. 'I guess that's another Saturday night of me watching *Strictly* in my pants.'

Rose laughs. 'Now there's an image.' Which, actually, it very much is.

'I'm kidding,' he says, then with a grin, 'I don't watch *Strictly*.'

Rose hesitates for a moment then forces the words out of her mouth before she can change her mind.

'Look,' she says in a rush, 'I've been invited to a party I don't want to go to at all. You'd be helping me out if you fancied tagging along, I mean,' she said quickly, 'as a friend.' Trying to ignore the fierce burning in her cheeks, she focuses on washing her own coffee mug for far too long. It is an agonising three seconds before Adam replies.

'That'd be great, actually,' he said. 'Yeah, why not? Better than sitting about in my pants with a takeaway.'

'Great!' Hard to quell the pleasure and relief that bloom through her. Pleasure at spending the evening with Adam and relief that she won't have to walk into that party alone.

For one unsettling moment, they simply grin at each other. Could he possibly feel as pleased as her? When he speaks again the moment slips away.

'Mind you,' he says, 'I've agreed without asking why you don't want to go. It's not a toga party or something is it? Fancy dress?'

Rose laughs. 'No, don't worry, nothing like that. It's just that it's an old colleague and, well, as they say, it's complicated.'

Adam regards her for a moment then looks away.

'Gotcha,' he says.

When Rose gets back to Highgate, she walks along to the high street to pick up some flowers and a bottle of wine for the party.

The evening is suffused with unexpected autumnal sunshine and people are making the most of this surprise gift by sitting outside the pubs and restaurants, even though all but a hardy few have warm jackets on.

She spends time choosing her items from the supermarket then wanders along the high street aimlessly until her attention is snagged by the window of a small independent boutique that is open late. It has been beautifully decorated with a display of paper leaves in a fiery riot of autumn colours that showcase the clothing in the window. A green dress catches Rose's eye. Silk, maybe? She's not sure. It has a lacy V-shaped neckline and short, delicate sleeves.

It's gorgeous. Rose doesn't have any reason to get dressed up that often but something about this dress calls to her. There's no visible price tag, which is never a good sign, especially not in a shop in Highgate. But on the other hand . . .

The thought of walking into that party – after her complicated history with Sam – isn't an easy one. If she can at least feel confident in how she looks, it might help. Plus, there's the fact that she is going with Adam. Even if it is impossible and wrong for anything to happen between them, the thought of him giving her an appraising eye causes her stomach to erupt in pleasurable butterflies.

Before she can talk herself out of it, she pushes open the door, which tinkles in an old-fashioned way. A thin, pale skinned woman about her own age glances up but doesn't say anything at all. This snootiness almost sends her right out the door again, because places like this annoy her. But she can see the dress from here and she walks over to the hanger to find one in her size. Fumbling for the hand-written price tag, she almost laughs out loud. Rose has never spent that much on one item of clothing. She needs to save her money to find somewhere better to live. But maybe she will just try it on for size and then can rule it out entirely . . .

Inside the changing room she slips her jumper and trousers off. Pulling the dress over her head, the silk seems to whisper as it flows down her body. It's a perfect fit. She steps out of the changing room to get a better look, conscious of her hot, socked feet that have been in sensible shoes all day.

'Oh, you look amazing in that,' says the woman who works there, her face quite lit up now. 'I think it's because you have the tiniest hint of red in your hair and that always looks good with green.'

'Thanks,' says Rose, feeling a little shy but pleased all the same.

'Want to take your hair down so we can get a better idea?'

'Oh, okay. I guess.' A little self-conscious, she releases her thick hair from its customary ponytail and fluffs it out around her face.

'Yep,' says the woman, nodding approvingly. 'Gorgeous!'

Rose can't resist a little smile at her reflection.

The sales assistant is right. She does look good in this dress.

When she steps out of the shop five minutes later, carrying the paper bag with the tissue-wrapped dress inside it, she has a little spring in her step. Rose is thinking about what to wear this with. She already owns a pair of knee-high chocolate brown suede boots with a heel that will go with it and a little jacket to wear over the top.

Back at The Squirrels, Rose can hear the sounds of a football match on the radio in the kitchen, so she bounds up the stairs almost two at a time to get into the bathroom for another shower without having to speak to Jimmy.

In the shower, she shaves all the places that need it urgently and ignores those that can wait, before stepping out and once again disappearing as much as she can into her long hoodie for the quick dash down the hall.

In her bedroom she props up her iPad and plays a Spotify playlist that will get her into a party mood while she attempts to do something with her hair. After spending so long with her hair straighteners that her arms ache, Rose is satisfied with the results. Her chestnut hair hangs in a smooth curtain for once.

She does her make-up and is just adding some red lipstick when she pauses. What if it looks like she is making a huge effort? What if Sam thinks it's for him? Which it kind of is.

What if Adam thinks it's for him. Even more true.

She stares back at her own reflection.

Sod them, she thinks. I'll wear it for me.

A few minutes later, she is ready to go. There is no full-length mirror in the room so she is forced to lift one of her legs up at an awkward angle to check the boots go with the outfit.

Satisfied, she has one final look in the mirror. Rose has been told she is pretty often enough, but this hasn't always been welcomed in the job she does. If anything, she errs on the side of playing down her looks. But tonight, she needs all the confidence she can get.

'Here I come, lads,' she says to her reflection. 'Not that either of you will care.'

Unfortunately, she isn't to be so fortunate that she will escape Jimmy entirely. As she gets to the bottom of the stairs, clutching her flowers and wine, he emerges from the kitchen. His entire man-baby head flushes red at the sight of her and his eyes widen, then narrow.

'Oh,' he says, 'you're all dressed up.' He manages to make it sound like she is guilty of an enormous amount of self-indulgence but doesn't disguise that he is getting a good look anyway. 'Where are you going?'

'Friend's housewarming party,' she says and feels a spasm of unreasonable panic that he might actually invite himself along too. She pictures herself walking into the party with Jimmy on her arm and almost starts laughing out loud.

'I found a mouse,' he says. 'In the airing cupboard. Quite dead.'

'Oh,' says Rose. 'That's good news.'

'Well,' he says mournfully, eyes lingering below the neckline of her dress and then doing a full body sweep. 'Have a good time.'

'Thanks!' she says. 'I'll certainly try!' and gets out the door before he can chat any further.

Out in the street, Rose walks towards the tube station. The temperature has dropped sharply since earlier, and she is soon shivering in the thin dress and inadequate jacket. But once on the train, she is surrounded by people heading out for the evening and the mood is infectious.

For once, it might be nice to feel like a normal youngish person living in London. Sometimes it feels as though Rose has entirely missed out on parts of her life that she should be entitled to. And it's all because of her upbringing. That house. Adele.

Tonight, anyway, she's determined to try and enjoy herself. Despite all the complicated feelings involved about a certain couple of policemen in her life.

12

Sam and Lucy live in Finsbury Park. Rose has arranged to meet Adam outside the tube station there.

She is on time but relieved to see he has already arrived, wrapped up in a warm-looking navy wool coat with a black scarf folded neatly at his neck.

An expression she can't quite catch passes over his face when he spots her, then he quickly looks away. She's never seen him this awkward before and is washed with worry that she has gone overboard; that he thinks she has dressed up for him and that she believes this is a date. It's as though someone has popped a pin in the buoyant confidence she had just been feeling, like a balloon that shrivels to nothing. She wishes she hadn't gone with the lipstick.

'You look a bit chilly,' he says. He seems to be avoiding looking directly at her, despite saying this, his eyes are fixed ahead. The only thing to do is to try and diffuse the weird atmosphere.

'Is it the clown-like red nose?' she says. 'Or the violent shivering that alerted you to this?'

Adam laughs loudly and gives her a warm look. Everything suddenly feels better. Rose finds it so gratifying, the way she can make him laugh.

'Would you like my scarf?' he says, unwinding it from his neck. 'I seem to have gone the other way.'

Rose is about to protest but he is handing it to her now and she's too cold to argue. The scarf smells of his aftershave. She thanks him and puts it on. Her unhelpful brain immediately plays a scene in vivid detail, where he gently puts the scarf around her neck and uses it to reel her in for a kiss. The image is so powerful, Rose can feel her cheeks warm.

Calm down, she tells herself. This isn't a bloody romcom. We're just two work colleagues who happen to be dressed up for the evening, that's all. Nothing more.

They start to walk down Stroud Green Road, passing people on their way out for the evening and tired-looking mothers hauling shopping bags and kids home.

'You said this party was complicated,' says Adam, 'Want to tell me about it? No pressure, obviously.'

Where to even begin? She imagines saying it out loud.

Well, we were half in love with each other but the ghost of the woman I called mother messed it right up, unfortunately. Life's a bitch, eh?

'It's a bit hard to explain,' she says instead. 'But let's say it was a friendship that got spoiled for various reasons.'

Adam seems to wait for a long moment before answering. 'Right, gotcha,' he says.

Sam and Lucy's new place is the bottom floor of a converted Victorian house in a cul-de-sac. When they ring the buzzer, the door opens and Ewa from Silverton Street almost shouts Rose's name before enveloping her in a massive hug. Judging by the slightly unfocused glaze to her eyes, she has already had a drink or two.

'I'm so glad you came,' she says, then her attention turns to Adam. Ewa is usually a low-key sort of woman, but the alcohol has evidently loosened her up considerably. She gives Rose a grin that is both congratulatory and vaguely lewd all at once. Ewa looks as though she might be about to say something hideously embarrassing, but luckily Adam saves the situation.

'Hi, we met before,' he says quickly. 'Rose and I work together.'

'Nice to see you, Adam,' says Ewa. 'But I'm off to the loo. I think coats go that way,' she vaguely gestures to the left. 'Go in the other way there and you'll find everyone.'

When they take their coats off in the dimly lit bedroom, Rose sneaks a look to see that Adam is wearing a light blue shirt that beautifully complements his dark skin, with black jeans. He smells amazing. Glancing over at her, he grins.

'You look very nice,' he says. 'If it's okay to say.'

'Thanks. So do you.' Rose can feel the colour staining her cheeks at his words. She wants to make a joke but can't think of one. She hurriedly gathers the wine and flowers.

There are quite a few people in the pale green, high-ceilinged living room already. Music fills the air, and a smell of new paint competes with delicious smells of curry wafting from a kitchen Rose can see through an archway.

Searching for a familiar face, she spies Mack talking to someone she recognises as a uniformed officer at Silverton Street. No sign of Sam or Alice.

'Rose!' The cry from behind makes Rose flinch in surprise and she turns, becoming enclosed in a tight hug that smells of perfume, cigarette smoke and hairspray.

'Zainab!' Rose feels her eyes prick as she hugs Sam's youngest sister back.

There was a time when Rose used to hang out with Sam's family so much, they felt like her own.

'You totally disappeared, you cow! Let me look at you.'

Zainab stands back and the two women regard each other, delight wreathing both faces.

Zainab is wearing a bright green sari edged with fuchsia pink that leaves one shoulder bare and her thick black hair is piled up on her head, with tendrils hanging by her cheeks. Her eyes are dramatically winged with eyeliner and her lips are the same bright pink as the edging on her sari.

'You look gorgeous,' says Rose.

Zainab makes a face. 'Mum says I look like a bloody strumpet.' She does a funny impression of her mum, who she is constantly in battle with, but adores.

'What are you saying about me, you terrible child?' Meera appears from the kitchen holding a huge casserole dish. 'I just think you'll be cold, wearing half a dress, that's all. And anyway, I don't even speak like that.' Her face lights up when she sees Rose and she hurriedly places the dish on a table that has been laid with bowls of rice, chutneys, breads and at least two other curries.

'Rose! We haven't seen you in so long!' Rose is enveloped in her third bone-crushing hug in five minutes. Warmth spreads through her. She is only now realising how badly she needs this. How she has missed it.

Introductions are made with Adam, and the flowers and wine are taken with thanks by Meera. Zainab says she will be back to 'hear absolutely everything' once she has made a call outside and Rose and Adam are soon furnished with drinks; beer for him, a large glass of white wine for her.

Alice and Sam have evidently both been in the kitchen and they emerge at once. Sam's face lights up. Alice's doesn't, although she manages a smile that doesn't quite meet her eyes.

'You made it!' says Sam and then glances with evident curiosity at Adam.

'I did!' says Rose. 'This is my colleague Adam Lacey. He was at a loose end and I invited him along. Hope that's okay?'

'Of course!' says Sam. 'Nice to meet you, mate.' They shake hands. Rose isn't sure if, despite her heavy emphasis on mentioning work, Sam thinks Adam is her boyfriend. Well, let him, she thinks.

'Nice to see you Rose and hi Adam,' says Lucy. Even though she is pregnant, she actually looks slightly thinner than the last time Rose saw her. Her large blue eyes look tired and her long blonde hair has been pulled back into a tight ponytail.

'Congratulations on the baby,' says Rose. 'How are you feeling?'

Lucy grimaces. 'A bit shit, to be honest. Sam wanted to cancel but I was determined we would go ahead with this. Oh God, excuse me a minute . . .'

She hurries out of the room.

'Oh dear,' says Sam. 'I'll leave her to it. She'll be okay in a minute. But it's not been fun at all. She's at twelve weeks now and we thought she would be better by now.'

Rose has no great desire to have children right now but all the same, the love etched on Sam's face gives her a bittersweet ache. Lucky Lucy, she thinks. Even if you have to puke ten times a day. Lucky Lucy, having all this.

'When my ex was pregnant with our girls,' Adam is saying, 'the only thing she could eat that didn't come back up again was Twiglets. She ate bags and bags of them.'

Sam smiles. 'Twiglets, really?'

'Yeah,' says Adam. 'It's something about the savoury, salty taste. Really helped.'

'We'll give that a go,' says Sam. 'Thanks!' He regards them both. 'So how are things going in the new job?'

She is saved by an arm around her shoulder.

'Alright kiddo,' says Mack. 'Scrubbed up well. And Adam! Since I saw you the other day I realised, we know some of the same people in Vice.' They shake hands, both smiling broadly.

'Is Rose telling you all about the fascinating world of compliance?' says Mack, meeting Rose's eye. She silently thanks him.

'I hadn't started but I'm very happy to!'

Sam makes a joking 'backing off' gesture with his palms up. 'It's okay,' he says, 'I'll take your word for it!'

The other two men start discussing a case they both worked on. Sam's expression turns serious again as he turns to Rose. 'Look,' he says, 'I know it's not for public consumption, so I wouldn't dream of asking you to discuss your new department. But anyone who worked on the Oakley case knows about it. You can't really keep stuff like that quiet in a nick, as you well know. But you can rely on our discretion.'

Rose feels a sense of relief wash over her. Who knows and

82

who doesn't know about UCIT within the Force is a constant source of worry to her.

'I wasn't sure what people knew but I'm glad I don't have to pretend with you.'

'You never have to pretend with me, mate,' he says and gives her a light punch on the arm. 'I really have missed you, you know. And Rose . . . '

No, she thinks, don't say it.

'About what happened before . . . '

Rose waves her hand in the air and almost knocks his bottle of beer onto the floor. She is momentarily conscious that Adam is watching their conversation from across the room, and this flusters her even further.

'Oh forget that!' she says, too brightly. 'We were pissed and it's all water under the bridge now. I mean, here you are, about to be a dad!' Hurriedly now, 'How are you feeling about that?'

'Terrified,' he says. 'Excited. Mostly terrified.'

'I think you'll be ace at it,' she says and clinks her glass against his bottle.

'Thanks,' he says. 'It's a hell of a responsibility. But I'm ready, I think.'

'I'm sure you are,' says Rose, fighting a wave of emotion as she looks at her dear friend, who hasn't been in her life for so long. When she glances across the room, Adam quickly looks away and says something animated to Mack, who laughs loudly.

The evening passes pleasantly. Rose talks to Mack for some time about his daughter, Caitlin, who suffered from anxiety that wasn't helped by the nature of her father's job. At the insistence of Meera, Rose has to try each of the curries. She is chatting to Meera and hoovering up a bowl of mouth-watering cardamom butter chicken when her living arrangements come up.

'Oh it's a bit of a nightmare,' says Rose. 'I'm stuck in a horrible place at the moment but everywhere is so expensive and I'm just not prepared to live out of London. It would be a nightmare for work and well, you just have to put up with a creepy landlord sometimes, don't you?'

'I don't like the sound of that at all,' says Meera with a grimace. 'I wish we had a spare room for you but it doesn't look like Zainab is ever going to move out.'

'Oi!' her daughter is weaving towards them as she says this. 'What bollocks are you talking about me now, Mother?'

Meera swoops her eyes. 'Dreadful child,' she says again as Zainab joins them. 'I'm just telling Rose I wish we had room to help her because she's in a horrible house share right now.'

'Much as I'd happily bunk up for you,' says Zainab, 'I wouldn't wish my living habits on you. But hey, Ma, what about that mate of yours? The one you told me about?'

Realisation dawns on Meera's face. 'Oh yes!' she says. 'Ness! I have a friend in Crouch End who is in the process of a divorce right now and she said something to me recently about wanting to rent out a room in her house. I mentioned it to this one because, well . . . ' she nudges her daughter, who laughs good-naturedly.

'It's almost like you want to get rid of me,' she says.

Meera laughs. 'As if I could! Anyway,' she continues. 'Ness doesn't really know where to start and wanted to rent it, in her words, to "someone nice". I can certainly verify that about you. Do you want me to put you in touch, Rose dear?'

Rose hesitates. 'It depends on what she would be asking, to be honest,' she says. 'Crouch End is quite an expensive place to live from what I've seen. I mean, if it's anything like Highgate, and it is, let's face it. I probably couldn't afford anywhere that isn't an absolute shit-hole, pardon my language.'

'Pardoned,' says Meera. 'I am inured to this after bringing up my potty-mouthed daughter. But I wouldn't worry about that. Ness isn't absolutely desperate for the money but just needs a bit extra now that her useless husband has gone. She's lovely and I really can't imagine her charging too much. She's always going on about how hard it is for young people in this city. Look, why don't I give you her number and you can have a chat and see what she says?'

Rose takes it gratefully, feeling a lifting of her spirits at the prospect of finding somewhere better to live than The Squirrels. She has to give a month's notice, but at least she would know she was moving out. But she's getting ahead of herself. It may come to nothing, so she decides to keep her feelings totally in check.

Adam is now talking to Zainab and if Rose isn't very much mistaken, the latter is in full-beam flirt mode. Adam looks slightly shellshocked but is clearly enjoying the moment from the way he keeps laughing. It's too hot in here. Rose suddenly feels the need for some air. Seeing Sam and Lucy so settled isn't as painful as she feared it might be but all the same, she can feel a sadness pressing in on her at being surrounded by so many couples. There isn't anyone here that she would like to get to know better. Well, apart from people she can't have.

It never ceases to surprise her that she can be ambushed by loneliness when she least expects it.

Rose goes out into the garden, which is small and edged with overgrown flower beds. There's a bench seat at the end and she picks her way across the grass to it to sit, which she does after a pat to check that it is dry. The sudden craving for a cigarette after almost eighteen months comes swiftly and brutally. Luckily it is far too cold to stay out here for long. Rubbing her arms and getting up, Rose glances up at the back door and the French windows of Sam's flat but a movement above catches her eye.

A tingle of shock passes over the crown of her head as she sees her, the woman who was standing behind her in the UCIT building. While she was in monochrome then in the reflection, now she is in full colour, wearing a pea-green leather jacket and her hair, in a cascade of ringlets, is a fiery red. She stands with both hands pressed flat against the glass as if trying to push her way out.

For a moment or two, she and Rose simply stare at each

other, then Rose hurries back towards the house and into the kitchen. She wants to get out of here. Right now. There is no way she can enjoy this party now. It feels like she's being stalked. She must look harried because Mack sees her pass through the kitchen and says, 'You alright, Rose?'

She makes a decision. There is no way she can enjoy this party now. It feels like being stalked.

'I think I'm going to make a move,' she says. 'I'm feeling a bit off.'

'Ah, that's a shame,' he says. 'We didn't even get to catch up on the case.'

'Yeah, sorry,' says Rose. 'Can't be helped.'

Sam, Zainab and Ewa all express surprise that she is leaving so early but she promises to catch up with all of them soon. Adam, who is in a conversation with an older woman Rose doesn't recognise, regards her carefully and asks in a low voice if she is alright and if she would like him to come with her. She declines the offer and repeats the lie about her reasons for leaving. She's clearly not doing a great job of concealing the fact that she is upset and it takes ages to properly extricate herself and be out the front door.

If she was thinking straight, she might be warmed by so many people worrying about her. That several people in that house really wanted her to stay.

But she isn't able to focus on that right now.

Because while she may have got rid of Adele's spectral presence, it appears that Rose now has another unwanted visitor from beyond the grave.

13

Questions run around her brain all night and when she does drop off, she has disjointed dreams involving Silverton Street and her childhood home, which are somehow one and the same place.

The sweet death smell seems to coat the inside of her nose and mouth as she comes to in the morning. So much for Jimmy's dead rodent disposal. Maybe it has simply become part of the fabric of this house now. Thank goodness she didn't drink enough to be hungover. But she hurries to the miserable shower and lets the hot water run over her scalp for so long that there is a knock on the door.

'Can you hurry up please?' The voice is terse. It's Zofia, the other tenant.

'Sorry!' she calls and hastily turns off the water before getting dried and brushing her teeth. Everything about this place feels mean and parsimonious. It's only then that she remembers the flat in Crouch End. She was so thrown after seeing that red-haired woman, she totally forgot about this exchange.

It's probably already gone, she tells herself, as she hurries past the disapproving face of Zofia in the hallway and makes the dash to her room. It sounds far too good to be true. And anyway, when does Rose get that kind of luck? A good flat simply falling into place? Best not to get any hopes up.

But when she calls the number a few minutes later, still in her dressing gown, the plummy-voiced woman at the other end of the line sounds delighted to hear from her.

'Oh good old Meera!' says the woman. 'I was just this morning thinking I'd have to go through the whole business of putting this online but it's such a rigmarole, isn't it? So much nicer to have someone who has come from a personal recommendation. What do you do, my love, for a living?'

'I'm a police officer,' says Rose and waits. This isn't always received warmly and even though the other woman doesn't immediately sound like the criminal type, she almost holds her breath for a moment.

There's a throaty giggle. 'Well, I shall have to mind my ps and qs a little bit then.'

'No, no, not at all,' Rose says hurriedly.

'I'm only kidding, darling,' says Ness. 'Look, can you come over this morning? We can have a coffee and get to know each other a bit. You can take a look at the room and see if it's the sort of thing that might be of interest?'

'That would be great,' says Rose, a hopeful feeling expanding inside her.

Ness gives her the address and they agree to meet at eleven thirty. Rose decides to get out of the Squirrels early. She can have breakfast then walk to Crouch End, which is less than half an hour away with a direct road all the way.

While she waits for a bacon and egg and roll in a café on the high street, she sips her Americano and opens a notebook. It's a personal one, rather than her official investigator's book. This work is private.

She decides to be methodical about this, even if what she is writing fills her with a strange sort of prickly shame.

All Rose ever wanted was to escape from her childhood, with its endless grieving punters coming through the door to be systematically fleeced by Adele.

But while Adele was a total fraud, who lied to her clients about the supposed links she created with their dead loved-ones, Rose felt presences in the house from the time she was around ten or eleven. It wasn't often, but it happened enough for her to understand it wasn't normal. At that age she was already canny enough to know that it would be a terrible mistake to reveal to Adele that she had this ability. She could picture all too well how quickly it would have been exploited.

She never really saw fully formed people, as she did with Adele later, then Gladys the tea lady and now whoever this red-haired woman is. It was more about sensing something cold and some-times seeing fleeting movements in the corners of rooms, like a sort of half shadow. But whether she likes it or not, it appears this is something she is stuck with and like the good police officer she is, she needs to think about it in a methodical way.

She starts writing notes.

Red-haired woman — who is she? Not my mother. Seen photos of her and she looked different.

Someone connected to UCIT or to Adele? Both possible? Unsolved UCIT case?

Or someone who worked with Adele and Bigham? Victim of something connected with them?

Connected with what I thought I saw that night growing up?

She pauses and shudders afresh at the memory of herself digging up the back garden. It was probably one of the lowest moments of her life, when she felt as though her past was never going to stop being a yoke around her neck. It's the reason her living arrangements are unsettled; while contemporaries are settling down in couples and she can't bring herself to have a proper relationship with someone. She can't risk having the unpleasant visitation she had the night Sam stayed. Since then, Rose's only sexual liaison has been a fairly soulless hook-up via a dating app.

No. She can't go on like this. But how on earth can she find out more? It seems impossible without access to any tangible information or a contact.

Her breakfast arrives and Rose begins to eat, feeling her spirits revive with each bite. Abandoning the notes, she spends a bit of time looking at social media and the news app, then has a second cup of coffee.

After a while she pays and heads off towards Crouch End in the weak sunshine.

As she walks up Shepherd's Hill, it's hard not to be on edge, ever looking out for the red-haired woman. But the only encounter she has is with a *Big Issue* seller sitting outside the Waitrose in Crouch End. She buys a magazine after going into the shop for some paracetamol for a low-lying headache that is probably a consequence of too little sleep.

Amberley Road is a further ten minutes on, heading in the direction of Finsbury Park and by the time she has walked up a long and quite steep hill to the number she wants, she is sweating inside her jacket.

When she arrives at number 107, she stops outside for a moment. She's half tempted to turn around again because, well, it's lovely. There's no way she is going to be able to afford to live here and it's only going to hurt more to see inside.

Rose isn't very good with houses but thinks this is probably Victorian. It's very large and made from a warm red brick edged with white. There is a central pointed gable at the top over big bay windows and the front door is made from beautiful stained glass. The garden is well tended and it's only then she realises someone is crouching behind the hedge to her right.

A head pops up. The woman in her fifties beams broadly at her. She's wearing a floppy light green hat and clutching some secateurs.

'Ah, did I forget the time?' she says in a loud, cheerful voice. 'Goodness me, I'm always doing that.'

'Hi,' says Rose. 'I'm Rose Gifford.'

'I'm Ness Rossetti,' says the other woman. 'Well, technically Rossetti isn't my name anymore, but I think I'm going to hang onto that because it's a damn sight nicer than Braithwaite, which I was born with!'

Rose isn't quite sure how to respond but it seems it's not necessary because Ness is still talking.

'Come on,' she says, 'I was just cutting back my laurel, but it can wait. Let's go in and get to know each other!'

Ness is one of those people who has a very petite top half and a wide bottom half, as though two totally different physiques have been attached together. She is wearing a denim jacket with the sleeves rolled up and a flowing silvery skirt over her wide hips that has mud splatters on the hem. Her feet are in a pair of wellies.

'We'll go round the back,' she says and opens a gate to the side.

They walk down a path at the side of the house, past a greenhouse and a shed to a back door, which Ness opens.

'Let me get these wellies off and wash up,' she says. 'You come in and sit down.'

She shucks the wellies off her feet by the back door and goes to the sink to wash her hands.

Rose crosses the terracotta floor tiles to a long wooden table and sits down. There are a few newspapers on the surface, along with an iPad, a book, some glasses and what looks like a large knitting basket with a rainbow of balls of wool inside.

She looks around the kitchen, which is painted in a bright yellow. There is an old dresser that has a mishmash of old plates along with a pile of paperback books, some clothes and post. The whole room has a comfortable, loved sort of air, nothing like Rose's childhood home, or The Squirrels. This looks like a place that has contained a lot of happiness. Rose can feel it, warming her through.

'I'm sorry it's such a bloody mess in here,' says Ness, turning back to look at Rose. 'I'm not the tidiest person.'

'Oh neither am I really,' says Rose. Then, flustered, 'I mean, I'm not bad to live with. I'm not dirty or anything like that.' She immediately cringes inside. Why does she get so awkward when she likes people? Because she already likes Ness and this house. It's almost painful, knowing that there is even the slightest chance this could come off.

Ness regards her for a moment with merriment in her small, dark eyes and then bursts out laughing.

'Sorry,' says Rose. 'I think that sounded a bit weird.'

'Not at all darling,' says the other woman. 'If I was writing the ad I probably would have put, "Bit messy but-not-actually-dirty tenant required".'

This makes Rose laugh and any tension she was feeling melts away.

'Now, coffee or tea?' says Ness. 'Too early for wine, I suppose?'

Rose smiles. 'Maybe a bit,' she says. 'Could I just have some water please?'

'Of course!' says Ness. She makes tea for herself and brings Rose a glass of water.

'Now then,' she says, sitting down at the table and looking at Rose with a smile. 'I'll tell you a bit about me and then if I haven't massively put you off you can fill me in on you, okay?'

'Okay,' says Rose, smiling uncertainly.

'So I am only recently here on my own,' says Ness. 'I brought up four children who are all over the place now, but come back and forth. I was married for thirty years to a man I genuinely thought would be with me until the day I died. Then, four months ago, he told me that he had been very unhappy for a long time and was leaving me. Not for anyone else, he said, although that turned out not to be true. So as you can imagine, that was very . . . that was very hard.'

Ness produces a tissue from the pocket of her skirt and blows her nose loudly.

'I'm so sorry,' says Rose. 'That must have been really rough.'

Ness makes a sort of strangled sound and swipes viciously at her nose.

'No,' she says, 'I'm the sorry one. This is why I haven't properly advertised the place. I seem to overshare with everyone I meet lately. I cried in the back of an Uber the other day and I swear I frightened that poor man. He probably marked me down for it.'

'You really don't have to apologise,' says Rose.

'I've probably put you right off before we've even started though,' says Ness gloomily. 'I'm not usually this Weepy Willy, honestly, ask anyone.'

'You honestly haven't,' says Rose. 'And anyway, you're the one with the beautiful home. I should be trying to impress you right now, if only I knew how.'

Ness's face brightens at this. 'Well, so far you seem very lovely,' she says.

'That's very kind of you,' says Rose, blushing a little.

'Why don't you tell me a little bit about yourself, Rose?'

Rose hesitates, buying time by taking a sip of the water. 'Ness, I really don't want to waste your time,' says Rose. 'I have a feeling this is all going to be irrelevant because it's out of my price range. Can I ask what you'll be asking, before we go any further? I don't want to start getting my hopes up unnecessarily.' She follows this with a laugh that comes out too high and too sharp.

'That's very sensible,' says Ness. 'My kids have been pushing me on this. They say the room and use of the house could go for . . . ' She mentions a figure per week. Rose feels the disappointment settle like grey silt inside her. Just as she expected, there is no way she could afford that.

'But there is no way I'm charging that,' Ness continues. 'I am far too much of an old lefty to go about trying to fleece people in this city. There is far too much of that already, thank you very much.' She goes on to name a figure that is just within Rose's budget, even if it's a push. Relief is warm water inside her bones.

'I could definitely manage that,' says Rose.

'Great!' says Ness, tapping both hands on the table at once so her teacup rattles. 'So, what do you do for the police, Rose?'

Rose trots out her usual line about working for a division of the police that deals with compliance and training and it has the usual effect of somewhat disappointing the listener.

'Oh damn,' says Ness, 'I was hoping you were going to be one of the exciting ones, out catching murderers and so on.' Then, hurriedly, 'No offence!'

'None taken,' Rose laughs.

'Where are you living now, I suppose I should ask?' says Ness. 'And why are you moving if it's okay to ask?'

Rose tells her she had to leave the rented house she had grown up in fairly quickly after a new landlord took over and that she was currently renting a room in Highgate.

'Mum and dad not around then?'

'No,' says Rose. 'Just me.'

Sympathy floods Ness's eyes. 'Oh I'm sorry,' she says. 'You're awfully young for that. But tell me, why are you moving from your current place?'

Rose makes a face. 'It's a bit grim,' she says. 'For a start everywhere you go there are ceramic squirrels looking at you, I mean, literally hundreds of them. And secondly, the landlady's son is creepy. I swear he'd be a proper sex pest if he didn't know I'd arrest him on the spot.'

Ness's laughter rings out in the kitchen at this. 'Well,' she gets up from the table, 'I can't promise it's perfect here, but I can assure you I have neither ceramic squirrels nor sex pests. Let me show you around.'

14

As they walk around the vast, comfortable house, Ness offers a running commentary.

'I had my youngest son on that floor,' she says wistfully of the largest of the two bathrooms, which has a claw foot bath in it and pale blue walls. There is a large, framed tube map with jokey names for different lines. 'Hell of a mess, it was.'

They climb the stairs to the third floor. The house is nicer than anywhere Rose has ever lived but there are endearing touches that prevent it from feeling intimidating. In places the paintwork is chipped and Ness keeps apologising for rooms that could do with a 'freshen up', despite Rose's constant murmurs at how lovely it all is.

'This one, though,' says Ness, 'was done up fairly recently so I hope you like it.' She pushes open the wooden door and they step inside. Rose feels something swell inside her.

It's a large bedroom with delicate cream wallpaper that has a fine silver leaf design on it. The floorboards are painted white, and overlaid with a large, soft grey rug. A Chinese screen with a beautiful turquoise and black design is in one corner. There's a chest of drawers and wardrobe, all in slightly distressed white wood and the bed has a wrought-iron brass frame. It's covered with a patchwork quilt that looks homemade.

'It's wonderful,' says Rose. 'I really, really love it.' She's never seen a more beautiful room. She could cry with how lovely it is.

'Oh, jolly good!' Ness sounds genuinely pleased, as if there might be any doubt. 'I thought it might be a bit old-fashioned for modern tastes. It's all minimalist bollocks now isn't it? Now watch your head on that sloping roof. My poor daughter clonked hers on a regular basis.'

Rose walks over to the large dormer window opposite, which looks out over lines of roofs stretching into London.

'She won't be needing the room back at any time?' says Rose, turning back to Ness, who shakes her head, smile dropping momentarily.

'I sincerely hope not. She lives in Canada with her husband.'

'Oh, right.'

'There's another bathroom on this level too,' says Ness. 'It is much smaller than the one below, but perfectly okay for one.'

It's much more plainly decorated but still feels like complete luxury in comparison to the two bathrooms Rose has ever had before.

'It's all perfect,' she says. It's almost hard to breathe with the wanting.

'Look, Rose,' says Ness. Her serious expression makes Rose's hopes dive. But then, 'I like to think I'm a pretty good judge of character and I like you, I may as well say so. I was supposed to be seeing someone else this afternoon, but if your references are all okay, and you're happy to offer a month's deposit, the room is yours.'

Rose walks in a happy daze back down the hill, a feeling like helium in her chest, lifting her up so it seems her feet barely touch the ground. It's an unfamiliar feeling and she realises maybe this is happiness? Normality?

On cue the sun comes out for her and she smiles to herself, thinking about where she is at in comparison to this time a year ago, when the Oakley case happened. She is settling into

UCIT and no longer hankering for her old job, at least, not now she has seen Rowland again and realised nothing was ever going to improve there. Things are okay with Sam again and maybe she really will be able to hang out with him a little now and it won't be weird.

And finally, she has somewhere decent to live. Somewhere without ghosts? Her thoughts are tugged back to Red Hair but she resists, for now. Maybe she'll gather her courage and ask Moony if the woman's appearance rings a bell. It's possible she relates to a case UCIT did before her time. Better still, she'll ask Scarlett. Discreetly.

As she makes her way back towards Highgate, she processes the admin required before moving into the new place. She is on a month's notice from The Squirrels but can't bear to stay that long. Ness says she can move in as soon as she wants, once the deposit and first month's rent have cleared so Rose is going to take the financial hit and simply go. It would be even harder to stay for a month now she has seen the Holy Grail of 107 Amberley Road.

It's a pleasure to anticipate Jimmy's disapproval but if she has paid up, there is nothing he can do. Rose is working things out in her head all the way back to her current abode. The bedroom is so large, there is room for a desk in it, which would be handy if she wanted to do some work in the evenings. The kitchen table from her childhood home might be an ideal size and shape to go under the dormer window. Rose decides to divert to the storage facility where she has kept some items. About time she sorted through all that stuff, especially now she is putting the past behind her. Not least because the price of storage ratchets up after the first two months.

She goes back to The Squirrels and collects her car, which is parked about half a mile from the house as usual. The luxury of a driveway is almost more than she can take, which is all to come.

The storage facility is part of a big chain and based in a

retail park off the North Circular. The car park is almost full with weekend DIY shoppers or people with small children heading into the Sports Direct as Rose heads towards the brightly coloured square block of the building.

Inside, she scans the row of garage-like units with their yellow doors until she finds her number. Rolling the corrugated door up her good mood is slightly pierced for the first time since she left Crouch End. Why did she keep all this stuff? She had been in such a hurry to get out of the house she had grown up in that some of her decision-making had been led more by a desire to get stuff out of her sight than proper planning.

There's a bike she is pretty sure she hasn't used since she was about twelve, a standard lamp she doesn't even like that much but dimly imagined might come in useful in an unfurnished flat, a bunch of kitchen stuff and various boxes that are piled on the kitchen table at the back. Rose finds the table and is relieved to see it does look about the right size for the space in the new place.

She plans to dismantle it so she can get it in her car and has brought along a set of screwdrivers. It's not a large table and with the back seats down in her car, she is hopeful she can fit it in. She will put all the rubbish into bin bags and come back for that later.

She starts lifting boxes down from the top, puffing with the exertion, then snaps open the first bin bag, ready to be filled. The boxes are taped across the top so she uses her car key to slit the binding. Looking inside the first one it's a mix of old trinkets and apparent souvenirs from trips that must have been taken before Rose was born, because she certainly didn't go to Marbella, where the hideous china bull and toreador came from. Without any further ado, Rose pulls everything out of the box and tips it straight into the bin bag. It is a pleasing feeling. But when she gets to the third box, her breath hitches in her throat when she sees what's written on the side in very faint biro.

'Kelly'.

Such had been her haste bringing this stuff here that weekend, she hadn't noticed.

Rose's memories of her mother are so vague she isn't even sure they're real. She has a vague memory of someone who smelled nice reading her a story, but she can't be sure this was actually Kelly at all. Adele used to be so tight-lipped about her own daughter, as though she was too much of an embarrassment to be discussed.

Rose is keenly aware of her thundering heart as she rips open the box. Since James Oakley effectively stopped it with a syringe full of Midazolam, she often feels aware of the red throbbing in her chest that keeps her alive these days.

The first item she finds is a school picture of a girl who looks about six or seven. She is smiling shyly, lips parted enough for the missing front teeth to be visible. Her hair – the same auburn as Rose's own – is in two plaits at the sides of her head. A smattering of freckles dusts her nose, and her eyes are hazel, unlike Rose's blue. Rose finds herself transfixed by this little girl and murmurs, 'What happened to you, Kelly?' out loud before putting it to one side and peering in to see what else is in there.

She lifts out some workbooks that seem to have come from primary school, judging by the looping handwriting practice and scrawled number work. Why on earth did Adele keep these? She never bothered to keep anything from Rose's own childhood, as far as she can tell. Kelly was never spoken of, apart from dismissively as a drug addict who overdosed and ruined her life, which is what Rose had always believed to have happened.

There are a couple of CDs in there – *Now That's What I Call Music! 1988*, and *Dirty Dancing: The Original Soundtrack*. Rose hesitates for a moment before adding them to the bin bag. Next is a battered paperback of *Lace* by Shirley Conran, which looks very well thumbed, then a complicated spotty hairband with a big bow on the top. Very eighties. Into the bin bag. But when she pulls out a scarf in soft lilac wool, she pauses and then, without even deciding to do so, lifts it to her face. Disappointing that there is no smell, but it was unlikely after all that time. She digs further into the box, daring to hope there may be a diary, but instead her fingers find a small circle of plastic.

'Baby Gifford D/O/B 09/09/91.'

Rose is almost winded as she stares down at the band that would once have encircled her own tiny wrist. Who kept it – Adele or Kelly? Someone did. That was the important thing. She swallows hard and puts the wristband into the pocket of her jeans.

At the bottom of the box there's further evidence that she was once loved. First, a pair of bootees in soft green wool. Then some photos. Rose stares at these with such hunger it's as though she is trying to sear the images onto her eyes. Here is a very young and very exhausted looking Kelly holding a newborn Rose in a blanket from a hospital bed. And here is one of Rose aged about two, dressed in a kilt and pink jumper, stout little legs in woolly tights. Kelly is wearing jeans and a black leather jacket and looking down at her daughter, her hair falling around her face. But you can see the indulgent smile curling around her lips.

Almost feverishly now, Rose digs in and pulls out more. Here she is as a baby in Kelly's arms. They're sprawled on a deckchair in what is clearly the back garden of the house she grew up in. Rose is reaching both hands to the air as if she could catch the sky.

She's crying now in great snotty gulps as she runs her fingers over these photos. It had felt all her life that she'd been an inconvenience, first to Kelly, then to Adele. But these pictures surely show she was loved once. It must have been Kelly who kept this box of special things.

There is only one item left now; a long strip of photos from a photo booth. It is face down and on the back Rose reads words written in flourishy handwriting.

Kelly and Orla. Southend.

She turns it over and her blood seems to turn to frozen sludge. For there, laughing next to her mother, is Red Hair.

15

Rose breathes as heavily as if she has been sprinting as she stares down at the strip of photos.

She's here. The woman who has been stalking her and may or may not be dead, is right here in front of her. And she not only knew Kelly, but was evidently a good friend, judging by the obvious warmth between them in these photos.

Kelly's hair is chin length here and bobbed and the other girl's distinctive curls are pulled into an explosive ponytail to the side. They both have sunglasses propped on their heads. The first photo seems to have taken them by surprise. Kelly stares wide-eyed at the camera while Red Hair only has the top of her head captured, evidently reaching for the machine to check it was working. In the others, she can be seen clearly. Her and Kelly stretch their mouths in exaggerated pouts. In the second to last picture, Kelly is blowing a perfect bubble of bubble gum and Red Hair – or, as Rose must now think of her, Orla – is looking at her mischievously. The final one shows Kelly with collapsed gum clinging to her chin and they both appear to be convulsed with laughter.

Rose looks again in the box, in case there is anything else she missed, but no, this is the last photo. She frantically roots through the remaining boxes, but they contain the same sort of Adele-related rubbish as the first one. One is almost entirely filled with a broken lamp. Rose shakes her head in irritation. She had been in such a state to clear the house she had literally chucked boxes into her car. But then, maybe somewhere in her subconscious she hoped to find gold one day. And she has.

Rose's mind churns. She forces herself to go through the motions of sorting the rest of the things and decides to take the bags of rubbish, and the Kelly box now. She can't face trying to dismantle the table and lug it back to the house. Maybe it's better to leave it there another week, until she is in the new place. She feels inexplicably exhausted; so wrung out she can barely haul the stuff back to her car and drive back. When she looks on her phone for the nearest dump, she sees you have to make an appointment and it suddenly feels over-whelming to try and think about this now.

Lifting the one thing she really wants, she leaves the storage unit and makes her way back to the car. Her legs feel like jelly and she badly wants to lie down on her bed and pull the duvet over herself. Preferably in the bed in the new place. But that isn't an option, so she turns on the engine and makes her way back to The Squirrels on autopilot.

Thankfully there's no sign of Jimmy as Rose hurries up the stairs to her room, where she dumps the box and stares at it for a few moments before climbing onto the bed.

She's asleep within minutes.

Rose doesn't dream. It is as though her brain has reached some sort of threshold and is kindly taking time to reboot itself while she naps.

She comes to with the outrageous volume of her ringing phone near her head on the nightstand. Blurrily, she reaches for it, but it has stopped. Sitting up, she can see she has been asleep for an hour. It is now five o'clock There are two messages, both from Scarlett. The first one came this morning; she must have somehow missed it. It is inviting her over for dinner this evening.

The second one is just a plaintive, Pleeeeeeeaaaaase?!

Rose's mouth feels dry and foul after sleeping and she picks up the remains of a glass of water from last night and drinks it down in one go.

She feels tender all over with everything going on. Bigham's request to see her. The red-haired woman – Orla. Her mother.

Loneliness slaps her in a wave. She has spent her whole life avoiding sharing any of this with anyone and where has it got her? She has no partner and while there are several people she calls friends, she has never really let any of them get properly close. This has to be shared. She needs help. And Scarlett may be the perfect, non-judgemental person to do it with.

Sorry she types back. I'd love to come. Send me all the details

Scarlett lives in Loughton. Even though tomorrow is a work day, Scarlett has persuaded her to come by tube so she can have a drink, so Rose gets the Northern Line to Tottenham Court Road, then settles in for the journey out east. Normally, she would read her Kindle or listen to music, but she feels a sense of disconnection from the world around her, barely even paying attention when an argument breaks out between two middle-aged women over the etiquette of where a large suitcase has been placed.

Rose still hasn't decided for certain that she is going to share all this with Scarlett, who she likes very much, but whose wife she has never met. It feels like a leap to go from not even having told people close to her, to sharing it with a stranger.

But from the minute she arrives at the small, brick home in a row of identical houses and Scarlett opens the front door, Rose feels herself relaxing at the unbridled joy on Scarlett's face.

'I'm so excited!' Scarlett says while hugging her hard. 'I've been meaning to do this for ages and ages!' she says. 'And then this morning Maz says to me that she feels like cooking Beef Bourguignon, which takes about a day or something. Felt like something we should share with someone wonderful. I obviously thought of you!'

Rose's cheeks warm. She's not exactly used to this sort of attention. Horrifyingly, emotion wells and she almost squawks in an attempt to hide this.

'Thanks!'

'Anyway,' says Scarlett, giving her a slightly curious look. 'Come meet Maz. And you've been here far too long already without a drink. We're on margaritas. Hope you like them!'

Rose follows Scarlett down the narrow hallway and into a room where a living room leads into a kitchen with an arch of bricks.

Maz is tiny and slight, with short dark hair that forms a tufty peak at the front, and a line of earrings in both ears. She's wearing a Clash band T-shirt and jeans. A tattoo of an angel's wings can just be seen poking out of the back of her T-shirt at the neck. Her eyes are merry and bright as she beams at Rose.

'Hey!' she says. 'I'm chuffed to buggery to meet you finally. Been badgering this one about it for ages.' Her accent is strongly northern to Rose's ears, although she doesn't have the knowledge to narrow it down further. Maz comes over and hugs Rose warmly.

'It's lovely to meet you too!' says Rose, handing over the wine and flowers she has brought with her. 'I believe you're the goddess who keeps us in baked goods at work.'

Maz beams. 'Do me best,' she says. 'Right, you get us all drink, Scar, and we'll be at the table in a few minutes.'

The small living room is cosy, with heavy, flowery curtains drawn closed and dark maroon walls. Some sort of realistic fire dances and flickers behind glass. The round table at the top of the room by the kitchen is set with napkins and cutlery. A circular candle holder with star-shaped sconces sends flickering warm lights across the tablecloth.

A female singer with a soulful voice is on low in the background and the overall effect of being here makes the space between Rose's shoulder blades loosen.

She's quickly handed a large margarita and takes a long sip;

the sharp lime and tequila spreading warmth through her instantly.

The two other women buzz about in the kitchen for a while, gently bickering, while Rose sips her drink.

'Right, I think that's us ready,' says Scarlett after a few moments, coming in with a dish full of crusty bread, warm, judging by the sweet smell wafting from it.

Maz carries over an orange Le Creuset pot, clutched tightly between oven gloves and places it on the table, before beaming at Rose and Scarlett.

'Come on,' she says, 'let's tuck in.'

The food is delicious; tender, falling-apart meat and rich, fragrant sauce. Rose closes her eyes in bliss for a second as she eats.

'See, I told you this one needs feeding,' says Scarlett to Maz.

Rose laughs. 'Is it that obvious? I'm crap at looking after myself . . . '

Scarlett chews her food thoughtfully for a moment before replying. 'No,' she says. 'I just think you put the job first.'

Touched by this, even though it is a little wide of the mark, Rose smiles and takes a sip of her drink, realising it has been refilled at some point without her even noticing.

'Well, this is the kind of looking-after I could get used to,' she says. 'The food is amazing, Maz.'

Maz does a little modest bow with her head.

'So what are your thoughts about the case, then?' says Scarlett.

Rose's eyes flick to Maz and then back. It feels wrong to discuss it in this environment. Scarlett must immediately pick up on this because she says, 'Oh don't worry about Maz. She would never share anything.'

'S'true,' says Maz, through a mouthful of food. 'I'm the only hairdresser in the world who gets asked where they go on holiday, rather than the other way round.'

Rose laughs, partially reassured.

'Yep,' says Scarlett. 'My wife isn't good at small talk and

never gossips, which can be bloody annoying sometimes, frankly.'

'Oi!' Maz grins. 'I don't know why you find it all so fascinating, is all,' she says. 'In my experience, most people are dicks.'

'Fair point,' says Rose. 'And in answer to your question, Scarlett, I have no idea what to think about this case at the moment. Is it even a murder? Are these other deaths in the woods completely unconnected, other than by location? I'm not even certain the doll means anything.' She hesitates. 'Do you know about that?' This is directed at Maz, who nods.

'Scar's way of decompressing from the job is to put all the horrible images into my head instead.'

Scarlett laughs loudly. 'Would you prefer I kept it all inside and let it fuck me right up?'

'Well, no . . . '

'Shut your gob then.' The two women grin at each other. They're clearly besotted and being around them is like sitting near a source of warmth, even despite the slight envy it stirs inside Rose.

'I've been thinking loads about the setting for all this,' says Scarlett, reaching for the jug of margarita and, realising it's now empty, nodding at Maz, who reaches behind to the counter for a bottle of red wine.

'I'm not sure I should have any more on a school night,' says Rose but it lacks conviction. Maz regards her so sceptically, one perfect eyebrow neatly raised, it makes Rose laugh.

'Maybe one then.'

'Attagirl,' says Maz.

'Anyway,' says Scarlett. 'I was reading up on the psychology of woods and forests, just in case it had any bearing, and it was interesting stuff.' She goes on to talk about how these settings are believed to tap into the most primeval parts of ourselves. 'Humans,' she says, 'have evolved to want two fundamental things apparently. We want a sense of refuge, and we want to be able to see ahead to what might be coming at us.

Some academic put it really well. What was it again?' She screws up her forehead in concentration. 'The most comfortable places are where you can see without being eaten and eat without being seen.'

'Blimey,' says Maz. 'Hopefully no one is getting eaten in a North London park.'

'But the thing is,' says Scarlett, on a roll now, 'is that woods are the absolute opposite of that. You don't feel enclosed in a safe way, and you can't really tell what's out there. They bring out all those deep-rooted fears. And let's face it, we've been telling stories about them for years and years, haven't we? I mean, everything from *Little Red Riding Hood* to *The Blair Witch Project*.'

'Frightened the crap out of me, that film,' says Maz, reaching for another slice of bread. Rose has never seen it. She avoids horror films for the reason that there's enough darkness lurking around in real life, thank you very much.

'Anyway,' Scarlett says, earnestly, 'what I was wondering was, is someone trying to make use of the setting?'

'What do you mean?' Rose pauses with her fork halfway to her mouth.

'Well, if you are someone who finds that sort of place spooky, and let's face it, many of us do, maybe you're more primed to react to, I don't know, some attempt to scare you.'

'Do you mean like getting her all spooked and then forcing up that platform?' says Rose.

'Maybe,' says Scarlett. 'I mean, I don't know how. What I mean is, maybe the setting is important because someone is trying to make this look supernatural when it . . . isn't?'

There's a moment of quiet before Maz breaks it with a loud guffaw.

'Blimey,' she says. 'Who are you and what have you done with Scarlett Clark?'

Scarlett laughs and nudges her with her elbow. 'I do try and look for rational explanations first!' she says.

Maz gives Rose a jokey, doubtful look. 'Hmm . . . '

'I really do!' says Scarlett, outraged. 'I just think we need to look beyond them more often, that's all.'

'Which is why you work for UCIT,' says Rose with a smile.

'Which is why I work for UCIT!'

There's a moment of quiet, broken only now by the scraping of forks on plates as everyone eats their last few mouthfuls.

'Enough of this work talk now,' says Maz. 'Who's got room for pudding?'

Scarlett groans and protests.

But Rose is still thinking about what Scarlett said.

Could someone be trying to create a sense of the supernatural around a murder for reasons of their own? But if so, why?

They move away from the table after finding room for a delicate lemon tart, made from the lightest, flakiest pastry Rose has ever eaten. Somehow, another bottle of red has been opened. Rose is on the sofa next to Scarlett; both have their socked feet on the coffee table. Maz is cross-legged like a pixie on a giant, fluffy beanbag that threatens to swallow her whole.

Rose feels cosy and full. She's aware that she has passed her tipping point of thinking about work tomorrow. She can't remember the last time she felt so . . . safe? It's all she can do not to ask if she can move in with the two women right now.

'So, are you still in East Barnet?' says Scarlett.

Rose reaches for her glass of wine, mostly to delay having to respond. Scarlett briefly came into her old home during the Oakley case and although she didn't say anything directly, Rose wondered if she had picked up on Adele's presence.

She takes a deep breath. 'I'm living somewhere else at the moment,' she says. 'But the most brilliant room has come up in Crouch End and I'm moving there soon.'

The delight on Scarlett's face tells Rose everything she needs to know. She fills the two women in on the house and Ness and they make suitably appreciative noises.

Then she swallows. Her mouth is suddenly dry and she's conscious of the alcohol seeping into her bloodstream.

'You, um, came in that time, didn't you,' she says to Scarlett.

It hasn't really been framed as a question, it feels more like opening a door with rusty, stiff hinges.

'Yeah,' says Scarlett. 'I hope you don't mind me saying but it felt . . . off.'

Rose nods. 'It is,' she says very quietly. 'Definitely off.'

To her horror, her eyes suddenly flood with tears. She gulps down some wine, too fast, to try and hide this.

Scarlett and Maz are watching her but with kindness emanating from both faces. Rose knows they're waiting for her to talk.

So she does.

She starts, haltingly at first, with her upbringing. About Adele Gifford, the woman she called Mum, who had no maternal skills at all. About the punters who came and went and finding out exactly what kind of business was being run in more recent times. She tells them about Terrence Bigham. And about his request to see her. At first it feels like forcing the words out and then they come in a flood that surprises even herself.

'Shit,' says Maz. 'That is a lot to deal with.'

Scarlett regards her with a fond expression, but says nothing. Rose struggles to meet her friend's eye because she somehow knows what Scarlett is thinking.

But she can't get this last part out.

She finally looks helplessly at Scarlett, who takes hold of her hand and squeezes it hard.

'So why would you even want to speak to that piece of shit?' says Maz. 'I mean, don't you want to leave it all behind?'

And there it is. Finally. It is time to tell another person about the haunting by Adele and all the unanswered questions choking her life like pondweed.

When she finishes she swipes at the tears coursing down her cheeks. From somewhere tender inside, a harsh laugh rips out of her.

'There you go,' she says. 'That's how crazy I am.'

'Fuck off, are you!' says Maz with such heat that Rose looks

110

at her in surprise. 'Look, I've lived with this one long enough to understand that some people have abilities I don't even understand. And personally, I think it would be bloody awful. I can tell from meeting you just this evening that you're a really top lass with no bullshit about her. So if anything, you have all my sympathies about this . . . whatever the hell it is.'

Rose's voice is stoppered by gratitude for the words of this fierce, kind woman in front of her. No wonder Scarlett adores her.

Scarlett squeezes her hand again. 'Look,' she says, her voice feather soft, 'I can only tell you what my gut feeling is here. Or at least, what I would do if I were in your shoes.'

Apologetically, Rose pulls her hand away to get a tissue from the pocket of her jeans. Blowing her nose loudly, she manages a watery laugh.

'Go on, then,' she says. 'What would you do?'

Scarlett regards her for a moment. 'I'd go to Brixton,' she says. 'Look that bastard Bigham in the eye, and demand some answers.'

16

Rose's hangover is so immense, even her hair follicles hurt. Her eyes are like a pair of boiled sweets that have been sucked to a sticky mess then spat out again.

She's already been sick, and it's only 7.10 a.m..

After her outpouring last night, they somehow moved onto the bottle of tequila. She can't remember much of what they talked about after this, beyond an outrageous story from Maz about an incident in her hometown of Manchester with a rude bouncer and a full pint of Guinness. She dimly remembers her telling Scarlett she loves her and getting a heartfelt reciprocation, then repeating this with Maz. She thinks the evening ended with the three of them putting on YouTube videos of Beyoncé and singing lustily along but she's not exactly sure.

In the morning all Maz manages to say is, 'Fookin' 'ell, someone has used my head as a football.'

Scarlett, on the other hand, is her perky self, offering tea and coffee and humming along to the radio in such a way that it's an actual insult to Rose's aching head.

Maz, sensing Rose's feelings, murmurs, 'My wife's basically a Viking.'

Rose borrows some clean underwear and a toothbrush. The small amount of make-up in her handbag is no match for her face though. They finally pull into the UCIT car park after a journey in which Rose had to plaintively ask Scarlett to stop talking so she could rest her head on the window and stare balefully out in peace.

In the office, she heads straight for the coffee. Only caffeine, painkillers, and sugar are going to get her through this day.

Adam arrives shortly after, looking so healthy Rose almost dislikes him for the first time ever.

He takes one look at her and says, 'Shit, what's up with you?'

'Spent the evening with Scarlett and Maz,' she says, huskily; even speaking hurts right now.

'Ah,' says Adam. 'That explains it. You don't want to go drinking with Scarlett. I learned that the hard way.'

Scarlett's laugh peals across from her desk. 'You're all light-weights,' she says cheerfully. Rose winces at the volume and reaches for the ibuprofen on her desk. Paracetamol alone is not cutting it.

'What you need,' says Adam, 'is a nice trip out. Come on, let's go and relive our schooldays.'

'Ugh,' says Rose, downing the rest of the can full of sugar Coke she picked up on the way. 'You're going to have to drive. My car's at home and anyway, I'm probably still over the bloody limit.'

In Adam's car, which is even less tidy than Rose's, Rose closes her eyes for a little while. She only realises she has fallen asleep when her chin jerks hard onto her chest and her eyes snap open.

Swiping at her mouth and praying she hasn't been drooling, she looks over at Adam, who starts to laugh.

'Feeling better?' he says.

She ponders this while she finds a mint in her handbag. 'Maybe a tiny bit,' she says.

'The big guns of a bacon sandwich are in order,' says Adam. 'We'll have to get one after.'

'Maybe,' says Rose. Food is still a little frightening.

'So why did you head off so early from the party?' says Adam. 'I was surprised you didn't stay longer.'

Rose steals a glance at him. He sounds . . . disappointed? She tells herself sternly not to read anything into this.

'Ah, I just had a bit of a headache,' she says.

Adam smiles. 'But not as bad as today's, I'm guessing.'

She winces. 'Not even in the same universe.'

Woodfields School is one large building with lots of tinted glass and a series of arty sculptures along the walkway to the main entrance.

Inside there is a reception area where a skinny girl in a hijab with a decidedly greenish pallor is sitting with her arms hunched around her knees. Rose regards her nervously. If the girl is sick, she's not convinced she won't follow suit. It could be absolute carnage.

'Mum's on her way, Asma,' says the middle-aged woman with a wide-set, kindly face behind the counter. 'Not long to wait now. If you think you're going to be sick, try and run outside first.' Then, 'How can I help?' to Adam and Rose.

Adam introduces them and says they have made an appointment to see the Deputy Head, a Mr Derek Reynolds.

'No problem,' says the woman with a smile and gets them to sign in and take visitor lanyards.

It's only a couple of minutes until Reynolds appears. Although the mother hasn't arrived yet, poor Asma has managed to keep it together.

Reynolds is a trim man in his fifties with short grey hair, a beard and glasses, wearing suit trousers and a smart shirt and tie. He extends a hand and introduces himself before suggesting they head to his office.

The bright, airy corridors are quiet apart from a few students as they follow him up a staircase and into a small, cluttered room.

'Thanks for seeing us, Mr Reynolds,' says Adam. 'Nice school you have here. My daughters' one looks very shabby in comparison.'

Reynolds looks pleased as he beckons for them to sit at two chairs in front of his desk.

'Please,' he says. 'Call me Derek. And thank you. When I started as a trainee here in the nineties it was a bit of a dump, to be honest,' he says. 'But the whole thing was rebuilt ten years ago and I must say, it's nice having all this light, although it turns into a bit of a greenhouse in the summer with all the glass.' He pauses. 'Now then,' he says, 'I believe you wanted to ask about some students we had in the late nineties. I've checked and all of the students mentioned were here at the same time, according to our records. I only remember Alex Weston though. He was a bit of a cheeky chappie, as I recall. Not bad, but tended to push his luck a bit.'

Rose hesitates. 'I'm afraid I have to tell you that each one of those students is dead; most recently Suzette Armstrong. It's actually her death we're currently investigating.'

Derek sits back in his seat so hard the legs scritch on the floor. He takes off his glasses. 'Oh dear,' he says. 'Oh dear. How? They must have all been only in their thirties now.'

He puts his glasses back on and regards them. His face is a little paler than it was before.

'Well, Ms Armstrong had a fall that may or may not have been an accident,' says Adam. 'Alex Weston was stabbed a few years back, and Haniya Shah drowned after walking on an icy lake. But there's something else we need to mention. All three deaths took place in Elford Country Park.'

'Oh my God,' says Derek. 'That's . . . well, that's very strange and also shocking. I mean, if it had been cancer or car accidents or something it would be a little easier to understand. So you're saying that at least two of them might have been . . . murdered?'

'Yes,' says Adam. 'That is possible. We're wondering if you can help us find out if there is some significance to the location? Or about any connections the three young people had? Were they friends?'

'I don't think I'm going to be able to give you that sort of information because I didn't teach them. I'm the longest serving teacher here too. The location means nothing to me. I mean, I know it's near here but I travel in from Walthamstow every day and don't know much about this area. But look,' he sits back in his chair, 'I know someone who might be able to help here. I'll just be a moment.'

He gets up and hurries out of the office. Adam looks at Rose and nudges her with an elbow.

'Doing okay?' he says. 'There's a waste-paper bin right there if you're going to spew.'

Rose's head has begun to pound again and she can feel a light sheen of sweat has broken out on her skin in a greasy layer. It seems to be unbelievably hot in the room and she just hopes she doesn't reek of tequila.

'I'll bear it in mind,' she murmurs.

They are left for easily fifteen minutes, by which time Rose is almost dropping off.

Derek bustles back into the room, accompanied by a small, rotund black woman with a frosty expression, holding a sheet of paper.

'Sorry we've been a long time,' says Derek. 'This is Glenda, our longest serving member of the support staff. She has an almost encyclopaedic knowledge of this school. I've explained why you are here and she has been to our records room to have a quick dig.'

Glenda greets them with a curt nod. Rose can imagine the short shrift any badly behaved child might get. Even Derek looks a bit scared of her.

'All those students worked on the Elford Park Outreach Project,' she says.

Rose looks at Adam, feeling her pulse quicken. 'What was that?' she says.

'It was a community project where students from the school helped with the construction of the visitor centre in the park. The teacher who ran it was Mr Buckley, but I'm afraid he died about ten years ago. There was a piece in the local paper, which we put in the newsletter at the time. Have a look.'

Rose takes the piece of paper from her. It is headed 'Woodfields School Newsletter November 1998'. There's a short article about the visitor centre being created but it is the photo that now pins Rose's attention and sends a prickle up the back of her neck.

It shows a group of people standing in front of the visitor centre. There's a middle-aged man wearing a body warmer and wellies, with his foot on a spade clutched between gloved hands. Another man is in the shot, hands on his hips and an arrogant bearing about him. It is clearly a younger Malcolm Reece, looking remarkably similar to how he looks now.

He claimed not to know Suzette Armstrong yet he had not only met her before, but the other two people who died in that park.

'So you said the teacher who ran this has passed away?' says Adam. 'Is there anyone else at all who might know about it?'

Glenda shakes her head. 'No, Alan Buckley wasn't married or anything so there is no widow. And it was his pet project in the school, which he pretty much ran alone. That's all I can tell you, I'm afraid.'

'Do you remember him talking about the project?' Rose addresses this to both Glenda and Derek. The latter shakes his head slowly.

'I wasn't especially aware of this at the time, I'm afraid,' he says.

Glenda is frowning; obviously searching her memory. 'I do remember him mumbling something about it being more trouble than it was worth a few times. But he didn't elaborate on why, I'm sorry.'

Rose looks again at the image in front of her. There are two teenage boys and three teenage girls, some standing a little awkwardly, while others smile full beam into the camera.

Underneath, the caption reads: '*Malcolm Reece from the*

117

Elford Heritage Committee, Alan Buckley from Woodfields School and his students: Ryan Brodie, Haniya Shah, Alex Weston, Leah Duffy and Suzette Armstrong.'

Seven people, all linked by this project. And four of them are dead.

'How did Mr Buckley die?' says Adam.

'Oh it was very sad,' says Glenda. 'He had lung cancer.'

Nothing sinister there then.

'Okay well thanks for your time,' says Adam, starting to get up. 'Before we go we'd like to ask if you have any contact details for Leah Duffy and Ryan Brodie?'

'We can only give you very old details of course, but yes that should be easily done,' says Glenda.

'Thanks,' says Adam. 'We'll be needing those immediately.'

'Oh.' Glenda frowns. 'Okay.'

'Thanks,' says Adam. 'As soon as you can.'

Adam's clearly thinking the same thing as Rose. Someone might be picking off the young people in that picture. And if so, the two still alive could be in serious danger.

17

THE DARK HISTORY OF ELFORD PARK
Chapter Two

. . . and so the story of Alice Goode is, sadly, not a unique one. In a time when death patrolled the streets of London every moment of every day, terrible mistakes like this would not have been uncommon and the cost of a human life was low. Why, then, did the story of this ordinary twelve-year-old girl, struck by tragedy in a world where tragedy was commonplace, find its way into popular culture?

Let us examine the facts as we know them, from the limited information available. According to John Marfield's book *Candles: Lighting the Dark Throughout History*, Thomas Goode was a well-known tallow chandler, making candles from the carcasses of animals. It was a low-grade profession, although necessary, but such was the stink that the fashion shifted towards using whale blubber and paraffin wax, as the seventeenth century progressed. Thomas Goode's fortunes, already not great, would have declined too. In June of 1665, Samuel Pepys, that great chronicler of seventeenth-century life wrote, 'I hear that the plague has come to this city.' It wasn't long after that he wrote, 'Great fears of the Sicknesse here in the City, it being said that two or three houses are already shut up. God preserve us all.'

But the only account of what happened to Alice Goode's family comes from a book that was a lesser-known first-hand account of the Great Plague. Matthew Quincey, a physician, wrote his 'Hiftorical Account of the Peftilence' booklet in 1700. (Author note: I have translated the arcane English into readable form.) He talks of a 'family of seven in the Spitalfields area who were taken within a day.' The deceased Goodes were taken to be buried as one but one of the children, known as Alice, was not dead. She was one of many who would be put into a coffin and buried alive, for reasons of great error or belief in preventing contagion, it is not known. Their bodies were carried out to the newest of the burial places north in the environs of Middlesex.

It wasn't until later in the seventeenth century that the nursery rhyme was first noted and is believed to be local to the area that was once part of Middlesex and is now a popular park in the country's capital city.

18

While they wait for the addresses they head back to UCIT to brief Moony on their findings. Rose has gratefully replenished the painkiller level in her bloodstream and drunk more coffee. The screaming headache brought on by last night's debauchery is now more like nagging; not going anywhere today, but no more than a dull ache.

They are all staring at the photo on the whiteboard.

'This is starting to look very interesting now,' says Moony. 'Good work, you two. Three people, who knew each other and spent time at Elford Park, all went on to die under criminal or unusual circumstances in that very location. It strikes me this is more than coincidence. I mean, we could be looking at a potential serial killer here.'

'Agreed,' says Adam, and Rose murmurs her own assent.

'What are we thinking about this Malcolm Reece character, then? I'd love to get him in but we have absolutely no grounds to arrest him. He's going to need to speak to us voluntarily. I guess he could have forgotten but Suzette is a relatively unusual name, surely? I mean, wouldn't you remember if you'd met someone called that?'

'We'll have another word with him,' says Rose. 'In person. I want to see his reaction when we bring this up. And we're just waiting for the last known addresses for Ryan Brodie and

Leah Duffy. Scarlett might track them down first but either way we'll get over there too.'

'Good,' says Moony, a gleam in her eye. 'I think you need to have a word with them both just in case someone, for whatever reason, is targeting people from that project. But before you go, there's something else. We've had the reports back from Tech on Suzette Armstrong's laptop and had a long phone conversation about it. And it was absolutely riddled with something called Ratware.'

'Bloody hell, what's that when it's at home?' says Adam.

'It's a very nasty type of malware,' says Moony. 'Basically, someone planted a ton of spying software on her computer. They were pretty much in control of her life.'

'Wait,' says Rose, sitting up straighter on the sofa. 'So all the stuff that was supposedly happening to her could have been done by someone else?'

'It absolutely could,' says Moony. 'It's sophisticated stuff. But some of it was relatively low tech. For example, look at this.'

A picture appears on the screen of a Twitter account. It's called @SuzettA and shows a close up of Suzette Armstrong, apparently on a beach in big sunglasses, with a wide smile showing white teeth.

'This is her real account,' says Moony and scrolls down. 'She posted a little bit about mainstream political stuff; telly programmes, complaints to big companies about service issues. The usual sort of thing you see on this site, which I've never really got, incidentally. Always feels like a bunch of idiots shouting at each other.' She gives a dismissive sniff. 'Anyway, I digress. Once our people understood what was going on, they went looking on social media and this is what they found.'

She clicks to another slide. It looks almost identical.

'Isn't that the same account?' says Adam, frowning.

'That's what you're supposed to think,' says Moony, clicking again. 'But look, here are the two usernames together.'

The screen shows @SuzettA and @SuzetTA side by side.

'Wow, you wouldn't notice that difference would you?' says Rose.

'You certainly wouldn't,' says Moony. 'And if followers of her old account are all followed by this new one, then messaged to say she has had to switch to a new account, she wouldn't even know. And if that account starts retweeting gently unsavoury or controversial Tweets, which this one does, after a while she is going to lose friends.'

'But wouldn't people say something?' says Rose.

'They might,' says Moony. 'But when it's done subtly like this, most people would simply think, "I didn't know she held those sort of views" and gently move away. And the victim might never even know about this other account.'

'Wow,' says Rose. 'That's pretty clever when you think about it.'

'It is,' says Moony. 'And when someone wants to take it up several notches there is even more serious damage that can be done. And was done here. I'm talking about a nasty piece of malware called a key logger.'

Moony goes on to describe how Suzette Armstrong's entire life online was visible to a hacker. Key stroke logging, she explains is where a piece of buried malware literally records every single line of text typed by a victim. 'So it completely bypasses the security you might have for say, bank details or anything else that, because the breach happens from the moment you touch the keys. It also reveals every single word that you might write in a diary, or privately to a friend.'

'And someone did this to Suzette Armstrong?' says Rose.

'Yep,' says Moony. 'But working out exactly what damage was done is too big a job. All we can say is that someone, somewhere, decided to mess with this woman's life.'

'So someone was out to get her,' says Adam, 'even if they didn't have anything to do with her death.'

'Yes,' says Moony. 'And I'd like to know who that is. Speak to her husband and contacts again please. And I doubt this is possible but see if you can get hold of the computers of Alex

123

Weston and Haniya Shah. I'd be extremely interested to know if they too had anything like this nastily bubbling away without them realising.'

'Already asked,' says Rose. 'And it's a no-go on getting their gear.'

'Hmm, shame,' says Moony. 'One thing's for sure,' she adds, still staring at the whiteboard. 'Sophisticated computer hacking is very much the remit of the real world,' she says. 'There is a flesh and blood human behind all this.'

Malcolm Reece's face visibly falls when he opens the door and sees the two police officers outside.

'Oh,' he says. 'You're back.'

'We are,' says Adam with a friendly smile. 'Is it okay if we grab another five minutes of your time?'

'Well, we're having lunch,' says Reece. 'It's not really convenient right now.'

'We could do it at the station later if you'd prefer?' says Rose. They can't make him go without arresting him so she is relying on the fact that he might not realise this.

He lets out a laboured sigh. 'Okay, if you must, come in then.' He holds the door back and they enter the hallway, which smells strongly of some sort of dish with a whiff of the school dinners about it.

'Come to the kitchen,' he says and leads them into an old-fashioned kitchen with lots of brown tiles and a vast pale Aga.

There is a round table with one leaf flattened against the wall and sitting there is a rather startling looking woman in perhaps her fifties or older. She is very thin with whitish-grey hair that hangs almost to her waist and she's wearing a thick, quilted dressing gown. In her hand a spoon is poised halfway between a bowl of brown soup and her mouth. Her wrist looks thin enough to snap with the effort. She regards the new arrivals with large, very pale blue eyes.

'This is Mary, my wife,' says Reece. 'Mary, these are the

police officers I told you about, who are looking into that woman's fall at the weekend. You know, I mentioned it?'

'Hello,' says Rose, attempting a smile, even though the woman's almost unblinking gaze and overall demeanour are quite unnerving. Her eyes are two lamps fixed especially on Rose. 'We're sorry to disturb your lunch but we won't take long, I promise.'

'Where are your manners, Malcolm?' she says in a voice that sounds like it could be carried away by the slightest breeze. She has the slight trace of an American accent. 'You haven't offered the police officers a drink or a seat.'

'Sorry, sorry,' says Reece, looking oddly flustered. 'Please sit. Can I get anyone tea? Coffee?'

'No, no, we're fine, but thank you,' says Adam, taking a seat.

Reece slides into the chair by Mary, but his whole body appears tense, as though he might leap up at any moment.

'We just wanted to ask you again whether you recognised the name of the woman who died on Saturday,' says Rose to Reece. 'She was called Suzette Armstrong.'

Reece seems to make a show of thinking about this but the pinkish tinge to his cheeks betrays him.

Mary is staring at her husband, her lips slightly apart. A small pink tongue flicks across her dry lips.

'No, no. I don't think so,' says Reece.

Adam produces a photocopy of the school newsletter. 'It's just that you met twenty years ago, Mr Reece. Look.' He places it in front of Reece, who looks at it for far too long.

'Ah,' he says eventually. 'I had no idea. That was a long time ago. So she was this young woman here, yes?' He points to the smiling Suzette in the photo.

'That's right,' says Adam.

Mary is still staring at her husband.

'I only vaguely remember the schoolchildren,' says Reece. 'They weren't involved in the visitor centre project for very long.' He glances at his wife.

'Malcolm enjoys helping young people,' she says. Reece shoots her a quick look. It's an oddly jarring thing to say and everyone else appears momentarily thrown before Adam breaks the silence.

'So just to confirm, you can't remember anything specific about these young people even though they were here, according to the school records, for two weeks from the end of October to the second week in November in 1998?'

'I'm not saying I don't remember anything about them,' says Reece testily. 'I mean, I remember that they spent most of the time mucking about. I don't think any of them really had any interest in history or conservation. I basically left it up to their teacher to control them and got on with my own work.'

'What sort of mucking about?' says Rose.

Reece frowns. 'Oh just general teenage tomfoolery,' he says. 'Sitting around chatting and larking about. I mostly ignored them.'

'Mr Reece,' says Rose, 'it's not only Ms Armstrong who is no longer around. We need to tell you that two of the other young people pictured there have died in unnatural circumstances.'

Reece looks at his wife, who stares back at him.

'We're not exactly sure whether these deaths are linked,' Adam continues. 'But if they are, and if someone is targeting this particular group, then there has to be a possibility that you too might be in some sort of danger.'

Reece is silent for a moment then lets out a sound that is almost a guffaw.

'Danger?' he says. 'I assure you I'm not going to be doing any climbing of trees.'

'We can't really be more specific at this time but I'd advise you to check your computers and phone. Ms Armstrong was the victim of a vicious hacking campaign before she died and it would be advisable to be aware of this. Just be wary, okay?'

Reece nods, looking confused. Mary is now robotically eating the horrible-smelling meaty soup with tiny slurps, as if they aren't there. She seems to be in a world entirely of her own.

'What was the nature of your work for the visitor centre, Mr Reece?' says Adam. Reece's shoulders seem to lower slightly at the question, and relief at the topic change takes over his expression.

'It was a special display on the folklore of the park,' he says. 'It's a bit of a hobby of mine; the unusual history of this place.'

'What's so unusual about this park?' says Adam.

Reece sits forward, eyes bright. 'Well, for example,' he says, 'did you know there's believed to be a plague pit in the woods? You can find the spot by an ancient hornbeam tree, which is in itself something notable. There are all sorts of things here, including a bunker from the Cold War, which has been boarded over now because the council are too lazy to make a feature of it. But there is so much history here.'

'We read about the Alice Goode story,' says Rose.

Reece regards her with new interest. 'Oh yes, that was a big part of it all. It's a fascinating legend and—'

'Some say she is the custodian of these woods,' says Mary, interrupting him.

They all turn to look at her.

'And that she still wanders here, protecting us all.'

No one, not even Reece, seems quite sure how to respond to this.

Then Mary speaks again, turning the great orbs of her eyes upon her husband. 'I'm not feeling well, Malcolm,' she says, suddenly sounding like a little girl.

Rose and Adam exchange glances.

'I'm sorry,' says Reece. 'But I think we will need to get on with our afternoon now.'

'We'll leave you to it then,' says Rose, getting to her feet. 'Thanks for your time. I think we left you contact details last night, so don't hesitate to get in touch if you feel worried about anything, or you think of any further information from working with the Woodfields students, okay?'

Outside, Adam is already walking away when Rose, still by the door, stops and hisses, 'Wait!'

She can hear raised voices inside the cottage but, frustratingly, no actual words.

Adam watches, a curious look on his face. 'What are you doing ?' he says quietly.

She raises a hand to silence him but simultaneously, all goes quiet inside the cottage. Walking over to catch up with Adam, she murmurs, 'I have a feeling our visit has caused ructions at *Casa Reece*. I could hear them going at it in there.'

'What were they arguing about?'

Rose shakes her head in frustration. 'I couldn't make out a word.'

'Hmm,' says Adam, as they start to walk back to the car. 'That's interesting. Especially because we've just been comprehensively lied to.'

'Yep,' says Rose. 'I think he remembers those kids very well.'

'So do I,' says Adam. 'But for now, let's go speak to the two still standing, shall we?'

Leah Duffy's last address is a grey pebble dash, semi-detached house only minutes away by car from Elford Country Park.

They knock on number seventy-two and after a few moments a woman in her fifties opens the door and regards them suspiciously. She is plump and tired-looking, with greyish blonde hair and watery blue eyes. A drab beige cardigan sits over a faded T-shirt. In the background a dog gives a single shrill bark.

'Hello?' she says, blinking as though she has been asleep. 'Can I help you?'

'We're sorry to bother you,' says Adam. 'We're looking for Leah Duffy?'

The woman blinks several times, as though warding off a wave of emotion.

'I'm afraid that won't be possible,' she says, her eyes darting from Rose to Adam and back again. 'Who are you?'

Adam introduces them and says they are carrying out some background investigation into the death of a woman who went to school with Leah and simply wanted to ask her a few questions.

The woman takes a second before replying. 'Well, I'm afraid my daughter's no longer around. She passed away eleven years ago.'

Rose can feel Adam dart a quick look at her, but she keeps her gaze ahead.

'I'm so sorry to hear that,' she says. 'Am I speaking to Mrs Duffy?'

'It's Ms Duffy,' says the woman, a little softer now. 'Sandra. You can call me Sandra, but why are you asking about my Leah?'

'Is there any chance we could come in for a few minutes, Sandra?' says Rose. 'It really would be a help and we promise not to take up too much of your time.'

Sandra gives a little shrug. 'No problem,' she says. 'I'm on holiday anyway. I was having a sleep, which probably isn't a great thing in the day.'

'That sounds nice,' says Adam as they follow her down a hallway painted in magnolia. 'Who do you work for?'

She names a large, well-known shop. 'I hadn't really booked to do anything, but I was owed a bunch of holiday,' she says, 'so I thought I'd just use it to catch up on some stuff. Please, come and sit down.'

They go into a medium-sized kitchen with a round table that has a fruit bowl containing a single banana. It's neat and tidy, with matching tea, coffee and sugar containers on a surface. A small black dog with one white ear lies curled like a comma in a basket by the back door. It raises its head before giving two thumps of its tail and going back to sleep.

'Good boy,' says Sandra fondly, then, 'right, please take a seat.'

They all sit at the table. There's a packet of cigarettes on it. A radio plays a middle-of-the-road classic in the background and it's otherwise so quiet, a clock above the sink seems to tick loudly.

Rose's impression is of a self-contained space; a little colourless and sad. But then she thinks about her own current abode and can see this would be a palace to have on her own.

'Thanks for this,' says Adam. 'As we mentioned, we're looking into a death that happened at the climbing centre in Elford Park at the weekend. Did you hear about it?'

'I did!' she says with a shudder. 'I was away visiting my auntie in Norfolk at the weekend and one of my neighbours told me about it. I don't really understand what happened though. I've always had the horrors about the thought of those climbing places. You wouldn't catch me doing it, but I'm not sure if that's how she died?'

'We're still getting to the bottom of it all,' says Rose, sidestepping her curiosity. 'The woman's name, if you don't already know, is Suzette Armstrong. Does that ring any bells?'

Sandra stares at her, eyes widened. 'Should it?'

'It turns out she went to school with your daughter,' says Rose.

'Oh blimey,' says Sandra, frowning. 'It was such a long time ago.'

'What about these names?' says Adam and then reels off the other three in the photo.

'I remember Haniya,' she says with a smile. 'She was a nice girl and Leah was quite friendly with her. I vaguely remember an Alex? But as I say, it really was a long time ago.'

'Would you mind if we asked how your daughter passed away?' says Rose.

Sandra gives a small, pained smile and lowers her gaze. 'It's okay,' she says. 'It was her heart.'

When she raises her eyes again, it's clear that saying these words cost her every time. Her expression is filled with pain, regret and something else that is almost a bit defiant.

'We're so sorry,' says Rose. 'That must have been incredibly difficult.'

'Yes, it was,' says Sandra. 'And, well, she was a troubled soul, my daughter. Just couldn't really cope with the world, you know?'

'We do,' says Adam. 'Unfortunately, we see that a lot in our job.'

'I bet.'

'Is it okay if we show you something?' says Rose and brings up her phone to show Sandra the picture from the local paper.

Sandra laughs, her expression momentarily soft. 'I do remember that!' she says. 'I think it was a great treat to be allowed out of school. But Leah was mortified to be in the paper!'

'So you don't remember whether she was close friends with these people here?' Rose continues.

Sandra shakes her head. 'No,' she says. 'Not as far as I know. But the truth is that we weren't super close then and she didn't tell me a lot. She was at that secretive age, you know?'

'The unusual thing about this, Sandra,' says Rose, 'is that as far as we know, only one of the young people here is still alive.'

Sandra's head jerks up at this. 'Really? That's awful. Even *Haniya*?'

'Yes, even Haniya,' says Adam.

'How?' Sandra's hand is at her mouth. 'What happened to her?'

'She had an apparent accident at the park,' says Adam. 'Two of the people here had accidents there and one, Alex Weston, was murdered. We're trying to work out whether these deaths are in any way connected beyond their location.'

Sandra pulls the sides of her cardigan together, as though a chill has passed through her. 'That's very sad,' she says. 'Really terrible news. I thought Leah would have been the only one.' Then, in a quieter voice, with a visible shiver, 'It's almost like, Christ, that year group was cursed or something.'

'Interesting choice of words,' Adam murmurs as they get into the car five minutes later.

'Yeah,' says Rose.

They're silent for a few moments before Rose speaks again. 'But you know what?' He looks over at her. 'While I'm prepared to think outside the box in this job,' she says, 'I think actual curses might be a bridge too far.'

'Me too,' says Adam.

Rose starts the engine. 'Tell you what, I'm interested to speak to the only Woodfields student in that picture who's still alive, that's for sure.'

'Me too,' says Adam. 'Let's go find this Ryan Brodie.'

19

But as they are getting into the car, Rose's phone rings. She answers it.

'Is that DC Gifford?'

'Speaking.'

'It's Josh Simmons here. We met the other day?'

'Hi Josh,' says Rose, looking at Adam and raising an eyebrow. 'What can I do for you?'

'I'm not sure if this is something I should be bothering you with or not . . . ' He sounds uncertain.

'Why don't you tell me?' says Rose. 'Honestly, it's fine to get in touch.'

'Okay,' says Josh. 'It's just that we had a bit of an incident earlier on.'

'What happened?'

'Well this lady had been quite nervous about doing the course and it took a lot to get her up there. Then she was about to go on the zip wire at the end of site five and she looked down. This bloke walking past on the ground did a sort of broken neck, hanging gesture at her. Do you know what I mean?'

'Yes, I think I do,' says Rose.

'It really upset her, anyway,' says Josh. 'She wouldn't come down and got a bit hysterical.'

'Do you know who this person was?' says Rose. 'The guy

who did the gesture? It wasn't Malcolm Reece, by any chance?'

'I've no idea,' says Josh. 'We were too busy trying to calm her down and get her off there. But I have her number from the booking details if you want to speak to her?'

Rose hesitates for a moment and then asks for the number, which she writes down, plus the exact time it happened.

'Honestly, though,' says Josh, his voice full of frustration. 'This is the last thing we need. Customer numbers have dropped off a cliff since . . . since what happened. People seem to be spooked now, like her death had something to do with us.'

'What was that about?' says Adam when her conversation is over.

'Apparently someone did this,' Rose demonstrates what Josh described, 'to a nervous customer. Probably someone with a sick sense of humour. I'd like to know if it was our Mr Reece up to his tricks.' She pauses. 'And if not, who else feels the need to spook the customers of Crazy Climbz.'

However, that proves to be slightly harder than they'd hoped. There is no sign of anyone at his parent's house, nor at the address Scarlett manages to get a little later with further digging.

It turns out that Ryan Brodie is a man who spends a good deal of time on social media. He enjoys taking selfies, particularly if he can get his naked, gleaming torso into them.

'God, look at the state of him,' says Rose, looking over Scarlett's shoulder at an image of him on Instagram that has made Scarlett giggle for a solid minute. He has his head back and his lips parted as though in ecstasy, eyes closed, and his hands gently tugging down the top of his shorts, revealing a tanned stomach so honed it has its own complex topology.

'Nothing?' says Scarlett mischievously, looking up at Rose. 'I mean, I have a good excuse.'

'Nope,' says Rose, popping a Quaver into her mouth and crunching loudly. 'He looks like a right plonker.'

'Right, well, in addition to being a model and personal

trainer,' says Scarlett, 'it looks as though he works at this bar here.'

She points to a picture of him behind the bar while a pair of blonde glamazons take a selfie from the other side.

'Good work,' says Rose. 'What time do they open?'

'Six,' says Scarlett.

'Right, we're there.'

At five thirty, Rose and Adam wait outside a bar called Rodeo Drive, near Turnpike Lane on Green Lanes.

They ring the bell.

A middle-aged woman with close-cropped white-blonde hair and tarantula lashes opens a window and informs them they're closed.

'We're police,' says Adam. 'Nothing to worry about but we're looking for one of your barmen, Ryan Brodie? Is he here?'

Her eyes scoot between Rose and Adam and then back again.

'Has he done something?' she says, her accent hard to define. 'Because he's on a warning for timekeeping and if he has . . .'

'No, nothing like that,' says Rose. 'It's just an enquiry about a case. We won't take too much of his time.'

The woman sighs heavily and then disappears into the gloom before there are sounds of bolts and locks being released on the other side.

'Come on in,' she says. 'He's in the downstairs bar. You can go down.'

The bar relies on a good deal of red velvet curtain on the inside and has a shabby look at this time of the day. They walk down a staircase and into a smaller bar, where a lingering smell of sweat and beer hangs in the air.

Ryan Brodie is standing behind the bar, staring into his phone. He has thick wavy black hair that's swept back from his forehead, a beard and bright blue eyes in a tanned face.

'We're not open yet,' he says, unsmiling.

'It's okay,' says Rose. 'We're not here for a drink; we're

police. We just wanted to have a quick word with you if that's okay?'

Brodie's eyes do a little dart towards the stairs behind them, as though he might suddenly bolt away. 'Why?' he says.

'We'll explain,' says Adam, with a pleasant smile that isn't returned. 'We're speaking to Ryan Brodie, yes?'

'That's right.'

'This is a strange sort of enquiry,' says Adam. 'But can I show you a photo?'

Brodie nods briskly, suspicion bristling off him.

Adam shows him the picture from the local paper on his phone. Both Rose and Adam watch his reaction closely. His eyes stay fixed on the picture as though he is trying to place it but his Adam's apple bobs hard in his throat.

'Do you remember that?' says Adam, still watching his face.

'Yeah,' says Brodie. 'It was something I did at school. Can't remember much about it. Why are you asking?'

'Do you remember this person here – Suzette Armstrong?'

'Maybe,' says Brodie, now fixing his eyes firmly away from the photo on Adam's phone.

'Well, I'm sorry to report that she died at the weekend,' says Rose.

For a moment he is absolutely still. 'Shit,' he says. 'Really? Suze is dead?' His eyes are wide and he looks almost winded by this news.

'You do remember her then?' says Adam. 'Because you sounded like you weren't sure before?'

This earns him a filthy look.

'Yeah, I remember her now,' says Brodie. 'We hung out a bit.' He seems to have regained his composure and stands a little taller. 'What happened to her?'

'She fell, or was pushed, from a twenty-metre platform at a treetop climbing centre,' says Rose, then, watching Brodie carefully, adds, 'in Elford Park, weirdly enough, where this photo was taken.'

Brodie looks as though he's going to say something, but seems to stop himself, licking his lips before replying.

'That's awful,' he says. 'I'm sorry to hear it.' He wipes his hands semi surreptitiously on his muscled thighs and licks his lips once again.

'Yes, her family are devastated, as you can imagine,' says Adam. 'But the weird thing is, that you're the only surviving student in that photo, which seems extraordinary for people so young.'

Brodie stares at Adam. 'Is that right?' he says after a few moments. 'That's really weird.'

'Isn't it?' says Rose. 'Only one person on here was murdered as far as we know. Alex Weston? Do you remember him?'

Brodie nods. 'I did actually hear something about Alex,' he mumbles.

'Right,' says Rose. 'But Haniya Shah and Suzette Armstrong both then died in ways that raise questions.'

'We just wanted to know if there was anything at all you could tell us that could shed any light on that, Mr Brodie? Anything at all?'

Brodie clears his throat loudly then shakes his head. 'I really have no idea at all what might be going on there,' he says. 'I'm sorry I can't help.'

Rose and Adam regard him for a moment longer. The shutters are not so much down as welded shut.

'Sure? Anything at all, even if you think it seems unimportant?' says Rose.

Brodie shakes his head. 'No,' he says. 'Can't help. Sorry.'

He doesn't look sorry. He looks as though he can't wait for them to leave.

'One final thing, if we can trouble you,' says Adam and flicks to another photo on his phone, which he then holds up to show Brodie.

Brodie frowns, suspicious, then reluctantly drags his eyes to the screen.

The effect is instantaneous. The light caramel of his fake

tan seems to grey. His eyes widen and he breathes out one quick huff of air, not a sigh, not a gasp, but something in between.

'What the fuck's that?' he says, his voice a little strangulated.

'Two of the people who died had these twig dolls on or about them, which we thought was a bit strange. Does it mean anything to you at all?'

Brodie shakes his head, briskly but his eyes are wide.

'Not a thing, sorry.'

'Are you sure,' says Adam. 'Do you want to take another look? Only because it seemed as though you reacted to that picture?'

'I'm sure.' Steely now. 'Only reason I looked like that was because whatever that is is as creepy as fuck, that's all. I don't know why you're showing me. I haven't done anything wrong. I know my rights. I don't even have to have this conversation with you, so I'd like to get on with my job now.'

'Mr Brodie,' says Rose, her tone more serious now, 'we think you might be in danger. We don't understand why, but if you do . . . well, sharing that information with us could help us to protect you and sort all this out.'

Brodie's chest, tightly enclosed in a bright white T-shirt is rising and falling rapidly.

'You seem a bit distressed,' says Adam. 'We do want to help. Why don't you tell us what this is all about and we can help.'

But Brodie is somehow pulling himself together right in front of them and the gaze he gives Adam is unflinching.

'I'm alright,' he says. 'I can look after myself.'

Rose and Adam share a look. This isn't going anywhere, clearly.

'Now if you'll excuse me . . . '

'We'll leave you our details, if that's okay,' says Rose. 'In case you think of anything?' She slides a contact card across the bar and Brodie's eyes flick to it and then back up again.

'We'll let you get on,' says Adam. 'But Mr Brodie?' Brodie

looks at him. 'We suggest that if someone contacts you and asks to meet in Elford Park, you give us a ring first, yeah?'

Brodie's Adam's apple bobs again in his throat like a cork in water. He doesn't reply. For one brief moment, something very much like terror flashes in his eyes.

20

Outside, Adam lets out a low whistle. 'Wow,' he says. 'What the hell happened in there?'

'I think we just frightened the shit out of that guy,' says Rose.

They get back into the car.

'I know,' says Adam. 'He was seriously spooked. When he saw the twig doll, I thought the big man was actually going to cry. And he clearly knew Suzette Armstrong too.'

'Tell you what,' says Rose, starting the engine and pulling away from the side of the road. 'I think we should keep an eye on him, don't you?'

'Yep,' Adam is already tapping at his screen. 'On it.'

Rose calls Rowland once they get back to UCIT and gives her a long and full update on where they are.

'Thanks,' says the other woman after a brief silence. 'I'm going to push for fast authorisation on the phone observation for Ryan Brodie and let me know if there is anything else you need. I think this man might be in serious danger, even though I don't understand how any of this fits together.'

'Neither do we yet,' says Rose. 'But we're working on it.'

The rest of the afternoon is spent pounding the phones but they don't get much further forward.

Neither Rufus Armstrong, nor Suzette's close contacts, have any insights into who may have maliciously planted the software on her laptop. Rufus had been quiet for a few moments after Rose described what they had found, and she realised he was crying. She waited it out until he was able to speak again.

'All those times,' he finally said, in a thick voice. 'I moaned at her for buying shit online, it's possible that was someone else?'

'It is possible, yes,' Rose says.

'I accused her of being a drunk once,' he said, very quietly now. 'That she couldn't remember buying twelve bottles of champagne we didn't need, or a dress she didn't even like. I didn't believe her.'

'Can you think of anyone at all, even in your wider circle,' says Rose, 'who has the kind of job or background that would make this kind of technical thuggery possible? Any tech experts at all?'

But the answer was no. They mainly, it seems, knew people working as journalists, PR professionals or lawyers. No one with a techie background. And it isn't, according to what they have seen in the report, the kind of thing someone can do from consulting YouTube.

The team have also been ploughing through the general registry docket for the Weston murder. This is the file containing all the interview notes on the case and other paperwork. Nothing seems to chime with this case though, other than the location of the death.

The tiring work isn't helped by Rose's hangover, which is of the variety that comes with a second wave in the afternoon.

Sneaking a glance around the office to check no one is looking, she briefly lowers her head into her hands and gives a barely perceptible groan. Staying like this for a few moments, it's all she can do not to drop off.

'Psst!' Scarlett is by her desk. She places a packet of Maltesers in front of Rose.

'What the hell have you done to me, Scarlett?' says Rose. 'I'm not sure the damage can be undone by Maltesers.'

'You're welcome,' says Scarlett with a grin. 'But hey . . . ' She gives a quick glance around and then lowers her head closer to Rose. 'That thing we discussed,' she says. 'About a certain person in prison?'

Rose feels her chest whump with stress at the memory of letting all this spill out. 'Oh that,' she says.

'Yes, that!' says Scarlett, emphatically now. 'I have a feeling that you aren't going to act on it and I want to make sure you do it. It's now or never, Rose.'

'God,' says Rose. 'I wish I'd never told you now.'

'Well, that's as maybe,' says Scarlett, 'but I think you should put the request in right now, while I'm standing here, before you lose your courage.'

'You're so bossy!' Rose manages to laugh, even though this whole conversation makes the pain in her head worse.

'It has been said,' says Scarlett, before tapping the table with her finger for emphasis. 'But I promised Maz this morning that I'd badger you about this so you'd better get on with it.'

'Alright!' says Rose. 'Alright! You're not going to shut up about it otherwise, are you?'

'You'd better believe it, sistah,' says Scarlett with a wink before finally going back to her side of the office.

Rose stares blankly at her screen, lost in thought. The thought of seeing Bigham makes her sick in her stomach. But Scarlett is right.

It's now or never. With a resigned sigh, she opens a new email. The quickest thing is to organise a legal visit, but she needs an inspector's authorisation for that. She's going to have to go back to Stella Rowland and make something up about remembering Bigham after all.

Rose winces. This just gets better.

Adam interrupts her thoughts. 'Hey, look at this,' he says.

Rose and Moony go over. Adam's screen shows the cell site information for Ryan Brodie.

'Thought I'd just have a little look at where our Mr Brodie is at,' he says. 'And look . . . look at the towers he's pinging. Here, here and here.'

'Wait!' says Rose, 'Is that . . . ?'

'Right in the middle of that space is Elford Park.'

Rose feels a lift of excitement in her stomach. 'When he was meant to be starting a shift?'

'He's gone to the woods,' says Adam. 'Now why on earth would he do that?'

'I don't know,' says Moony, who is listening in, eyes bright. 'But get over there right now. He might be in danger.'

'But we're talking about the biggest woods in London,' says Adam. 'How can we find his exact location?'

'We can check ANPR for his car,' says Rose. 'Unless he's on foot, we might be able to see where he parked.'

They quickly find that Brodie has passed a camera on the north side of the park, close to an entrance they haven't seen before.

'God,' says Rose, as they get out of the car into icy rain. 'Why was this a good idea again?' She is wearing a waterproof coat, but it isn't that warm and she immediately begins to shiver.

Adam grimaces and pulls the hood of his jacket over his head. 'If it's any consolation,' he says, gesturing across the small car park to the only other vehicle here, a white Range Rover, 'that's definitely his car, according to the info Scar has sent over.'

'Let's go,' says Rose, chafing at her arms, her cheeks already starting to tingle with the cold air. 'I suppose we just have to look now.'

They follow the narrow, rough track, careful not to trip on raised roots that would be easy to miss at night. The trees seem even more imposing than in daylight; towering and crowding around them. The light from their torches catches tree trunks that flash bone white. Rose's shoulders hunch inside her coat as the rain drums down but it's not only the weather that makes her want to draw in; to protect herself. She wonders what it is about woods, that bring out these childish fears? Every scritch and scratch sounds menacing. Like a thing that wants to eat you up. Stop it, she tells herself, almost wanting to laugh at where her imagination is taking her. Now and then they catch the bright orbs of watchful animal eyes in the darkness. Rose has to fight the odd feeling she had before, of being watched. It's probably just the atmosphere, she tells herself, but her eyes dart constantly around her, her body tensed.

They keep going on through the miserable rain until Adam stops and puts a hand out to halt her movement.

'I can hear something,' he whispers. 'Let's turn these off and try and go quietly.'

They creep forwards, relying only on the little bit of moonlight peeking through a cloud like lace on black velvet until they can see a man – Ryan Brodie – sitting on the cut-off trunk of a tree. He is drinking from a bottle of what looks like some sort of spirit and muttering to himself.

Then he gets to his feet in a rush and says, 'Fuck it, fuck it, fuck it,' before turning his back on them and heading off into the trees.

They follow, making more noise now, but Brodie doesn't seem to notice as he squats down low to the ground.

'I think we go in,' murmurs Adam.

'Wait.' Rose stops him with her hand. 'Let's see what he does.'

Brodie has completely disappeared from sight.

It's disconcerting and a little surreal; as if the woods have simply swallowed him up. Rain drums a steady rhythm on Rose's hood and her heart pounds. She can't feel her toes but forces herself forwards as Brodie emerges, carrying something they can't see properly.

When it comes into focus, Rose's throat constricts.

'That's it!' says Adam. 'Let's go!'

They run over, shouting Brodie's name, and he looks up with a wild cry.

He is soaked through and panting. His face has streaks of dirt on it and he makes a stricken sort of sound in his throat as he drops the thing he's holding onto the ground before falling to his knees and cradling his head in his hands.

21

Horror rises in Rose and she covers her hand with her mouth.

It looks, at first, like the remains of a child, wrapped in old cloth. But as she forces her feet forward, her brain immediately rearranges what she is looking at into a different picture.

It's a child-sized doll made from branches, twigs and cloth. Wrapped in its makeshift shroud, it appears to be wearing a stained apron and a cap made from once-white cloth. It's both faceless and unnervingly human.

'What the hell is that, Mr Brodie?' says Rose a little breathlessly.

Brodie says something through his fingers.

'What did you say?'

His head snaps up. His eyes are hard and his expression closed-down, even though he is visibly trembling all over.

'Nothing,' he says. 'I didn't say nothing.'

'I think you did say something,' says Adam. 'I distinctly heard the words "making it stop". Making what stop? Did someone tell you to come here?'

Brodie gets to his feet. Despite his rather pathetic and bedraggled state, he now radiates belligerence.

Rose takes a step towards him. 'This is serious, Mr Brodie,' she says, trying to stop her voice from shaking with the cold that feels like it has eaten into her bones. 'We need to know if we're dealing with multiple murders connected to these woods and for your own safety, you need to tell us what's going on.'

'Arrest me then,' says Brodie, chin lifted.

Rose exchanges a look with Adam. Brodie clearly knows the law. They have no way of compelling him to talk to them without taking that action. They have no grounds to arrest him for the suspected murder of Suzette Armstrong. Rose wishes causing a police officer to spend their evening being soaked in the rain was an offence, but it isn't as yet.

'No, I have nothing to say. Leave me alone. I'm going home,' says Brodie, and starts to walk past Rose and Adam but Adam calls his name and he turns.

'I'm afraid you're not going anywhere,' says Adam. 'We have reason to believe that you've been consuming alcohol. We can't let you get back into that car without checking exactly how much.'

'Fuck's sake!' Brodie kicks at a stick on the ground. 'Bloody breathalyse me then! I'm not over the limit, I can tell you that right now. I only had about two sips.'

'We don't routinely carry breathalysers, Mr Brodie,' says Rose. 'We're going to have to get some uniformed officers to bring us a machine. And that means you're going to have to wait with us, I'm afraid.'

Brodie looks for a moment as though he cannot stand being inside his own skin. He makes an anguished face and turns one way, then the other, before running a hand over his rain-sodden face.

'Fucking hell,' he says but quieter now. 'Get it over with then.'

He starts to move away from what's at his feet. 'Not so fast,' says Adam, turning to Rose. 'We need to take that thing, whatever that is, with us. It might be evidentially relevant to this case. One of us is going to have to sit with him while the other comes back with an evidence bag.'

'Shall we toss a coin?'

*

147

Five minutes later, Rose grudgingly trudges back the way they went to find Brodie to collect the twig doll as a piece of evidence. She is now so wet that her coat has been completely breached. Her bra clings to her soaking wet skin and she is so cold her teeth are chattering together like one of those wind-up joke sets.

She has the peak of her hood up to try and keep the rain out of her face and with the poor visibility, she thinks at first she is only seeing the pale trunk of a tree. But then it moves; a white flash ahead. A deer? But no, it wasn't the right shape. Whatever it was, it was on two legs, not four.

Stopping where she is, her hand snakes to her phone in her pocket.

'Is someone there?' she calls but there's only the pattering of the rain all around, a little lighter at last. Breathing more heavily, from the shock and the cold, she forces herself on, eyes scanning around her for the person she saw. She wonders if it was Red Hair but why would she not show herself?

When Rose reaches the spot, at first she thinks she must have made a mistake. No, there's the bunker and the huge, ancient tree with its thick roots. She looks around in confusion.

The large twig doll, which had been lying right here, has gone.

Rose is still trying to process this confusing fact when she hears the first gunshot.

22

For half a second she thinks it might be thunder, then she is down on her belly on the filthy wet ground, arms over her head as instinct and training kick in.

She switches off the torch immediately and the darkness is shockingly all-encompassing until her eyes begin to adjust. Fumbling in her pocket for her phone, she pulls it out then immediately drops it in the mud. Swearing under her breath she picks it up and tries to wipe the muck off the screen.

Fear rises into her throat when she sees that there is no coverage here, deep in the woods. Will Adam have heard it back at the car? Unlikely. It sounds close and he is just as likely to think it's thunder.

Rose scoots on her belly across the ground towards the bunker and then turns round, scrabbling backwards with her feet until she has her back up against the stone wall. She tries her phone again. Nothing happening.

Listening hard, she can only hear the drip-drip of leaves shedding their burden of water now the rain has finally stopped.

She waits, thoughts churning in her mind. She can't get backup and she has no idea how long it will take Adam to realise something is up. There haven't been any further gunshots though. Could it be safe to move?

It occurs to Rose now that it might be a poacher. She has

read there are deer in the country park and while it is strictly prohibited to hunt them, it can't be ruled out. Was it some idiot trying to shoot animals, unaware that a police officer was trying to gain evidence?

Feeling a tiny bit reassured by this thought, Rose waits a few moments more then gets slowly to her feet, wincing at the viscous mud clinging to her bottom, knees and even on her chin from when she first threw herself down. Despite how filthy, cold, tired and hungover she is, her senses are on the highest alert as she walks back. The whole way she can't help feeling like there is a target on her back and the clattering of her heart only starts to slow when she sees the car park appearing through the trees. There's a squad car parked next to Adam's with two uniforms inside. The door is open. Adam is standing by his car, arms crossed. Ryan Brodie gets out from the passenger seat of the squad car, his expression thunderous. He spots Rose and mild curiosity passes over his face for a moment at her appearance, before his brow clenches in fury again.

'Fucking waste of time,' he says. 'Knew I wasn't over the limit.'

Adam exchanges a few words with the officers inside the car then pats the roof to signify they are all done. It's only then that he registers the state of Rose.

'What the hell happened to you?'

'I'll tell you in a minute,' she says, clenching her teeth to stop them chattering.

'Can I go?' says Brodie.

'You can,' says Adam, but he doesn't take his appalled eyes off Rose. 'But can we drop you somewhere?'

'No thanks,' says Brodie. He reaches into his pocket and brings out cigarettes and a lighter. 'I'll make my own way.'

He starts to walk away and towards his car when Rose calls to Adam, deliberately loud. 'I tried to get the doll but it had gone.'

Brodie stops dead; his shoulders hunched as though he is about to ward off a blow. It's obvious he is listening carefully.

'Gone?' says Adam. 'Are you sure?'

'Quite sure,' says Rose. Brodie turns, very briefly, to look at her. There's no mistaking the emotion in his eyes. Rose has seen it before. It's the kind of fear someone experiences only when they believe their life is in danger. It's terror in its purest form, stripping the person back into someone as ageless and vulnerable as a newborn.

'Let us protect you, Ryan,' she says.

He looks as though he is going to speak then only shakes his head before climbing into his car and gunning the engine unnecessarily aggressively. In moments, he is gone.

'Christ, gunshots?' says Adam a few moments later inside the car. Rose is trying to wipe some of the mud off her with pieces of kitchen towel Adam keeps in the back of the car, but it isn't really doing anything.

'We need to call it in,' says Rose, but the cold has got her in a grip now and she can't properly control her voice.

'There's not much point now,' says Adam. 'But we'll log it tomorrow. It was probably a poacher. Look, I'll drive you home. And take this.' Adam struggles out of his rain jacket. Underneath he has on a navy blue fisherman's jumper over a white T-shirt. He peels off the jumper and Rose can't avert her eyes as a flash of brown skin at his waist briefly appears.

She turns her head away, cheeks suddenly aflame. 'No, I can't take that,' she says. 'You must be cold too.'

'Yeah but you're probably in a bit of shock too,' he says. 'Whatever it was, it felt like someone was shooting at you. I'm not arguing about this.' He pauses. 'And you were drinking with Scarlett last night so you're in shock from that too. Now I'll turn the other way and you put this on.'

Rose doesn't reply. She wants to laugh hysterically. Strip her top off, here? It might be something she has imagined doing with Adam many times but not like this.

Unable to think of a response, she meekly takes the jumper. Adam puts his coat on over the T-shirt and gets out of the car.

'I'm going to stand right over there,' he says. 'Shout when you're done.'

He goes to stand a good four metres in front of the car, his back turned to her.

Rose hurriedly peels off her sodden coat and the shirt and cardigan underneath, which are damp and almost steaming in the warm air of the car heater. She's wet to her bra but can't quite bring herself to take that off, although the idea of doing it and simply waiting for Adam to turn around is so intensely erotic – despite her miserable state – she feels a bolt of pure heat between her legs.

But instead she pulls the warm jumper over her cold body and breathes in the smell of it before calling out, slightly feebly, that she is ready.

Adam looks slightly awkward when he gets back into the car and doesn't meet her eye. Illogical though it may be, she can't help feeling that she has somehow transmitted her thoughts as surely as if she had said them.

The drive home seems to take a long time.

23

Rose calls Rowland first thing to update her on last night's events.

'So you had what was potentially an important piece of evidence,' she says when Rose stops speaking, 'but you lost it? Am I right?'

Rose swallows. Rowland has always had this effect on her, making her feel like the teenager who would get hauled into the head's office now and then for some real or perceived misdemeanour.

'It had *gone*,' she says. 'We had no way of transporting it safely and believed at the time that we had the chance to go back and properly collect it.'

'Right.' The word seems loaded with criticism. 'Well, I'm not happy about any of this right now. We seem to have a link between a bunch of mysterious deaths and this setting and so far we have very little explanation for it. We have no idea what drove Suzette Armstrong off that platform to her death. We haven't made a single arrest. Please get back to me with something concrete as soon as possible.'

Rose comes off the phone feeling dejected. She looks across the office at Adam, who is speaking to someone on the phone. She's still cringing about the oddness in the car last night and has replayed in her mind whether she could possibly have done something that could be misinterpreted. There's definitely an odd atmosphere at the moment.

Almost as though he senses her eyes on him, he partially turns his head and Rose immediately switches her eyes to her screen. An email has come in from Brixton Prison.

Her request to see Terrence Bigham has been authorised. She is to be there tomorrow at 10 a.m.. She closes her eyes for a moment and covers her face with her hands. It's so much faster than she hoped.

'Hey,' Adam is by her desk and she jolts. 'You alright?'

'Fine, yeah, fine,' she says and fusses with her pen, willing herself to stop being so weird.

Adam gives a slightly confused smile before speaking again. 'I rang that woman who was frightened at Crazy Climbz yesterday.'

'Oh yeah?' Rose's interest takes over and normality is resumed.

'Yeah, it's one Demi Galanis, who was there for her son's birthday. Apparently she hated every minute of the experience but was forcing herself round. She'd got to the end and was gearing herself up for that final zip wire when she looked down and this guy was standing, watching her. She said he had an odd smile on his face then sort of shook his head warningly, before doing that broken neck thing. It really upset her.'

'What did he look like?' says Rose.

'Very tall,' she said. 'At least six foot five, although she is only five two and was looking down from a height so I don't know much store you can put in that. But he had a very straggly beard and short-cropped hair too and that's not the best bit.'

'Oh yeah?'

'Turns out he was helpfully wearing a fleece that was recognisable to her from local walks there,' says Adam. 'He's one of the park keepers.'

*

a troubled childhood. His father was terrible bully.' She winces. 'I used to hear him shouting in there and worry so much for Sharon, Kyle's mama. Then he finally left and took all the money with him.' She makes a loud tutting sound with her teeth. 'They had to move to the Lake District and I don't see him for years and years. It was a lovely surprise when he turned up at my door again.'

There's a sound of the front door opening in the hall and her face brightens again. 'Here he is now!'

The man who appears at the doorway appears to be all glower and beard. Not quite the giant he'd been portrayed, he is still at least six feet two and broad with it, in an old Army jacket and jeans with thick-soled black boots. His hair is cropped very short and he has one of those long wispy beards that comes to a point and has, in Rose's opinion, never looked attractive on any man, ever. His eyes are full of hostility as she and Adam rise to their feet.

'Who the hell are you?' he says, northern accent detectible.

'We're police,' says Rose. 'DC Gifford and DC Lacey. It's nothing to worry about, Mr Jenkins. We just wondered if we could have a word?'

He narrows his eyes and then speaks to Mrs D without moving his gaze from the two police officers in front of him.

'Give us a minute, Mrs D, would you?'

'Of course, of course,' says the old lady, rising painstakingly to her feet. She slightly falls back into the seat and Jenkins is right there, surprisingly fast for such a big man, gently helping her up. She beams at him.

'Thank you,' she says. 'I'm a silly old sausage.'

'No you're not, Mrs D.' The affection in Jenkins' expression quite transforms it.

After Mrs D has left the room, Jenkins goes back to glaring.

'Shall we sit down?' says Adam.

'No, you're alright.'

'Okay, then,' says Adam. 'No problem.' All three are standing awkwardly in the middle of the room.

Rose makes the snap decision to get straight to the point. No amount of buttering up is going to work on this one. There will be no 'just a little chat' here.

'There was a complaint about someone intimidating a customer of Crazy Climbz and they match your description, Mr Jenkins,' says Rose.

Jenkins' reaction is totally unreadable for a moment. Was he expecting something else? Then he guffaws and slaps his leg.

'Intimidating? What the hell was I doing then?'

'You made a noose gesture to a woman who was struggling on the highest of the platforms,' says Adam. 'Which wasn't a very sensitive thing to do, was it?'

Jenkins sighs, all humour gone now. 'Maybe,' he says, pronounced 'mebbe'. 'Not a crime though, is it. If you're daft enough to pay good money to throw yourself off summat like that then I don't have much time for you.'

'Bit insensitive though,' says Adam. 'Are you aware that a woman died after falling from that platform a week beforehand?'

Jenkins merely shrugs.

'Well, you work at Elford Park,' says Rose. 'So I'd have thought you were certainly informed that a suspicious death occurred there.' It's only now she realises that Jenkins hasn't looked her directly in the eye the whole time she has been here. Only at Adam.

'Yeah, okay, I heard about it. Just not sure if it's got owt to do with anything, that's all.'

'Do you approve of the Crazy Climbz centre, Mr Jenkins?' says Adam. 'I mean, do you believe it should be there?'

'Couldn't care less either way.'

'Have you ever engaged in any vandalism towards the centre?' says Adam.

Jenkins rolls his eyes. 'I haven't, no.'

Rose takes a small, controlled sip of air in through her nose. This is pointless. 'Where did you go to school?' she says. Jenkins frowns and for the first time, his eyes – light green – meet Rose's. Then away again.

'Why?'

'Just tell us,' says Adam.

'I went to school in Barrow,' he says. 'Doubt you'd know it.'

'Here though,' says Rose. 'Mrs D told us you started life next door.'

For a fragment of a moment a look of chilling dislike passes over his face. 'I went to Chase Grove primary and then had one year at Woodfields,' he says.

'And how old are you, if you don't mind me asking?'

'I do mind,' he says. 'Because it's none of your business but I want to get on with my day so I'll tell you. I'm forty two.'

'Do you recognise these names at all?' Adam reels off the names of the three dead people but Jenkins says he doesn't know them.

It's clear they're not getting anywhere. After a handful more questions, they are back in the car.

'They won't have had any crossover in the school at all if he left after year seven,' says Rose, pulling away from the side of the road. 'He's a bit of a prick but I'm not sure he's of any interest to us.'

'Let's run him through the PNC,' says Adam. 'Just in case anything comes up.'

24

Rose comes through the front door of The Squirrels and takes off her coat. She is longing for a quiet evening in front of the telly in her own place. Fat chance of that.

After the visit to Jenkins, it had been a long day of painstakingly going through the General Registry Docket of all the details from Alex Weston's murder, and the scant details they have on record about Haniya Shah. Phone calls have been made to friends and family from a list provided by her brother, but so far nothing has come to light. Everyone in the team has been looking at finding a connection between these three deaths but as yet, they are meeting dead end after dead end.

The one moment of interest came when they immediately found a hit on the PNC for Kyle Jenkins.

He had a conviction for common assault after punching an anti-hunt protestor at a fox hunt in Cumbria, before the ban in 2005. There was nothing since then.

Rose carries the ready meal she picked up on the high street into the kitchen to find Jimmy sitting at the table with a huge plate of pie, mash and gravy in front of him, a napkin stuffed into the neck of his salmon-coloured jumper.

'Hi,' she says trying to keep her head down and signal that she isn't up for any chat.

He looks up, chewing ruminatively for some time before replying.

'Hello, Rose.'

His eyes brighten with the desire to bore her about something. She recognises the signs. Rose hurries over to the microwave and puts in the macaroni cheese. Maybe she can cook this thing and get out of here before he starts.

'I had an appointment yesterday.'

Too late.

'Is that right.' She doesn't bother with the uptick of a question mark.

'Oh yes,' says Jimmy. 'I think you will find this interesting in your role as an officer of the law . . . '

Rose keeps her eye on the slowly revolving microwave tray as Jimmy launches into an account of meeting with the council about what he believed to be the 'highly inconvenient' new cycle lanes in some areas of the borough.

The pasta tray goes round and round.

When he finally draws breath, she turns to see him looking expectantly at her.

'Sorry, what was that?'

Jimmy makes a huffing sound and pinches his nostrils with his fingers. He's one of those people who is always fiddling with his nose, then touching every surface around him, much to Rose's disgust. She keeps picturing items in the kitchen being covered in a sticky layer of bogey.

'I wondered if you felt there was any possible element of illegality in it all?' he continues.

She frowns. 'In what, cycle lanes? I don't think so.'

Jimmy sighs as though he is the one needing infinite patience in this conversation.

'Not the cycle lanes, *per se*,' he says, as though explaining something to a child. 'I'm talking about the altercation I had with the cyclist and the abuse I suffered as a consequence.'

'Oh,' says Rose, mentally trying to pull back remnants of

161

what he was talking about. She dimly recalls something about 'extreme rudeness'.

'When you say abuse, what do you mean?' She hurriedly removes the container from the microwave, almost burning her fingers in the process and pours the contents into a bowl. She's never been much of a cook but one of the resolutions she had for leaving her childhood home at last was to learn how to do it. Unfortunately, there is nothing about this depressing little kitchen, with its ceramic squirrels on the windowsill and light brown splashback tiles that makes you want to hang around. Particularly if there is any chance of Jimmy being in there as well.

He's not done yet, evidently.

'I was told to "eff off,"' he says. 'Except not using those words, when I pointed out that I had every right to cross a road and that a cyclist should look out for pedestrians.'

Jimmy has gone quite pink at the memory of this terrible injustice.

'I'm afraid that if someone saying eff off was a crime,' she says, 'we wouldn't have time to deal with any of the really important stuff.'

Jimmy's expression sours. His eyes run up and down her body, as though disappointed in her but needing to have a good look just in case.

'I would have thought protecting decent members of the public and making them feel safe was an important part of your job.'

'Oh it is!' says Rose cheerfully, to confuse him. 'Now, if you'll excuse me...'

He opens his mouth to say something else. Rose is out of there, getting a whiff of his musty shirt smell as she goes.

But it's not only her landlord who is putting her off her food, as she sits in her bedroom with her miserable meal balanced on her lap.

It's the thought of sitting opposite Terrence Bigham tomorrow morning in Brixton prison.

*

Rose dreams about the red-haired woman, Orla, soaking wet from the rain, flitting through trees and always just out of reach.

In the morning, her stomach is in knots. Rose has been face-to-face with a good number of bad men and women, over her career so far. But this feels different. She thinks about the febrile atmosphere in the house coming from Adele before Terrence's visits. The smell of heat blasted hair and spray, perfume and endless cigarettes when she got ready. Patsy Cline records playing loudly. The way Rose would be under strict instructions not to interrupt or bother them when he was there. She was kept separate from him then, only passing as he arrived or when she was heading upstairs with some miserable evening meal that comprised of toast in one form or another. There was an arrogant air about him and a whiff of aftershave that always lingered too long the next day.

The big question is, why does he want to see her all these years later?

Rose arrives at Brixton Prison early for her security check. She told Moony that she has a doctor's appointment this morning. The chances of her boss finding out the real reason for Rose's absence seem slim. Moony knew Bigham back in the day, but Rose feels there will be too much interest in what she is doing today. She wants to be in full control of when she tells her. Her phone distracts her with a notification from her banking app. The deposit and rent to Ness, paid already, have come up as a credit. Some annoying glitch has obviously happened and Rose tiredly adds it to the list of things to sort out later.

Inside the entrance for non-family visitors, she fills out the paperwork and shows her security authorisation before stepping through the metal detector and waiting in the anteroom to be collected.

After about ten minutes, a stout woman in her fifties with blue-black hair in a severe bob comes through the security door and greets Rose in a friendly way. She has the battle lines around her mouth of the hardened smoker and a gravelly voice to match.

'You're here to see our Terry?' she says, her accent Liverpudlian.

Rose is washed by a desire to say, 'No, there's been a mistake. I need to go.'

'That's right,' she says, instead. Her stomach pitches.

'I'm Wendy,' says the prison officer. 'Come with me, love.'

Wendy takes Rose through a series of doors, aided by the clanking metalwork at her waist. Wendy asks no questions and merely whistles quietly as they go. Rose is grateful for the lack of chitchat. Her mouth is dry, and her palms are damp, as though all her bodily moisture is in the opposite places to where it should be.

'Okay, love,' says Wendy. 'You're in here. Just knock once you're finished. One of us will be outside.'

'Thanks.'

Wendy opens a door to a small meeting room adorned with only a table with two grey bucket chairs.

One of them is occupied by a small, trim man with a few thin whisps of hair across a scalp that has reddened patches in places. He wears dark-rimmed glasses and has small, watery blue eyes that immediately come to life at the sight of her. She doesn't really recognise him as the man who used to visit.

'I'll leave you to it,' says Wendy and goes out closing the door behind her.

'It's good to see you!' says Bigham, thrusting out a hand to be shaken as though they have both rocked up at a barbecue.

'Little Rose Gifford. All grown up.' His eyes roam over her face and down her body. She curls her toes inside her boots but meets his gaze with a stony expression.

'Nice,' he says.

'It's DC Gifford to you,' she says. 'I want to know why you asked to see me, Mr Bigham.'

His face falls in a deliberately exaggerated way, as though she has let him down. 'Come come, Detective Constable Gifford,' her title said with so much sarcasm she tenses even further. 'Can't we have a nice little chat when we go back so far? I mean, I've known you since you was this high.' He gestures somewhere around the level of his knees. Then he lets out a wheezing laugh that turns into a bubbly cough.

'Sorry about that,' he says, once he has recovered again. He pulls out a tissue from his grey trackie bottoms and wipes at his eyes. 'I'm just trying to picture what your dear grandmother would say if she knew you'd gone over to the dark side!'

Rose doesn't reply but merely regards him evenly. *Don't let him get under your skin.*

'Oh, come on!' says Bigham, jovially. 'You must see the funny side! Old Adele had, shall we say, *views* on the filth.' He smiles, revealing a row of teeth yellowed with age. 'No offence.'

'None taken,' says Rose. 'But why do you think I joined?'

Bigham laughs loudly at this and slaps the table. 'Good on you,' he says. 'Nice to see a bit of spirit about you, girl.' He pronounces this, 'gel'. Then, 'You seem to have changed a lot. You were like a little shadow, slinking about in that house as a kid. Adele wasn't much of a maternal presence was she? Always watching everything, you were.' His smile has slipped away now and his eyes are as cold as two marbles. 'Used to wonder how much you saw.'

Rose stares back at the man across the table, unflinching.

'Why am I here, Mr Bigham?'

'Oh please,' he says. 'Can't a couple of old friends go by first names?'

'Happy to call you Terry, Terry,' says Rose. 'You can stick with DC Gifford.'

Bigham suddenly looks tired as though sheer bravado was holding him upright and he can't be bothered anymore.

'I thought we could help each other,' he says. 'For old-times' sake.'

'Firstly, we have no "old-times' sake", Terry, and secondly, what could you possibly do for me?'

Bigham sits back in the chair so the legs squeak against the stone floor.

'Don't you want to know what happened to your mum?'

His voice, although feather light, gives Rose an unpleasant jolt. 'And even,' he grins again, 'who your dad is?'

He starts to laugh, a rumbling sound deep in his chest turning into a cough that wracks his whole body for a few moments.

Rose's mind whirls.

Wiping his mouth, he smiles at her and waggles his bushy grey eyebrows, as though waiting for her to work something out.

'Lovely girl, she was, Kelly.'

Rose's body reacts before her brain in the form of a wave of nausea she manages to swallow down.

No. He's not . . . He's not saying . . . ?

She swallows and looks him square in the eye. The only thing to do is style this out, front foot forward, even though she feels like she literally might vomit up her disgust at any moment.

'Are we having some sort of Darth Vader moment here, Terry?' she says. 'Is that what's happening?' He takes a moment to understand then laughs loudly before his face falls serious again. It's like weather passing swiftly, with sunny periods you can't trust.

'Wouldn't you like to know?' he says softly.

No, no, no, she thinks, not if that is the answer. *Please don't let that be the answer.*

Rose swallows and reaches into her handbag. There's nothing to lose now.

'What happened to Orla?' she says and slaps the photo of her mother and the red-haired woman on the table.

Bigham leans over and looks at the picture. 'Oh, that silly little tart,' he says with a sniff. 'Couldn't handle anything. She was the cause of all the trouble in the end.'

'What happened to her?' says Rose, leaning forward and staring directly into his eyes. 'Did you kill her, Terry?'

Bigham makes a scoffing sound. 'Kill her?' he says. 'Nah, she managed that all by herself by sticking needles in her arms. She was a silly girl.'

'What do you mean about causing all the trouble?'

Bigham smiles thinly, his eyes narrowed. 'Now, now, I'll tell you all of it,' he says, 'about Orla and about Kelly. And more. I've got nothing left to lose now. But I want something in return.'

'What?' Rose sits back in her seat and regards him.

'I'm dying,' he says. 'Oh, not quickly, unfortunately. I've got early stages of lung cancer but it might take a while before I'm sick enough to warrant a nice hospital bed. But I want to be moved nearer my eldest daughter, to Gartree. It will be a comfort for me to know I'm nearer family.'

'I don't think that's going to happen,' says Rose. 'Also, I think you like playing games with people and this is all just a waste of my time.'

Bigham's smile drops completely now. 'I'm not playing games, Rose,' he says and she can't help feeling a little shiver of discomfort at the way he says her name. 'In return, I'll give you all I know about two missing people. One of them being your mother. Wouldn't you like to know if she's still alive, Rose? Maybe she's out there right now and all it takes is a word from me that she's safe at last and she can come back.'

'She's alive?' Her voice is firm, even though internally she wants to shriek and grab this man by the collar, screaming into his face.

Bigham shrugs. 'Like I say, talk to your bosses. Tell them what I want. But there's a condition.'

'What's that then, Terry?' But she knows what it is before he even opens his mouth.

'I'll only speak to one person.' He smiles. 'That's you, Detective Constable Rose Gifford.'

She doesn't respond straight away. Outside the room there are shouts and catcalls and metallic sounds of clanking doors.

'Well, I'm not sure that's going to work,' she says after a few more moments. 'Something like this requires a lot of paperwork.'

He crosses his arms and sits back in his chair, evidently done. 'Make it happen,' he says, his tone flat. 'That's all I'm saying for now, but we'll talk again, little Rosie.'

Rose gets to her feet and hurries to the door to alert Wendy. Bigham begins a harsh whistling through his teeth.

When she recognises the tune, her neck prickles and she whips around to look back at the man sitting at the table, a satisfied expression on his face.

'Trying to tell me something, Terry?' she says, managing to keep the wobble from her voice.

Bigham gives her a yellow grin. 'We'll talk soon, yeah?'

Wendy opens the door and Rose gets out of the cell. Her chest feels constricted as though all the oxygen has been sucked out of her lungs.

Why was he whistling that particular song? 'The Teddy Bears Picnic'. The one that starts, 'If you go down to the woods today, you're sure of a big surprise.'

25

THE DARK HISTORY OF ELFORD PARK
Chapter Three

. . . and over the centuries, since Alice Goode may or may not have been buried beneath Elford Woods, along with so many other poor souls, the area has developed a rich source of folklore. There are many legends associated with this area. For example, if you park your car at the hill on the far northeastern corner of the woods at dusk, it might start rolling upwards.

Likewise, if you go wandering in the woods at night, you may fall prey to a whole array of strange sightings, from a headless woman riding a horse, a phantom coach and horses or a pack of black dogs that bring bad luck.

But it is the legend of Alice Goode that has perhaps grabbed the imagination most. There have been many supposed sightings of a girl in a rough woollen dress and apron wandering the woods, holding a doll and weeping. It is unclear when people started to suggest this would curse the person who witnessed the sight. But what if there is another explanation? The feminist historian Jessica Moriarty has written that Alice

Goode is a protector of these woods and looks out for, as she puts it, 'all the lost girls; the ones who have been ignored, the ones who have been abused, and the ones who are simply left behind'.

26

Rose receives a voicemail as she pulls into the car park at UCIT that makes her heart plummet into her lower belly.

It's Ness, sounding flustered and upset.

'Oh, hello Rose,' she says. 'I'm calling to tell you, oh gosh, I feel awful about this . . . ' She breaks off to blow her nose loudly. Is she crying? 'But you know I made that comment about my daughter in Ottawa? Well, it was almost as though I tempted fate because she's here, with the kids, after having a catastrophic row with her lovely husband. She doesn't know how long she'll be here and even though I told her about you and how gorgeous you are, she has made me feel very guilty at even thinking about bringing someone into the house while she needs her mum. I'm so sorry, Rose. I really did want you to move in, but it might not be the best time. I've repaid you. I hope you got it okay?' She sniffs again. 'I can't tell you how bad I feel about this.'

Yeah, thinks Rose, putting the phone back into her bag and squeezing her eyes shut. *But you don't feel half as bad as I do.* The disappointment feels so acute, Rose finds her shoulders rounding as though to ward off another blow. Tears rush to her eyes, and she angrily swipes at them, cursing herself for daring to hope that something so good, so easy, would fall into her life.

Now she's going to have to tell Jimmy and beg for the room for longer. Feeling about three times her age, Rose gathers her things and goes into the office.

After making herself a coffee she looks over at Moony, who is frowning at her computer screen and turning a pencil rather skilfully through her fingers. Her stomach flutters in anticipation of having this conversation and for a moment she considers leaving it. Letting Bigham stew and never acting on his request.

Then she pictures the times she found a spectral Adele sitting in the living room, dressed in that horrible fur coat and wringing her hands with their sharp, thick talons, tears falling down her insubstantial face. It took Rose a very long time to understand that Adele was trying to tell her something. Maybe she didn't want to understand. But something happened involving Orla and Kelly and if Rose doesn't find out the truth, she is never going to be able to live a normal life.

She takes a deep intake of breath and walks over to Moony's desk.

'Can I have a word, Sheila?'

Moony peers at her over the top of her glasses. 'Got more creepy dolls for me?'

'No.'

'Thank God for that. Not sure I can take any more of those.'

Rose manages a weak smile. 'No,' she says. 'It's . . . it's about something else. Can we talk privately?'

Moony regards her for a moment longer and then pushes herself back from the desk in one swift movement of her wheeled chair.

'C'mon then,' she says. 'We'll go into the interview room.'

Rose feels the curious eyes of Adam and Scarlett as she and Moony swipe out of the main office.

They go into the interview room and sit down at the table.

Sheila taps her hand on the table, silver rings banging in a way that never seems to bother her but makes everyone else flinch.

'So, what can I do for you, Rose?'

There's nothing for it, Rose thinks, but to plough straight in. 'You know Terrence Bigham?' she says.

Moony's eyebrows shoot up, the movement corrugating her forehead. 'I certainly do,' she says. 'I was in the team that brought down that toe-rag in the end.'

It was only on their last big case that Rose discovered Moony had known both Adele and Kelly, and been aware of exactly what kind of house Rose had been brought up in. Rose had been furious enough to want to leave UCIT when this came out, because she was convinced that Moony had ulterior motives for hiring her. But she had been persuaded otherwise. Still, the eagerness on Moony's face at what feels like rummaging around in the worst parts of Rose's past does not feel good.

'I'm sorry I told a white lie this morning, but I needed to get my head around what was happening. He asked to see me. Bigham, I mean.'

Moony sits back in her seat, tipping it at the legs so she wobbles slightly and has to right herself with a hand against the table.

'Well, well, well,' she says. 'What did that delightful individual want to talk to you about, exactly?'

'He claims,' Rose says carefully, 'he wants to tell us, me . . . he wants to tell us how to find two missing people. One of them being . . . '

'Your mum,' says Moony softly, finishing the sentence. Her always sharp eyes momentarily soften. Rose scrunches her fists under the table. Please don't say anything too nice, she thinks. She can't handle it today.

Luckily, Moony doesn't say anything else for a moment, but looks off into the distance, clearly mulling all this over.

'And in return?'

'He's sick,' says Rose. 'Got cancer apparently. He wants to move prisons to be nearer to family. Gartree, I think he said.'

Moony nods slowly. 'Not the biggest ask in the world.

Thought he might be wanting to change categories or something and that ain't happening. Maybe he wants to get this off his chest as much as anything.'

'Hmm,' says Rose. 'There was definitely a feeling of him . . .' she pauses, 'relishing the whole thing though.'

Moony grimaces. 'Horrible little man,' she says. 'But I have a feeling I know who the other person is. A man called Ronnie Bentley who was well known in the club scene and totally disappeared.'

Her eyes flick back to Rose's face. 'And Kelly, your mother. I'd very much like to know where she went and what happened to her.'

'He suggested,' Rose has to break off to steady her voice with a fake cough. 'He sort of hinted that she might be alive.'

Now the look on Moony's face is most definitely one of pure sympathy.

'Did he now?' she says quietly. 'Well, knowing how trustworthy that walking scrotum is, I wouldn't put too much store by anything he says.'

'Yeah, that's what I thought,' says Rose. Disappointment tumbles through her innards anyway, for the second time today.

The fact that Kelly has never shown herself to her has meant she always held on to a tiny hope that she was still alive somewhere. But Moony's reaction just now suggests otherwise.

'Okay,' says Moony. 'Well, if he says he will only speak to you, I need to know whether you have done the CHIS handling course?'

Sadly, Rose has indeed done the Covert Human Intelligence Source course. It was her first thought when she was back in her car after meeting Bigham. She would have had a ready excuse if she hadn't been trained to this level. Someone else would have to have done it.

She replies that she has.

'In that case,' says Moony, 'I'll get this rolling. Are you happy to do it?'

'I wouldn't say happy is the right word,' says Rose. 'But yes. I think I have to.'

Moony's gaze is sympathetic. 'I guess you do,' she says softly.

Luckily Rose doesn't get long to obsess about this because more telephone evidence has arrived from Suzette Armstrong's phone and Adam has found something.

He calls them over, excitement sharp in his voice.

'So the deleted messages are here,' he says, 'and it's obvious that Suzette was having an affair with someone who didn't use their name but repeatedly left a Fox emoji at the bottom of their exchanges . . . it made me wonder if that was a name. But anyway,' he hurries himself on, 'the number turns out to belong to . . . guess?'

Rose and Moony exchange glances.

'Not Reece?' says Rose, with a grimace as Moony says, 'Ryan Brodie?'

Adam points to Moony. 'You win.'

'Wow,' says Rose, 'sly dog. He was quite convincing when we told him she had died too. I bet he knew.'

'But that's not all,' says Adam. 'On the night she died, she received this message. "Babe. I need to CU. URGENT. Woods. Our spot." Then the Fox emoji.'

'Right,' says Moony. 'That's good enough for me. Go arrest him but you'd better update Her Majesty straight away.'

There is no dedicated custody sergeant or overnight cell at the UCIT building so 'Her Majesty' – AKA DCI Stella Rowland – instructs Rose to bring Brodie to Silverton Street.

They find him at his flat, a newish building on a main road in Lewisham. He answers the door half asleep and smelling of booze; dressed only in a pair of white boxer shorts, the line of his stubble looking less sharp than the other night.

'What the fuck?' he says when he sees them, snapping from blearily hungover to wide awake in a moment.

'We'd like to talk you,' says Rose, 'Ryan, or should I say . . . Fox?'

His eyes widen and he places his hand against the door, as if to steady himself.

'Ryan Brodie,' says Adam, 'I am arresting you on suspicion of the murder of Suzette Armstrong. You do not have to say anything but it may harm your defence if you do not mention, when questioned, something that you later rely on in court. Anything you do say may be given in evidence against you.'

'No!' says Brodie. 'You've got it all wrong! I would never have hurt Suze!'

'Plenty of opportunity to explain down at the station, Mr Brodie,' says Rose. 'You can tell us all about you and "Suze".'

27

It feels strange being back in one of the interview rooms at Silverton Street, especially with Adam at her side. She's keenly aware of the eyes of Rowland in the Observation Suite and can't help remembering when she went too far with a suspect and Rowland made her feel like her career was over.

She has to force this thought out of her mind. Not good for the confidence.

They go through the formalities. Brodie has asked for a solicitor, a good-looking man in his forties with salt and pepper hair, called John Bird.

'Look, I am going to tell you everything,' says Ryan. 'But you need to contact my girlfriend, Jade Kurti. She can tell you exactly where I was on Saturday night.'

'We'll do that,' says Rose. 'Now why don't you tell us about you and Suzette. When did you start seeing each other?'

Brodie sighs heavily. 'I delivered a takeaway to her.' He looks up. 'I'm trying to get my personal training business up and running but it was a quiet patch so I did a few weeks for Uber Eats. I was delivering a curry and it turned out it was to her.'

'Must have been a surprise,' says Adam. 'You'd had no contact since school?'

'None at all,' says Brodie. 'She went off to Oxford or wherever and when I saw her around the place after that she was a bit snooty. Had changed, you know? But we were really close when we were kids and then we went to the same secondary school and well, we were together on and off all the way through.' He pauses. 'But she was so chuffed to see me. Tried to get me to come and have a drink but I was working. Anyway, I went back the next day and well,' he shrugs. 'You know. We always were good together. Like that, I mean. We were each other's firsts, if you really want to know. And so we just sort of started up again.'

'What's the fox thing all about?' says Adam. Brodie looks down at the table and the tops of his tanned cheeks go a little pink.

'We were both into *The X-Files* when we were kids,' he grunts after a few moment's silence. He looks up and shrugs. 'I was Fox Mulder and she was Dana Sculley.'

'What about her husband?' says Rose. 'Did he know?'

Brodie makes a face. 'Probably,' he says. 'I mean, they were in one of those open relationships. She gave the impression they did their own thing to some extent.'

Well, he never mentioned that, thinks Rose.

'Why did you contact her and ask her to go to the woods that night?' she says.

'What?' Brodie looks at her, then Adam. 'What are you talking about?' He turns to his solicitor. 'What's she talking about?'

Rose reads out the message.

'I never sent that! You have to believe me!' He looks like he might burst into tears. 'I was at Jade's mum's sixtieth all evening in Tottenham! You can check it out.'

'We are doing that.' Adam sits back in his seat and crosses his arms. 'But I think it's time you explained why you went scrabbling around in the woods the other night and what that doll is all about. Don't you?'

Brodie slumps and puts his face in his hands. When he emerges again his cheeks are stained pink through the caramel of his tan.

'I feel like a dick,' he says. The silence this is met with seems to force him on. 'It was just some stupid shit we got into as kids.'

'When you worked on the school project at Elford Park?' prompts Rose.

'Yeah,' says Brodie. 'That doll was in the visitor's centre. We called it Scary Mary and we used to move it around to freak each other out. Suzette found out there was meant to be some ghost of a girl in the woods and she got a bit obsessed with it all. It was just a bit of fun, really.' He takes a sip of water, his hand almost imperceptibly trembling.

'But when we hooked up again,' he continues, 'Suzette started talking about it again. Said she felt like she kept seeing that bloody doll.'

'Seeing it?' says Adam. 'Seeing it where?'

'Once at the bottom of her garden at night,' says Brodie. 'And once she thought she saw it in the back of someone's car, looking out at her.' He catches – and misinterprets – their expressions. 'I know, I know,' he says. 'It sounds nuts. But she started going on about how she felt like she was constantly being watched. And then . . . ' his face crumples for a moment and he pulls himself back together. 'This happens. She's dead.'

'What do you think happened to her?' says Adam.

Brodie rubs a circle into the table with the tip of one finger, staring down. 'I think she had a breakdown and threw herself off that tower.'

'None of this explains what you were doing the other evening,' says Rose and the big strong shoulders of the man before them become a little more rounded.

'I just needed to know it was still there, that was all,' he says, his voice small.

'Can you explain what you mean?'

'It sounds really stupid,' he says. 'But I've started having that same feeling Suze talked about . . . like someone is watching me. And then I thought I saw the bloody thing in someone's car, looking out at me. Just like Suze said. I needed to know it was where I last saw it.'

179

'And when was that?' says Rose.

Brodie frowns. 'Back when we were kids on that project. I don't really remember why we did it but for some reason it ended up getting stuffed in that bunker.' He shrugs. 'Like I said, it's all really stupid. I feel such an idiot for what I did the other night. But I can tell you that I would never, ever hurt anyone. Especially not Suze.' His voice cracks. 'Especially not her.'

Rose's phone vibrates and she glances down to see a message from Moony.

Brodie's alibi solid. Lots of witnesses. There from late afternoon to after midnight.

'Well, we've had to let him go but he's still very much a person of interest,' says Rowland a little later, once Brodie has been released. 'I still don't really understand the significance of this bloody doll.'

'Neither do we, yet,' says Adam. 'But we're trying hard to find that out.'

Rowland sighs. 'Okay,' she says. 'Off you go, then. But don't waste too much time chasing legends. There are plenty of real villains out there.'

'Clear what she thinks of UCIT, then,' murmurs Adam once they are on their way back to Reservoir Road.

'Oh yeah,' says Rose. 'I think that may be what caused the beef between her and Moony.'

'That,' says Adam with a quick grin, 'or the fact that they have such extraordinarily cuddly personalities. A match made in heaven, or what?'

Rose barks with laughter in response.

'Blimey, that's spooky,' says Adam, looking down at his phone. 'Think I just conjured her up.' He answers the phone and listens, then turns to Rose, eyes widened. 'On it,' he says, ending the call.

'What?' says Rose.

'She's been looking at Alex Weston's phone records. In the period before he was murdered, there was a flurry of calls to a certain number. It's registered to, wait for it. . . ' he mimes a drum roll, 'Mrs Konstantina Diamandis.'

Excitement fizzes inside Rose and all thoughts of chocolate fade. 'Right,' she says. 'Let's go and have another chat with our Mr Jenkins.'

28

Mrs D takes some time to come to the front door and when she does, her face shifts from curiosity to concern in a moment.

'Oh dear,' she says. 'Has something happened to Kyle?'

'It's nothing to worry about, Mrs Diamandis,' says Rose. 'We just needed to speak to him again if that's okay? Is he at home?'

'He's not here, I'm afraid.'

'Do you know when he'll be back?' says Adam. 'We really do need to talk to him.'

The old lady chomps her teeth and looks around; she seems a little distressed.

'Oh dear,' she says again. 'I don't know if I should . . . ' She breaks off the end of her sentence.

'Don't know if you should what?' prompts Rose gently.

'It's just that I'm not supposed to tell people about his other place, you see,' says the old lady, hand fluttering at her neckline.

Rose and Adam look at each other quickly.

'His other place?' says Rose.

'Yes,' says Mrs D. 'He mainly uses it for storage and so on and he has some valuable belongings so he doesn't like people knowing about it. I'm not meant to tell anyone. I mean, I only know about it because I was in the car with him once and he had to make a stop there.'

'Mrs Diamandis,' says Rose, 'we're the police. I can assure you that any knowledge of Kyle's belongings is very safe with us. And it's very important that we find him.'

Mrs D looks from Rose to Adam and back to Rose again. 'Is he in some sort of trouble?'

'We just need to speak to him,' says Adam one more time. Mrs D hesitates for a moment and mutters something in Greek under her breath, then nods.

29

They follow the Great North Road out of the outskirts of the city into Hertfordshire. The details given by Mrs D are a little vague, with no specific address, let alone a postcode. But from what they can gather, it's located on a patch of land near the trainline that takes commuters from inner London to the market town of Welwyn Garden City.

The sky seems to open up as they cross the M25, the dual carriageway slicing its way through fields richly green after the rain, the leaden sky opening up around them.

'I'm very interested to see what sort of valuables . . . ' Adam makes air quotes around the word, 'Jenkins is so worried about.'

'Yeah, me too,' says Rose.

'Hey,' says Adam suddenly. 'I meant to say, is it a coincidence that the weird doll is called Scary Mary? What with Reece's wife, who I wouldn't call scary as such . . . '

'No,' says Rose thoughtfully. 'What about Weirdy Mary?' They both break into childish snorts.

'Let me introduce you to my friends Weirdy Mary and Pompous Malcolm,' says Adam in a stupid, high-pitched voice that makes Rose laugh hard from her belly. It's nice. Maybe the intense strageness of the other evening was all in Rose's mind. She sneaks a quick glance at him and feels a warmth pass through her. She really does like him. It would be awful to spoil it. She drags her focus back to what he's saying now.

'But it's definitely interesting that Brodie called it that.'

'Where do you think it went, that doll?' says Rose. 'I mean, really? I presume you don't believe it's gone roaming around North London on its own like some sort of rustic Chucky?'

'Hmm, I dunno though . . . ' says Adam.

Rose shoots him an appalled look.

He bursts into laughter. 'I *love* winding you up about this stuff,' he says. 'No of course I don't! Someone's got that thing in their possession.'

'We didn't get long to look at it,' says Rose. 'But it was covered in crap and cobwebs. Took Brodie a while to get it out of that bunker. If someone was using it to scare Suzette Armstrong, I think maybe they made a replica?'

'Yeah, maybe. Anyway, let's get back to the Reeces' as soon as we can and get a look around.'

'I think we're getting close to Mr Jenkins' second home anyway,' says Rose. 'Maybe he can help shed a bit of light on it all, although after the other day, I have a feeling he's not going to welcome us with open arms.'

Mrs D's directions were to park in a layby opposite a pub called The Royal Oak and that the clearing where Jenkins' property was located was a bit further along to the left.

They get out of the car and walk along a little until they see a rough path, made only by footfall, leading off into a thicket of trees. It soon leads to a patch of ground with some sort of small, disused building on one side. It looks condemned but has reinforced security shutters over the windows. A path to the doorway has been deliberately cleared from the thick nettles growing on each side and the door is also substantial, with a large bolted padlock across it.

'Really going for the "keep out" vibe,' says Adam quietly. 'I'd like a look in there.'

A mobile home is perched on bricks at a right angle to the

185

building. When a train suddenly thunders past through the trees behind the dwelling, it's almost possible to see the structure shaking.

The mobile home is made from rusting pink and grey metal. Dirty curtains hang over the three windows and there's another reinforced door that looks very secure.

Rose knocks hard and hears sudden movement inside. The curtain on the nearest window is thrust aside and Jenkins' face peers out. His expression goes from furious to shocked.

'Hi, Mr Jenkins?' says Rose, 'Can we have a quick word?'

All is silent inside for a moment and then after a good deal of unlocking sounds the door is held open enough to reveal a slice of the man standing there.

'Who told you about this place?' he says. His bulk fills the doorway so his head is slightly bowed. From what Rose can see, he's wearing a T-shirt with a picture of a black, lozenge-shaped pill, which stirs something in her mind she can't place.

'We only need a minute, Mr Jenkins,' says Rose. His eyes slide away from her in a way that feels oddly disgusted and it all slots into place. The 'black pill' T-shirt is an emblem of the incel movement; the group of men who believe themselves to be 'involuntarily celibate' because most women are pre-disposed to reject them. It's a nasty world that has grown significantly online in recent years.

Rose feels her spine filling with steel and stands taller.

'We can talk at the station if you'd prefer,' she says and places a foot on the wooden structure that acts as a step into the property. Jenkins regards the foot.

'You'd best come in then,' he says and stands back.

The smell is the first thing that hits Rose; blood and shit and some other animal tang that makes bile rise in her throat.

A rickety camping table in the middle of the property seems to be covered in fur, blood and viscera. A large, curved hunting knife glistens red next to the remains of what must be, from the fluffy little tail, a rabbit. Draped around a chair is a waxed jacket, so stiff and greasy looking it's like a hulking headless man sitting at the table and waiting to be served the grim meal.

Jenkins' eyes are fixed on Adam, whose expression matches Rose's at the gore covering the table.

'What, you never seen what's inside an animal before?' says Jenkins in a mocking tone. 'Where d'you think your dinner comes from?'

'We're looking into a murder that happened in 2013,' says Adam, sidestepping his snark. 'A man called Alex Weston, who we mentioned to you when we met before. Did you say you didn't know him?'

Jenkins does a laughable impression of thinking hard before shaking his head. 'Can't say I do.'

'The thing is though,' says Rose, 'we found quite a few calls between him and the phone registered at Mrs Diamandis's house.'

'Maybe she called him then, I dunno. What's it got to do wi' me?' He reaches into a pocket with a filthy hand and pulls out a tin before extracting a rollie and lighting it. The sight of his large, bloodstained fingers near his lips turns Rose's stomach. The smell in here is appalling and isn't helped by a gas heater blasting out at the other end of the room. It seems to be coating the stink to her nose and throat linings. It seems she can't get away from the smell of death lately.

'It doesn't seem very likely though,' says Adam. 'Because she didn't know him at all. It seems more likely it was you, Mr Jenkins.'

'As I say, I know nowt about it,' says Jenkins. He sucks hard on the cigarette, his cheeks hollowing.

'Been hunting?' says Rose, looking around the space. Something is just visible on the pulled-out bed below a rough looking tartan blanket.

'Maybe.' *Mebbe.*

'Have you got a licence for that shotgun, Mr Jenkins?' she says, pointing at the barrel of the gun.

Jenkins goes quite still; the rollie pauses halfway to his lips. 'I have.'

'Could you show it to us, please?'

Jenkins sighs and goes over to a small filing cabinet that's green and rusty. He unlocks it and rummages around.

On top of the filing cabinet there are two piles of books. Rose scans the authors: Hemingway, Bellow, Nabokov, Updike, Mailer, Easton Ellis, Foster Wallace. All the dudes, she thinks, then a title snags her eye as Jenkins speaks again.

'Here it is. Wanna see it or not?'

She turns to look at the piece of paper he's holding and quickly scans it. It does seem to be a valid gun licence. Rose thanks him distractedly and looks back at the books again. When she spots what caught her attention before she feels a pulse of adrenaline in her chest.

A Dark History of Elford Woods is the title of the slim paperback. And the author is one Malcolm Reece.

Rose leans across and picks it up. 'Where did you get this from?' she says and holds it up so Adam can see it. His eyes widen.

'Dunno,' says Jenkins. 'Charity shop, I expect. That's where I get most of me books.'

'Do you know the person who wrote it?' says Adam. 'Because he lives where you work, basically. Must have bumped into him many times.'

Jenkins shrugs. 'Doubt it. Can't say I know many authors.'

'Why did you get it?' says Rose.

'I work in Elford Woods, don't I?' says Jenkins. He still hasn't looked at her once. 'Thought it would be interesting.'

'And is it?' says Adam. 'Learned much?'

'Haven't got round to it yet,' says Reece. 'So I wouldn't know.'

'Can we borrow it in the meantime?' says Adam.

Jenkins takes a drag on his rollie before replying. 'Nah, you should get your own copy, I reckon.'

She looks at Adam and it feels as though he is silently communicating the same thought. They're still going to need more to take him in.

'Before we go, Mr Jenkins,' she says, 'do you own the building over there?'

His eyes skid to hers for the first time and then scoot away again.

'Nah,' he says. 'Nowt to do wi' me.' As he lifts his cigarette to his mouth again, his hand betrays the tiniest tremor, so slight, Rose isn't sure if she imagined it.

'Okay, thank you then,' says Rose. 'I expect we'll see you soon.'

Outside a couple of minutes later, they both try to get a closer look at the other building. Rose turns to look back at the trailer and a dirty curtain passes over the window like a lid closing over an eye.

'I want to see what's in there,' says Adam quietly.

'Me too,' says Rose. 'Let's see if we can get a warrant and take a look.'

'And I think I'd like another chat with Malcolm Reece,' says Adam. 'Good spot on that book. I'll try and find out more about it while you drive.'

The book appears to be a self-published title from 1997, available on Amazon for what seems to Rose an astonishing sum of twenty seven pounds.

'Maybe he wrote it as part of the exhibition in the visitor centre,' says Rose. 'But I'd really love to know why Kyle Jenkins has a copy.'

'If it has lots of the folklore stuff, it could be used by someone wanting to carry out spooky shit in the woods.'

Rose turns to him. 'But you can get all that on the internet, surely?'

Adam gives a wide yawn. 'I suppose,' he says, his voice still slightly strangulated. 'It feels like everywhere we go we get a piece of a puzzle that does not match up in any way I can see.'

'No me neither,' says Rose gloomily. 'It's one of the most frustrating cases I've ever worked on. And I can't bear the thought of never knowing what drove that woman to climb to her death. Or what the hell is going on with these bloody dolls.'

'There's some kind of thread running through all this, I'm sure of it,' says Adam. 'I'm just buggered if I can see what it is.'

They get stuck in a traffic jam on the way back into London and by the time they are pulling into the car park nearest to the Reece property, daylight is starting to leach from the sky.

Walking into the woods towards the cottage, Rose's steps slow when sees it is in total darkness.

'Looks like no one is home,' says Adam. 'That's annoying. I hadn't really imagined this pair ever leaving the woods.'

'Yeah,' says Rose. 'There's that forcefield thingy around it for them, like the one in *The Hunger Games*.'

Adam laughs and then abruptly stops. 'Wait,' he says. 'The door is slightly open.'

He's right. The front door is ajar, as if left for someone to enter.

Rose knocks on it gently and calls out. 'Anyone home? Mr and Mrs Reece?'

Silence.

Rose makes a face at Adam and then gestures her head to signify entering the building.

Pushing the front door open, they step inside. The air is chill in the small hallway.

Adam calls out again as they head into the kitchen. 'Can't see a bloody thing in here, hang on, let me find the . . . ' He fumbles for the switch.

The scene before them floods with light.

'Oh shit,' says Adam as a distinctive metallic smell hits their noses.

30

Images all come at once, so it's hard to take them in.

The remains of the Scary Mary doll, dismembered on the kitchen table, its horrible face staring up at the ceiling.

Mary Reece on the floor in a long white nightie, curled around herself; pale head bent over her knees and thin, veined feet poking out that look almost blue with cold. Rocking slightly and murmuring to herself.

Malcolm Reece, slumped over the kitchen table, shaggy head sagging to one side so they can't see his face. But from the kitchen knife sticking out between his shoulder blades and the dark slashes congealing on his shirt, it is clear he is dead.

'What happened here, Mary?' says Rose.

Mary looks up. 'I killed him,' she says, in barely a whisper. 'I killed Malcolm.'

Rose takes a step towards her while Adam checks Malcolm for signs of life. He looks at Rose and shakes his head.

'Mary Reece,' says Rose, 'I am arresting you for murder . . .' She states the rest of the caution. 'Do you understand?'

'I found more pictures, you see,' says Mary, as if she hadn't heard. Her tone is almost dreamy. 'He tried to use the thing you said as an excuse. That someone planted them there. But I didn't believe him.' She gives them a small, surprising smile.

'I always believed him over the years, that was the trouble.' A pause. 'Anyway, it's all over now.'

She holds up her wrists, as meek as a child, awaiting the handcuffs.

Some time later, Rose, Moony and Adam are in Rowland's office at Silverton Street. Only a couple of familiar faces are there because a different shift is on duty.

The UCIT team have filled the senior officer in on everything they have discovered so far.

The atmosphere between the two older women is chilly but polite.

Mary Reece has been processed and seen by a doctor, because she was reaching the point of being dangerously cold. It turned out she had been sitting there for over twelve hours. After some warm food, drink and clothing, she has been confirmed as fit to be questioned.

'I'm happy for UCIT to lead this investigation,' says Rowland. 'Given that it seems to be so connected to your ongoing case into Suzette Armstrong, so I will take a backseat.'

'We'll watch the interview and you two can do it, okay?' says Moony.

Rose and Adam agree.

'Go off and work up your interview strategy and we'll get the ball rolling as soon as possible,' says Rowland.

A little later, Rose and Adam start the interview.

Mary has declined legal representation. She looks very small, sitting with bent shoulders in the oversized tracksuit she has been given. Her own clothes have been taken away and bagged up as evidence.

They start the tape and go through the procedure of date, time, and who's present before Rose kicks off.

'So, Mrs Reece,' she says. 'Do you want to tell us what happened?'

192

Mary nods, clasping her pale hands together in front of her on the table, the knuckles knobbled with arthritis.

'I knew what he was like from very early on, you see,' she says. 'I'm younger than him and looked even younger than I was. You should see our wedding pictures. I looked like a child.'

'What are you saying exactly?' prompts Adam. 'What do you mean "what he was like"?'

Mary turns her large eyes to Adam. 'He liked teenage girls,' she says. 'Always did. It was pretty harmless most of the time and I was able to pretend it wasn't an issue because he still wanted *me*, you see?' She stabs a thumb at her own chest. 'But since I got old and ugly, he has become so dismissive,' she continues. 'I used to dance in those woods and I was beautiful then. I know how much he wanted me. But when I danced the other night, he said some very cruel things. Very cruel indeed.' She pauses and takes a sip from the water glass in front of her.

Something chimes in Rose's mind. The flashes of white through the trees when she went back to get the doll.

'Mrs Reece . . . were you dancing in the woods two nights ago?'

Mary nods sharply twice and her bottom lip creases with rising emotion. 'Yes, for what will be the last time ever, I imagine.'

'Did you see anyone else?'

She looks at Rose, evidently surprised by this question. 'I don't think so.'

'Did you find the straw doll then?' says Adam. Mary's face seems to stiffen.

'I did,' she says. 'I hate that damned thing. "Scary Mary" they called it. Downright cruel.'

'Who called it that?' says Rose.

'Those schoolchildren,' she says. 'The ones you asked about. And Malcolm didn't see fit to tell them that was inappropriate at all. He thought it was funny. When I saw it in the woods

193

the other evening I felt . . . ' she pauses. 'It makes no sense really but I felt Malcolm left it there to upset me. To stop me doing what I wanted to do. I brought it back with me and threw it in his face but he denied everything.' She laughs. 'He was good at that. We both pretended not to remember what you were talking about yesterday when you showed us that picture of the schoolchildren. But it all came flooding back. The one called Suzette, who just died, she was a terrible little flirt with Malcolm. I used to tell him she was laughing at him behind his back – they all were – but he wouldn't have it. He claimed she was interested in the history of the woods and he liked to think of himself as some sort of wise old storyteller.' She gives a bitter little laugh. 'But really he just liked being near her. Smelling her.'

'Do you have any reason to believe anything sexual between Suzette Armstrong and your husband?' says Rose, mentally shuddering at Mary's comment.

'No,' she says. 'I don't think he ever touched her but he definitely wanted to. Her parents wised up to something being amiss and complained about him to the teacher. He was taken off that project after that. It was all water under the bridge but then we had a row that sort of continued. I looked at his computer, you see. There were pictures on there that he didn't deny he'd downloaded, but some really bad ones too – the girls looked so young. He tried to argue those had been planted but I could tell he was lying.'

'Mary, did you hear gunshots the other night in the woods? When you were dancing?' says Rose.

Mary gives a dismissive shake of her head. 'That wasn't anything to worry about.'

'How could you be sure of that?'

Mary looks down at the table and doesn't reply. This leads neatly into Rose's next question.

'Do you know someone called Kyle Jenkins?'

Mary looks at her quickly and then sighs. 'Yes,' she says. 'I knew where he was and was perfectly safe. You obviously know he does a little bit of hunting in the woods or you wouldn't have asked.'

We do now, thinks Rose, glancing at Adam.

'How do you know him exactly?' says Adam.

'From around the park,' says Mary. 'But he also helps us out, me and, um, me and Malcolm.' She shivers as if she has suddenly remembered that Malcolm is dead. That she killed him.

'Helps you out in what way?'

'He would bring some of the game he caught for Malcolm to cook,' says Mary. 'I have been vegan for ten years but Malcolm enjoyed cutting up these animals in our kitchen and taunting me about it. I didn't blame Kyle though. My husband's cruelty wasn't his fault. I think he is quite a troubled young man. He comes across as a misanthrope but I think he is a little misunderstood. He had a dreadful upbringing.'

'You say he helped you *both* out?' Rose prompts.

A great shuddering sigh goes through the other woman. 'I am in so much trouble now,' she says. 'I'm afraid I have little energy for protecting others. Look, he supplied me with my weed. There. He's only a very small fish in that world really.'

Rose writes herself a note to get onto CID re Mr Kyle Jenkins. It's definitely going to be worth having a look in that building next to his trailer, as they suspected.

'Can you talk us through the exact order of events from that night in the woods to stabbing Malcolm, Mrs Reece? Don't leave anything out, okay?'

In a voice as dry and whispery as the rustling of paper, Mary Reece describes what happened.

When she came back from what she called her 'final dance', she accused Malcolm of putting the doll there to upset her. He argued that he hadn't seen it for years and mocked her for going out in 'that state, at your age'. Mary grabbed the doll from him in a frenzy and ripped it apart with her hands. She claimed she wanted him to understand that she was a 'force' in her own right, and not some dried-out creature like that doll. She still had power. But he 'laughed and laughed' at this. 'I couldn't take the laughter,' she said. Then he sat down at the table where he opened his laptop and opened up the tab with the child porn. 'Right in front of me,' she said, still incredulous. He'd denied he had been looking at that page and went back to try and delete it. That was when she went to the sideboard and took the biggest knife from a block they'd been given as a wedding present thirty-five years earlier and drove it between his shoulder blades five times.

'I suppose I just sort of . . . snapped,' she said after she finishes this account. 'That's what people always say on TV don't they? I always thought it was one of those cliches but it really is how it felt. Something broke apart inside me. I think I'd just had enough.'

There's a short pause before Rose speaks again.

'Mrs Reece, do you know anything about the deaths of Suzette Armstrong, Haniya Shah or Alex Weston?'

Mary shakes her head. 'No,' she says. 'It's very strange they are all dead and I'm sorry about it. But it's almost as though they disturbed something in that place. Something they should have left alone.'

31

It has been raining in sheets of silver all the way and she has to park two streets away from the Squirrels. Head down into the filthy weather, Rose doesn't notice a loose paving stone that causes her whole shoe to fill with icy water. Plus, period pain is beginning to clench her insides like an angry fist.

Cursing, she turns the key in the front door and enters the house.

A mental picture of the airy cheerfulness of Ness's house breezes unhelpfully into her mind and she scowls it away.

The radio, tuned to some talk station is playing very loudly from the kitchen, muffling Rose's entry. She pokes her head in to look and witnesses a strange scene.

Zofia, dressed in a very short and tight dress, her feet pushed almost vertical in towering sandals, is standing near the fridge, holding a pint of milk and looking upset.

Jimmy is positioned between her and the route to the table, where Rose can see a bowl of Coco Pops awaiting its milk. He's muttering something Rose can't quite catch but whatever it is, it's clearly making Zofia extremely uncomfortable. Neither of them appears to have seen Rose.

'Can I get past please, Jimmy?' says Zofia. All glammed-up she somehow looks younger than usual, like a teenage girl who has gone overboard then spends the whole evening tugging her skirt over her thighs and licking off the lipstick.

What's more, she looks scared.

Rose could walk in right now and change the atmosphere completely. Instead, she waits.

'Of course you can,' he says in a low voice, but he doesn't move. He merely stands back against the sink so Zofia would have to squeeze past him.

'Plenty of room,' he says, and his oily voice is quite different from the one Rose has heard. He was never going to mess with a policewoman.

Zofia's face crumples as though she is fighting tears.

Rose has seen enough.

Maybe it's the thought of Malcolm Reece and his predilection for young girls, or Kyle Jenkins hanging out on vile woman-hating forums. Or maybe it's the thought of her mother and Orla being controlled by men like Bigham. Maybe it's just the long difficult day she has had. But whatever the reasons, fury detonates inside.

'What the *fuck* do you think you're doing?' she says, entering the kitchen in three quick strides.

Both Jimmy and Zofia visibly startle. While Zofia pales, horror-struck, Jimmy blushes puce, his eyes wide. The top of his bald head shines greasily under the strip light.

'Nothing,' he says, chin tilting in defiance. 'We were just having a little conversation, weren't we, Zofia?' The warning look he gives the trembling young woman in front of him proves to be Rose's tipping point.

Before she can even think about it, she's grabbing his hands behind his back and slamming his body forward over the kitchen table. Zofia gives a little scream. Jimmy makes a grunting sound of shock as his mouth is smushed open against the table.

Rose bends over so she has lips near his ear. 'You don't intimidate women, you little shit, do you hear me?'

He doesn't say anything, and she shoves him harder onto the table.

'I said, "DO YOU HEAR ME?"'

'Yes!' Jimmy squeaks. 'I hear you! I hear you! You're really hurting me!'

Rose's heart rams her ribcage but it's a good, cleansing sensation. She wants more of it and pictures herself slamming Jimmy's head onto the table a couple more times. Disturbed by how pleasing this image is, she lets go and stands back, her hands shaking a little.

Shoving past both of them, Zofia runs out of the room.

Jimmy stares at Rose with bug eyes, chest heaving. 'I've done nothing wrong!' he pants. 'I'll put in a complaint about you to your superiors. You can't assault innocent citizens like that in their own homes!'

'You,' hisses Rose, tapping her finger against the kitchen table for emphasis, 'can't scare women in their own homes!'

'I was doing no such thing!'

'I saw it with my own eyes!' Rose is yelling now. 'She was too scared to walk past you! Were you going to have a little feel as she went by? Was that it? A little accidental-on-purpose grope? Or worse, hey? Just her word against yours, eh? Maybe you would have done that to me too if you didn't know I'd arrest your shitty little arse for it!'

'You're disgusting,' says Jimmy, mouth pursed.

'No,' says Rose. 'You're the disgusting one here and you need to know that I'm watching you now, Jimmy. I'm watching you very closely.'

Jimmy mutters something she can't make out and then hurries out of the kitchen. Rose closes her eyes and tries to calm her galloping breaths as she looks around the grim little room, rain battering the windows. Her wet socks chill her toes and the period pain is now a determined, grinding presence. She gives a heavy sigh and leaves the kitchen, desperate to change out of her damp things.

Her mind spins. That was justified, right? But did she go too far? For some reason it's Mack she envisages now, giving her a slightly disappointed, raised-eyebrow look. She *hates* it when Mack does that.

Knocking gently on Zofia's door, she gets no response. But she can sense the presence of the other woman behind it.

'Zofia,' she says gently. 'It's me, Rose.'

'What do you want?' The voice is even curter than usual.

Rose almost laughs. Okay, maybe she was a bit heavy handed. But isn't Zofia just the tiniest bit grateful that she stepped in?

'I just wanted to make sure you're alright, that's all.'

Silence. Then, 'Am fine.'

'He didn't touch you?'

There's a frustrated sound from the other side of the door. It's like Zofia has screamed into a pillow; a muffled kind of anguish.

'Zofia?'

'No! No, for God's sake!'

'Look,' says Rose. 'Can I come in? To check you're okay?'

Movement behind the door. Then it opens a crack. Zofia peers out, scowling.

'I fight my own battles,' she says. 'I don't need you. I like this house. Is very convenient for my work. I don't see him much. Now you make things difficult here for me.'

Rose feels as though she has a slow puncture as she looks back at the young woman's defiant face. She shouldn't feel this way, having had loads of practice with ingratitude in her job. But is it possible she misunderstood something? No, there was no mistaking the vibe in that kitchen. She goes to speak again, and the door closes firmly in her face.

'Oh well,' she says. 'I'm glad you're okay.' As she walks down the hall, she mutters, 'You're bloody welcome.'

Back in her room, Rose lies back on the bed with one hand across her eyes and the other resting on her tender stomach.

She's exhausted and wired at the same time. And when is she going to eat something? Heading back out in the rain is a horrible prospect, but then so is going into the kitchen.

Remembering an apple in her handbag, Rose eats that, staring miserably at the peach anaglypta wallpaper. She thinks about Ness's lucky, lucky daughter, growing up with Ness as a mother in that beautiful, warm house, and being able to come back at the drop of a hat. It's hard not to hate her. She puts the apple core on the bedside table, before pulling the duvet around her until she is a human sausage roll.

Rose somehow drifts off, waking at 4 a.m. feeling sour-mouthed and stiff. She gets into her pyjamas and big hoodie and walks along the landing to the bathroom, where she uses the toilet and brushes her teeth.

It's as she is coming back towards her bedroom that she sees the envelope with her name on it that is propped by the door. She must have missed it when she came out.

The contents are no surprise.

Jimmy is evicting her immediately, on the grounds of 'unreasonable and violent behaviour'. And he is going to 'report her to the relevant authorities' first thing in the morning.

32

Rose doesn't go back to sleep.

Instead, she packs up her things, taking special care with the box of personal items that includes the photographs of her mother. Then she spends time looking for somewhere she can stay for the immediate future.

Jimmy has no legal right to throw her out like that. But the thought of staying here for another day is too dreadful to contemplate. Even being back in East Barnet with the spectre of Adele and her flea-bitten fur would be better than having to see that little creep every day.

And the thought is niggling at the back of her mind that he might act on what he said and report her behaviour. As she was off duty, he could have called the police himself, and the fact that he didn't is, belatedly, a big relief. He probably wasn't aware, thank God. But if she leaves immediately, as requested, it might deter him from taking this further.

In terms of where to go, her immediate thought is of friends and work colleagues.

Just a couple of nights.

You'll hardly know I'm there.

She can't do it. She hasn't spoken to Aisling, her one-time good friend from Hendon, for so long. Rose's issues and housing situation have effectively cut her off from friends she valued in the past. Scarlett and Maz would welcome her with open arms, but Rose knows for a fact that Maz's difficult mother is staying for a while and they don't have room. Mack? No, not after turning up in crisis so recently. Sam isn't an option and she can't ask Adam. No, not Adam.

But she quickly discovers that the cost of a hotel for a week, even a low budget one, is going to be unsustainable, especially when she is still having to pay for storage of all her other items and furniture.

A hostel it is, then.

She finds somewhere in Kensal Green, a backpackers place, that she could just about afford for two weeks, which seems like a realistic amount of time to organise and get in somewhere else. It's marginally cheaper to block book.

It looks absolutely soulless. Is this her life now? Each place she lives that little bit worse than the last? Aren't things meant to go the other way in this fourth decade of her existence?

But she doesn't really have a choice.

Checking in isn't until 2 p.m. but Rose has loaded her car by 7 a.m..

There's been no sign of either Jimmy or Zofia. She gives one last look at The Squirrels then starts the engine.

Goodbye and good riddance.

By 8 a.m., Rose is at her desk with a double Sausage and Egg McMuffin and a large coffee. It's quiet and in the bright sunshine that has followed last night's heavy rain, the room is flooded with a warm, apricot light for a change.

She forces her mind onto the case. They have absolutely nothing to link Mary to the other deaths in terms of evidence. The killer could still be out there.

And that means Ryan Brodie is in danger.

When she tries calling him though, his phone goes straight to voicemail.

Sitting back in her chair, she contemplates what to do next. No one is likely to be at the bar at this time so there's no point ringing there but she could go over to his flat.

She contemplates whether to wait for Adam, then gets up decisively, grabbing her car keys and bag.

Getting back into her car, Rose yawns. She's exhausted to her bones. But the prospect of laying her weary body down in that hostel later is enough to wake her up as she heads out onto the main road, the bright sun spearing her eyes.

When she knocks on the door of Brodie's flat, it opens so quickly, it surprises her.

'Oh. I thought you were Ryan,' says a woman in a black Lycra dress that clearly shows a pregnancy bump. She has bright blonde hair that hangs in a perfectly straight glossy sheet around her head, big blue eyes with heavy lashes and lips filler-puffed. But she looks distressed and her nostrils and eyes are pink tinged, as if she has been crying.

'Hi,' says Rose. 'I was looking for Mr Brodie but I gather he's not here?'

'No he isn't,' says the woman. 'He was meant to be at our scan appointment today and I don't where he is. He's not answering his phone.'

'I'm with the police,' says Rose. 'Did he say anything about talking to us?'

The woman blinks in shock. 'Is he in trouble?'

'We aren't sure,' says Rose. 'But would really like to talk to him.'

'You'd best come in,' says the woman and beckons her inside.

Rose introduces herself. 'And you are?' she says.

'Livia Kurti,' says the woman. She of the alibi, thinks Rose. 'Ryan and me, we're having a baby and he would never miss that appointment today, not on purpose.'

'When did you last see him?' says Rose, once they are in a small, tidy kitchen with shiny black worktops.

'Not since the day before yesterday,' says Kurti. 'Has something bad happened to him?' She is swaying a little bit and looks as though she might faint.

'Are you alright, Ms Kurti?'

'I'm just really worried,' says the other woman weakly, pulling out a chair and sitting heavily at the table.

'Look, let's make us both a drink and then we'll talk, okay?' Rose opens a couple of cupboards and finds tea, coffee and hot chocolate.

'Yes please,' says Kurti in a weak voice. 'Black tea.'

Rose puts the kettle on and starts to make them both a drink. Kurti watches her mournfully.

'You probably think he's a right jack-the-lad and that a baby isn't something he wants,' she says after a moment as the kettle comes to the boil. 'That he's got cold feet and done a runner or something. But I need you to understand how much he's changed. He's told me what he used to be like. But it's different with me and we both want this baby so bad. He's besotted before she's even born.' She bursts into tears. 'I found out we're having a little girl. He doesn't even know.'

Rose looks quickly for the bin so she can get rid of the teabags and offer Kurti a tissue. Finding a sleek Brabantia bin in the corner she presses the pedal with her foot and goes to throw in the two teabags.

But what she sees inside the bin stops her in her tracks.

Kurti apologises for crying, but Rose isn't listening.

She hurries to her handbag and pulls out some Nitrile gloves and an evidence bag.

'What are you doing?' says Kurti, voice rising. 'Shit, have you found something?'

'I don't know,' says Rose, pulling on the gloves. She opens the lid again and peers inside. On the very top is a wodge of damp kitchen towel. Just underneath is an item that is starting to become horribly familiar. A poppet doll, stick limbs twisted together. There's a piece of paper underneath that. Rose carefully places the doll inside the bag and reaches for the paper.

It's a small, white sheet that could come from a writing pad and on it, in neat handwriting, it says:

> *Alice Goode's a-weeping*
> *Soil upon her head*
> *Come and find her sleeping*
> *Down among the dead*

33

'We need to find him,' says Moony a little later, back at UCIT. 'I mean, it's just about possible he's got freaked out about what has been going on with his classmates and run off . . . '

'It is,' says Rose. 'But he's the last person alive of the group and that really worries me.'

'Yeah, me too,' says Moony, stroking her chin thoughtfully. 'Come on, let's do everything we can to find this bloke.'

His girlfriend reacted with a shudder but utter incomprehension to the doll and the note. She had no insights into either and been horrified when Rose told her what had happened the other evening.

'Think hard, Livia,' Rose had said. 'Does this ring any bells at all? Has he said anything about his schooldays to you that might shed light on this?'

But Livia had nothing to offer. She had gone to school in Leyton. All she knew was that Ryan had been a 'bad boy' at his own school, getting into frequent trouble but had straightened himself out when he got an apprenticeship at a garage. He'd given that up to become a personal trainer in more recent times.

She passed on details of all the friends and family she knows and while Scarlett works her way through that, Rose and Adam investigate Brodie's last known movements.

Midmorning, Rose gets a call back from her contact in CID. They have taken a warrant to the outbuilding by Kyle Jenkins' trailer and forced entry, where they discovered a bunch of unlicensed guns and a quantity of cocaine and methamphetamines they could relate to a major investigation. It looked like Jenkins was minding this property for other, bigger fish.

'We're very grateful for this,' said Mona Mukherjee from CID as she signed off, sounding so chipper that Rose came off the phone wishing they were having such luck on their own case.

Adam has the glazed look of someone watching a lot of CCTV coverage as Rose puts a fresh cup of coffee by his elbow.

'Thanks,' he says, sitting back for a moment and stretching.

'What have you found so far?' says Rose.

'There's a camera on the fried chicken shop right across from his flat, handily,' says Adam, picking up his mug and slurping distractedly. 'Look, wait a sec.' He brings up the footage. 'I started around the time he left us. He doesn't go back to work but goes straight home. Here he is, getting back at around 10.30 p.m..'

Rose watches Ryan Brodie, hunched in his probably-still-damp jacket, walking over to his block of flats and disappearing inside.

'He appears to be in there all night so I'm going to skip forward to see him coming out again.'

'No other exits?'

'No,' he says. 'Only this one.' He looks up at her. 'What about you?'

'I'm starting to look at the cell site stuff from Vodafone. Shall we get together and pool what we have in a bit?'

'Good idea,' says Adam. She starts to walk away. 'Hey,' he says, and she turns. 'Do you think he's alive?'

Rose makes a face. 'I don't know,' she says. 'I bloody hope we're not going to be too late.'

*

It's a tiring day, with a team of three people doing what would normally require more bodies. But by seven, they are assembled in front of the screen, which now has printouts of the faces and names of several people. Scarlett has been able to find pictures from defunct or active social media accounts.

Haniya Shah, Alex Weston, Suzette Armstrong, Leah Duffy, Ryan Brodie, Malcolm Reece.

All but one now dead. As far as they know, anyway.

There are also images of the twig dolls and the rhyme found in Brodie's bin.

Moony comes over, stifling a yawn. 'Update me with where we're at,' she says.

'So I managed to follow him after he left the house at 8 a.m. yesterday morning,' says Adam. 'And then I lost sight of him after a few streets. But he used his contactless HSBC debit card to access the station at St John's, and tapped out at Oakwood station just before nine. I lost him once he left the station and am still trying to find him on cameras near by.'

'Okay,' says Moony. 'And Oakwood station is . . . ?'

'One of the ones nearest to the woods,' says Adam.

'We need to go back and have a look there,' says Rose, rising slightly in her seat. 'That's been where everyone else has died. Something might be happening to him there right now.'

'It's huge though,' says Adam.

'What about his phone activity?' says Moony.

'That also places him in that broad vicinity,' says Rose, 'although it's hard to be precise. The cell towers that cover the country park also cover some of the surrounding neighbourhood.'

'Okay,' says Moony. 'What about you Scarlett? Anything to add?'

'I'm not sure,' says Scarlett. 'But I've been thinking about the apparent obsession with this Alice Goode legend. The rhyme is quite clearly referring to how she died – being buried alive, so the story goes. I'm wondering whether, if someone has intended harm to Brodie, whether it might involve something like that?'

'God!' says Adam, eyes wide. 'I hope not!'

'What was that bunker thing where Brodie was scrabbling about finding the doll the other night?' says Rose, her voice rising in panic. 'Could he be trapped in there?'

They all look at each other in horror for a moment before Moony slaps her hand down on the table, silver rings cracking like a thunderbolt against the wood.

'Go!' she cries. 'Every second might count here!'

They are halfway out the door before she has finished the sentence.

Backup is meeting them there: an ambulance from Barnet hospital and a squad car from Silverton Street. But a lorry has overturned on the Great Cambridge Roundabout and caused chaos for anyone driving the other direction to the woods from Rose and Adam. It could be a while until help arrives, even for the emergency services

Adam slaps the siren on the roof and it's blues and twos through traffic that is thickening in compensation of what is happening elsewhere. It's still slower progress than Rose would like when every single second might mean the difference between life and death.

She grips the wheel so hard her knuckles blanch and tries not to let thoughts of what might be happening to Ryan Brodie right now cloud her concentration. But it's hard not to imagine the sensation of being enclosed inside a tomb.

The panic as you realise how little air you have.

The realisation that your own panic is going to kill you faster . . .

For the first time she thinks about the story of Alice Goode, the plague victim, being buried alive in that stinking grave. Diseased, rotting bodies all around; the smell of death so dense it's thick on her tongue too.

It's hard to think of a worse way to die.

It's already starting to get dark. Mist hangs like thick white breath clinging to the ground as they burst from the car in the car park they used the other evening. Sirens can be heard in the distance; their backup. But they don't wait.

Running through the trees, it all feels a little more familiar now and they reach the bunker in a few minutes.

Adam jumps down into the gully near the entrance.

'Shine the torch in,' he says and Rose does so. Wire mesh covers the entrance.

Brodie had apparently broken this away from the side before and given himself room to squeeze through. Adam gets down on hands and knees and tries to follow.

'What can you see?' says Rose, squatting on her haunches behind him.

Adam is quiet for a moment before responding.

'He's not here. There isn't room to swing a cat. Nobody has been coming in and out of here, from what I can tell. There are too many cobwebs for that.'

'So the apparent sightings of it must be of a copy?'

'I think so.'

Adam scuttles forwards and Rose tries to angle the torch for a clearer view of what he is looking at.

What must once have been a room has been bricked up to create a narrow space that could just about accommodate a prone body.

With a grunt of discomfort, Adam starts to crawl backwards out of the space. He emerges and brushes at his knees, which even by the light of the torch are evidently wet and muddy. The shoulders and back of his grey rain jacket are streaked with dirt too.

'Nothing further in there,' he says.

Relief and a certain anti-climax mingle together as they hear the call of their unnecessary backup arriving through the trees.

'Where the hell are you, Ryan?' murmurs Rose.

They don't make any further progress back at UCIT and call it a day around 10 p.m.. Rose thinks about slogging over to

Kensal Green to that hostel and self-pity pricks her like a series of jabs with small, but sharp knives.

The hostel turns out to be clean enough but completely soulless. There's a kitchen-diner area with hard-looking seats and laminated pictures on the wall of the culinary delights on offer for breakfast, including 'Omlett' and 'Cupochino'. This does not feel promising.

The walls have been painted in an egg yolk colour that is presumably meant to be cheery but instead only emphasises the cold and institutional nature of the place.

Rose's room is tiny, with a brown-painted wardrobe and chest of drawers next to a basic looking bed. A sink and a shower cubicle that will be big enough for Rose but would be a nightmare for someone bigger, such as, say, Adam. The thought of Adam in the shower is a welcome distraction for a few moments as Rose unpacks the baguette, chocolate and crisps she's having for dinner. She can't face going into that kitchen and trying to converse with some cheerful Antipodean back-packer.

Rose props up her iPad and plays a dating reality television show that provides a sort of soothing white noise.

It has thankfully been a busy day, which has helped her ringfence some of the comments he made into no-go areas. For example, the suggestion he may be her father. What a terrible thought that would be. She contemplates getting a DNA test and feels such a wave of revulsion that she has to put her packet of crisps to one side.

Rose lies back on the hard bed and stares up at the ceiling, which is scabbed and flaking above the bed where there has evidently been a leak at some point.

Tears of self pity spring to her eyes and she rests her forearm across them, breathing heavily.

It's hard to imagine that such a young person would have had sex with Bigham with total willingness. Did he pay her when she was off her head on drugs?

Or . . . ?

No, she can't bear that. That she might be a product of rape or coercion is too terrible to contemplate. For a disorientating moment she feels a pang of nostalgia for when she thought her family history merely encompassed a mother who didn't want her and a grandmother who was a heartless old fraudster.

She sits bolt upright and swings her legs round onto the rough, blue institutional carpet. Get on with some admin. Don't sit here stewing.

Rose gets her laptop and props herself up on the narrow bed, attempting to get comfortable with a cushion behind her but not quite managing it. The TV programme runs in the background with a soundtrack of much shrieking and discussions of 'boundaries' and 'letting down walls'. Rose glances at it occasionally as she works through some admin she has been putting off, tutting once at the actions of the arch villain of the piece and trying to forget about anything else.

It's almost midnight when she realises there is an email she hadn't seen earlier.

At first she is too weary to register what she is looking at. Then her attention sharpens, and her heart starts to pound in her chest.

It's an email from the Professional Standards Unit, which is a team of officers based at the Basic Command Unit for Rose's part of North London. They are putting her on notice that they will be investigating her for potential Gross Misconduct following a complaint from a Mr James Burgess.

34

'Take a breath and run that by me again?'

It's seven o'clock in the morning. Rose has managed roughly four hours sleep after receiving that email and has been waiting for what seemed a respectable time to call the only person she can bear to share this news with.

'Like I said, they're investigating me for gross misconduct!'

It sounds like Mack is driving because there is a vague echo to her words.

'Hang on, kiddo,' he says. 'I'm just arriving at the station, let me park up.'

There's a pause. Rose chews on a thumbnail that begins to sting when the nail rips too far. She sucks the metallic wetness away and fights more tears.

'Okay,' Mack is back on the line. 'Tell me exactly what happened and where this came from.'

Rose tells him about the creepy vibes she had picked up from Jimmy since the day she moved into The Squirrels.

'Did he ever do anything inappropriate to you?'

'No,' she says, almost reluctantly. 'But I think that was only because he was a bit intimidated by my job.'

Mack doesn't speak but it feels like he is silently passing judgement. Rose feels a flash of anger. 'Look, as a bloke you can't possibly understand what it's like!' she says. 'We have to put up with that shit constantly!'

An imagined picture of Terrence Bigham and her teenage mother flashes up, unhelpful, but vivid. And Reece and Suzette Armstrong.

'Okay, okay,' says Mack hurriedly. 'I'm not denying that. I'm thinking about the sort of questions you might face later, that's all. Now tell me what actually happened.'

Rose goes through the episode in the kitchen, from when she saw Zofia's rabbit-in-the-headlights expression and frozen stance, to the moment she pushed Jimmy down onto the table.

'You lost your shit, basically,' says Mack.

Rose swallows the thickening emotion in her throat. 'Yeah,' she says in a tiny voice. 'That's about the size of it.'

There's a heavy sigh at the other end.

'What's going to happen now, Mack?' she says.

'It's hard to say,' he says. 'It depends on how far this Jimmy character wants to take it. I mean, if he wants to press criminal charges, you know that you'll have to face that just as any civilian would.'

'Oh fuck,' Rose gives a strangled groan and places her hand over her eyes.

'But he might not do that,' says Mack hurriedly. 'Look, it's a good sign that Professional Standards are handling this. It means a decision has already been taken not to pass this onto the IOPC.'

Rose nods. The Independent Office for Police Conduct would take this to an even higher level. It's some small comfort.

'And although they have gross misconduct as a starting point, this is still fairly low level stuff and the overwhelming likelihood is that it will be downgraded to misconduct.'

'What's the difference?'

'Big difference in outcomes,' says Mack. 'Gross misconduct can end in dismissal without notice but that won't happen if the outcome is basic misconduct.'

The word 'dismissal' looms across Rose's mind to the extent that, for a moment, she can't respond.

'Rose?'

'Yeah, yeah, I'm here.' Even though she distantly knew all this information, hearing Mack say the words out loud is making it hard to catch her breath.

'What will happen next then?' she manages to say. 'What should I expect?'

Mack goes on to explain the stages of this sort of inquiry. The PSU will now carry out an investigation, which will involve interviewing Jimmy, and Zofia too, and then interviewing Rose under a misconduct caution.

'You'll be entitled to support there from a Police Federation representative and maybe a solicitor too. They'll then decide if there is a case to answer or not and whether it's gross or just misconduct. There are different types of hearing for those.'

'Oh God.' Rose has been pacing the tiny room but now she sinks down onto the bed, forgetting how hard it is and getting an unpleasant jolt to the lower spine as she does so.

'Don't despair, kiddo.' Mack's voice is low and kind. 'There's the possibility the whole thing might be diverted into a "reflective practice review" process. That's basically about being sat down and made to have a good hard think about what you've done and why you won't do it again.' He pauses. 'You never know. That could happen.'

Rose thinks of Jimmy's puffed-up self-important face when he was complaining about the cyclist who was rude to him. This must be like all his Christmases have come at once.

'No,' she says. 'This dickhead will push for this to be a criminal enquiry, I know it.'

Mack is silent for a moment.

'This is a bit shit, isn't it?' she says. 'What a mess.'

Mack sighs. 'I'm running late and really have to get inside now, mate, but you know I'm always here.'

'Thanks Mack.'

'Chin up, Rose. It may not be as bad as you think.'

But it is. Losing this job is her very worst nightmare. What else does she really have?

Both Scarlett and Adam look up curiously when Rose asks if she can have another quiet word with Moony, for the second time in a couple of days.

It feels as though she had finally been opening herself up to being a real part of this team. And now she has secrets she can't bear to discuss more widely. Moony though, will find out anyway, and there is no point in putting this off any longer. It feels as though the ceiling is lower than usual today. As if the actual sky is pressing down on her.

Moony is low key when Rose tells her about the disciplinary proceedings, clearly having already heard. She doesn't come out with any platitudes about it all being alright and Rose is grateful. She simply says, 'Keep me posted' and they go back into the main office.

Rose keeps her head down but she can't concentrate. Moony disappears for a cigarette break and Rose can feel the pull of the desire for one like something physical. When Moony comes back into the office and resumes her seat, Rose goes over.

'Can I please steal one of those?' she says, pointing to the packet of Marlboro Lights on the desk.

Moony regards her for a moment without saying anything. Then she slides the packet and the lighter across the desk.

Rose hurries out to the back of the building, where there is a scrappy bit of grass and what was once part of a river, since rerouted and now basically a dry ditch.

She sits on a low wall there, wishing she had thought to bring her coat because although it isn't raining, there is a chill wind biting through the sleeves of her thin jumper.

Lighting the cigarette, she gets a dizzying head rush and a wave of nausea, swiftly followed by a sense of satisfaction. It has been a year and a half since she last smoked but it's the last of her worries right now.

The thought that Ryan Brodie might be in danger gnaws at

her. There is no real evidence he has been abducted but something in her guts tells her otherwise. This and all her personal problems churn around in her mind like clothes in a washing machine.

'Hey.'

She looks up sharply to see Adam coming round the side of the building. He's holding her jacket.

'Thought you might need this,' he says. He smiles but concern is evident on his face.

Rose forces a quick grateful grin. 'Thanks,' she says. 'It is bloody freezing.'

She takes the jacket and shrugs it on with the cigarette in the corner of her mouth.

'Didn't know you smoked?' Adam perches next to her.

'I don't,' she says, then grimaces. 'I'm not starting again. I'm having a bad day, that's all, and for some reason it felt like it might help.'

'Is it?' says Adam. 'Helping?'

'Yeah a bit, if I'm honest,' says Rose, and Adam laughs.

'Look, Rose . . . ' he says. She takes another drag and stares straight ahead. Bracing herself for this conversation. 'What's going on, mate?' he continues. 'You can tell me to sod off and mind my own business. I won't be offended.' Then he leans in a bit and nudges her with his shoulder. 'I'm saying that, but I don't really mean it, obviously.'

A combination of gratitude, regret and longing twist inside her. She can't speak and simply puffs on the cigarette. Hating herself for smoking it; loving smoking it.

'I'm a bit of a mess, Adam,' she says after what seems like a long silence. 'That's the truth of it. I think maybe I always will be.'

'I don't think you're a mess,' says Adam. 'And I don't think Moony, or Scarlett, or Mack for that matter think so. Or that Sam bloke.'

Rose blinks hard, gathering herself. 'I am though,' she says. 'I've gone and got myself into terrible trouble. I might lose my job.'

'Shit . . . what's happened?'

Rose can hardly bear to say the words so she forces them out quickly in three short sentences.

'I went for the creepy little shit who was my landlord. He was perving at a girl in the house and I lost it. And now he's reported me.'

'Ah . . . that's, well, that's not good,' says Adam, wincing. 'I'm sorry to hear about it. But you know, these things happen. It might not be the end of the world.'

She looks at him. 'You ever been reported?'

'Well, no . . . '

'Huh, thought not. But it's not just that,' Rose says, the words coming faster. 'I can't seem to find somewhere to live like a normal person of my age and I have all these . . . ' she laughs bitterly, '*issues*, I guess you'd call them.'

'What sort of issues?' Adam's voice is gentle.

Rose takes a shaky breath in and out and then throws the last bit of the cigarette onto the ground, where she grinds it into the grass with the heel of her boot.

'About my upbringing,' she says. 'There's stuff you don't know about me. Moony knows because, well, through the job. Turns out she knew all about me and my fucked-up home long before I ever thought I'd met her. And I told Scarlett really recently, only because she got me so drunk I almost went blind.'

Adam laughs. 'Yeah . . . drinking with Scar . . . big mistake, as I said.'

Rose presses on. 'But when I say my childhood was messed up, it was stranger than you can possibly imagine. I didn't grow up in a normal home with a normal mum and dad like other people did. All sorts went on in that house. And now someone from that past is going to drag it all out and I seem to have no choice about any of it. I feel like I'm in a car with no driver that's doing ninety on the motorway.' She glances at him. 'You ever had that dream?'

'Not sure I have, to be honest,' says Adam. 'Mine are more of the no-trousers-in-an exam variety. But that all sounds like a lot to deal with. I had no idea about your upbringing. I'm really sorry to hear it. You weren't . . . ' he pauses. 'Abused?'

'No,' she shakes her head. 'Not physically anyway. It was more like neglect, really.'

'Oh.' Adam seems unsure what else to say. 'Shit.'

'I'll tell you about it properly over a drink some time,' says Rose. 'It's a long story.'

'Anytime you want,' says Adam. 'But no pressure.'

She turns to look at him. He suddenly seems very close, and she finds herself unable to look away from those kind brown eyes. The distance between their faces is nothing. She can smell the mint of the gum he must have been chewing before he came out to find her. To check she was alright. He isn't looking away and the moment suddenly feels so loaded that Rose can hardly catch her breath. She's conscious of her smoky mouth and wants to seal her lips shut but she finds instead they are parting instead as Adam's mouth moves closer to hers.

He says 'Rose' so gently it's almost an exhalation.

There's a movement to the left and Scarlett is right there, next to them.

'You both okay?' Her voice is too loud, her presence unwelcome, for the first time since Rose has known her.

'Yeah, fine!' Adam sounds unnaturally bright as he shifts away a little from Rose, whose whole face and neck helpfully flood pink.

Her mind is reeling. He was going to kiss her. Was he? He was. *Adam was going to kiss her*. She is incapable of speech. Rose merely tries to force her eyes to Scarlett, who is staring at both of them with total incomprehension.

'Am I interrupting something?' she says. 'You both look weird!'

'No!' they both cry at once, which is evidently so unconvincing, the side of Scarlett's mouth twitches in supressed mirth. But thankfully, she says nothing. 'Well you both left your phones inside and Moony said to come and get you. We've got the DNA results back on the large doll. Best come in.'

Rose practically runs back into the building. The skin covering her entire body seems to be on fire.

35

Back in the office, they gather at the sofas. Rose's hands are still shaking slightly and she daren't look at Adam, although she feels his gaze on her at times.

'So,' says Moony, 'there was nothing useful on the small one found with Armstrong's body so whoever made it was careful. But we rushed through the test on the one at the Reeces', like you asked. And they found a bloodstain that got a hit on the database.'

'Oh yeah?' says Rose, focus coming back. 'What did they find?'

'Seems they matched on an arrest in 2003, from one Leah Duffy.'

'Okay,' says Rose. 'I suppose she might have handled it along with everyone else in that group?'

'Blood though,' says Adam. 'That interests me.'

'Remind me how she died?' says Moony.

'She had a heart attack, I think,' says Rose, turning to her screen and tapping. 'Yeah, I made a note. Double checked the death certificate and it was just as her mother told us.'

'Young for a heart attack, surely?' says Moony.

'She was,' says Rose. 'But it appears that years of alcohol and drug abuse took their toll. I think cirrhosis of the liver would have got her if her heart hadn't packed in, from what I read.'

'Okay,' says Adam. 'Let's go back and have another word with her mum.'

The atmosphere in the car is strained. To fill the awkwardness, Rose finds herself forcing conversation about the case. But she's talking too much, she knows it. Adam looks distractedly out of the window.

Finally, as they wait at traffic lights on the main high street through Southgate, he speaks.

'Look, Rose . . . ' he says heavily but she cuts him off with a too-bright, too-sharp laugh.

'It's fine!' she says. 'Let's just pretend it never happened!'

'Oh, okay,' says Adam quietly. 'Okay.'

'No worries then,' she says.

'No worries.'

It's a relief to park up and leave the claustrophobic vibe of the car.

When Sandra Duffy comes to the front door, her eyes widen at the sight of the two police officers.

'Oh my goodness,' she says. 'You're back. Has something else happened?'

'No, no,' says Adam. 'We're sorry to bother you Sandra, but we are following a few things up and wanted to ask if we could have a moment more of your time.'

She hesitates. 'It's not the most convenient time because I'm working, but look, I could do with a break. Come on in.'

'Thank you,' says Rose.

They follow her back into the kitchen. Two laptops are open on the kitchen table. She closes the lids and tidies them away before heading to the kettle.

'Drink?'

They decline and she fills the kettle anyway. Rose looks around the kitchen for the little dog but the basket is empty.

'Where's your dog?' she says. Sandra turns to look at her as she spoons coffee into a mug.

'Oh, asleep on my bed, I expect,' she says, turning back to make her drink.

'Sandra,' says Rose, 'I'm going to get straight to the point. We found something connected to the case that has your daughter's DNA on it.'

Sandra turns away from the counter, frowning. 'Leah's DNA?' she says. 'Where? How?'

Rose gets out her phone and brings up a picture of the doll. She holds the phone out towards Sandra, who takes it a little reluctantly before flinching.

'Yikes,' she says. 'What the hell is that meant to be?' she hands it back to Rose as though it has scalded her.

'It was part of an exhibition,' says Rose. 'It used to be outside the visitor centre and it seems to have had some meaning to the young people who took part in that school project in 1998 – the one in the photo.' She pauses. 'The one Leah helped with.'

Sandra's face is scrunched in apparent confusion. 'But how does it have my daughter's DNA on it? What kind of DNA anyway?'

'Blood,' says Rose. 'It had a small amount of blood on it that came from Leah.'

Sandra brings her black coffee over and sits down, gesturing for Rose and Adam to do the same. They sit.

'Well, this is all very strange and a bit upsetting if I'm honest,' she says. 'My poor daughter had a very hard life but I honestly don't see what any of it has to do with that woman's death at the climbing place. I mean, if that horrible thing was in the exhibition, then Leah could easily have scratched herself on it, couldn't she?'

'That's very true,' says Rose. 'But just so we can get a picture of how that period of time might relate to now, can you tell us a little bit about your daughter?' says Rose.

Sandra's shoulders round and she looks down at her mug. 'I'm not sure what to tell you,' she says. 'She was a troubled soul who took a wrong turn at a certain point and never really got back on her feet again. Got into a bad crowd in the final years of school and her life sort of imploded from there. And I—' she stops and takes a tissue from her pocket, which she dabs at her nostrils with, 'I blame myself, frankly.'

'Why's that?' says Rose gently.

'Because I had her quite young and wasn't around for most of her life,' she says. 'My own mother did her best but she couldn't cope, not really.' She looks close to tears and is breathing heavily. 'I suppose you had her DNA on record because she was arrested a couple of times.'

'She never said anything about the significance of this doll?' Rose presses.

Sandra shakes her head. 'No,' she says. 'But anything could have happened in that period of her life and I wouldn't have known a thing about it.' She looks down at her cup again and her nostrils flare with the deep breath she takes. 'I can't tell you how bad that makes me feel.'

There's a silence broken only by the ticking of the clock before Adam speaks.

'I think we have what we need for now,' he says. 'We'll leave you to get on with your work.'

They get up.

In the car, which they have had to park across the road, Rose gets out her phone and starts to thumb the keys at speed.

'What are you doing?' says Adam.

'I'm looking her up,' she says.

'Why?'

'I don't know many people who need two laptops,' says Rose. Then, 'Look' she says triumphantly.

She is holding up a LinkedIn page for Sandra Duffy. Her job description is Server System Manager.

'What's one of those when it's at home?' says Adam.

'Dunno, but sounds techie to me.' Rose's thumbs fly on the screen. 'Okay, it's the person who looks after all the main servers for a company.' She looks at Adam. 'So, like I said. A massive techie. Why didn't she say that when we asked?'

'Could be any number of reasons, not least that most people don't know what it means,' says Adam. 'But are you thinking she would have the knowhow and skills for installing all that ratware?'

Rose shrugs. 'I'm sure she would.'

'I guess,' says Adam. 'But what motive would she have? Her daughter's been dead for years. Some sort of revenge thing?'

'Maybe,' says Rose. 'And anyway, something in that house felt . . . off.'

'Off, how?'

Rose lets out a slow exhale. 'I can't explain it. It gave me an odd feeling. Like there was something . . . else there.'

It was a familiar one; the one she had so often in her childhood. As if someone was watching, out of sight. All her life she has resisted it; hated that she had this heightened sense. Whatever it is, she had felt it inside Sandra Duffy's house.

'Ay up,' says Adam, turning his head. 'It looks like she's on the move.'

Sandra Duffy is hurrying out of the house, carrying something wrapped in a blanket. As she turns their way, they see a pair of black and white ears peeking out of the top. She climbs into a black Fiat Uno parked on the road outside her house.

'She didn't say something was wrong with the dog, did she?' says Rose.

'Well, no . . . '

Rose shoots her colleague an irritated look. 'You think this a wild-goose chase?'

'God, I don't know, Rose!' says Adam. 'I'm just not as convinced as you are, that's all. But look, I'm behind whatever you want to do 100 per cent. We work for UCIT and if you say you have a feeling, you have a feeling.'

Rose looks over at her colleague and they meet eyes for the first time since the Almost Kiss. He smiles and warmth fills her chest.

'Shall we follow her?' he says, breaking the moment.

'Nope,' says Rose, starting to open the car door. 'We're going into that house.'

They run across the street and down the alley that leads to the back garden.

Rose looks at Adam as they contemplate the locked gate.

'Are we sure about this?' he says. 'Do we have reasonable suspicion to break in?'

'I do,' says Rose. 'And I'm already in the shit so who cares if we're wrong? You can blame me if you have to.'

'No chance of that,' says Adam then breaks open the back gate with two sharp kicks.

They rush to the back door.

'Stand back,' says Rose. She is holding an old metal garden chair, covered in scabbed white paint with a filigree of green mould.

Adam moves out of the way as Rose smashes the chair into the top of the kitchen door, which explodes inwards in a shower of glass.

36

November 4th 1997

Leah shivers as she crosses the main road. It's much colder than she expected and her favourite bomber jacket is scant protection from the knifing wind. Nan nagged her about wearing her winter coat before she left but she ignored her, mainly because she didn't want her to be right. Nan is so determined Leah won't turn out like her mum that she won't let her make any decisions for herself.

When she knocks on Haniya's front door, it's Rami who answers. He's holding a massive sandwich in one hand and the other is casually lying across his flat stomach, just above the waistband of his trackie bottoms. Leah's mouth goes a bit dry and she can't think of anything to say. Rami is three years older and even though he has quite a few spots, he still makes her go a bit funny. She manages to mumble a question about whether Haniya is ready yet. He turns and yells his sister's name, sounding vaguely irritated as if she has inconvenienced him by existing.

Haniya appears at the top of the stairs. She still has her uniform on and she's gnawing on a thumbnail in a familiar gesture. It's what she does when she knows she is about to say something unpopular. This is compounded by the fact that her eyes are aimed a bit to the side of Leah's face, as though looking directly at her would be uncomfortable.

'You ready?' says Leah briskly, pretending she isn't aware of any of this. Haniya hurries down the staircase.

'I don't think I'm coming,' she says in a quiet little mouse voice. 'I've got stuff to do here.'

'For God's sake,' Leah hisses. 'When are you going to stop being such a wuss? You promised I wouldn't have to go on my own! You *promised!*'

Haniya shushes frantically as her mother appears, carrying a stack of primary school exercise books.

'Oh hello, Leah!' she says. 'Haniya didn't mention you were coming over. Have you come to study together?'

'Hello Mrs Shah!' says Leah with a big smile. 'We're going to study at mine tonight if that's okay because my nan wanted me to be around? I said I'd walk Haniya over.'

'Well, that's fine,' says Mrs Shah, glancing at her daughter. 'Do stay together though, girls, okay? And if you ring me, Han, a bit later, I'll pick you up, okay? I'm just trying to plough through all this marking and don't mind an interruption.'

'No problem, Mrs Shah.'

The woman looks at her daughter, who is staring mutinously at Leah. 'Haniya?'

'Yes, Mummy. I'll call you later. I won't be late.'

Leah grits her teeth. She finds it embarrassing that Han calls her mother 'Mummy' like they're still in Year Three or something.

'Good girls,' says Mrs Shah with a smile. 'Be careful now and go straight to Leah's house. And give my regards to your granny, Leah.'

'Will do!' Leah knows her smile is plastered on but somehow seems to be getting away with it, even if her friend is giving her daggers as she drags on her duffel coat and scarf.

Outside the front door, though, Haniya stops dead. 'I don't want to do this, Leah. It's stupid! I don't know why you even want to be friends with those people. They don't really like us.'

Leah hides her wave of irritation by giving Haniya a grin and an elbow nudge.

'Come on, Han,' she urges. 'We never do anything fun! You have to admit they're a bit more exciting than anyone else we get to hang out with. And anyway, it's not true they don't like us, well me, anyway. Suze told me she'd come over and show me how to do my eye make-up like hers at the weekend.'

'Oh, *Suze* is it now?' Haniya's eye roll makes Leah feel cold anger in her stomach. 'And you just want to be near that Ryan,' she pulls a face as though even saying his name bothers her. 'He loves himself so much. I can't understand what you see in that bighead.'

Leah controls herself by concentrating on getting gum from her pocket, unwrapping it and popping it in her mouth. She offers the packet to her friend who shakes her head.

'I like him, that's all,' she says. 'He's been really nice to me since we've been doing this woods thing. Please, Han!' she pulls her friend by the arm and almost frogmarches her across the main road to where the dark mass of Elford Woods begin.

They trudge through the trees, which seem taller and more ominous than in the daytime. The moon is shining brightly tonight, which makes it simultaneously more spooky and less so. It's a relief to be able to see the way, but it means the trees throw night shadows down in the silvery light that look like all sorts if you let them.

Haniya mutters something Leah doesn't catch.

'What d'you say?'

'I said *this is madness*.' She gives Leah an imploring look. 'Look, Leah, don't you know they're laughing at you?' Haniya stops and turns to her friend. 'Why would that lot invite you out otherwise? Can't you see we're not their type of people?'

Leah tilts her jaw as the words jab at her.

'They're not laughing at me!' she says. 'They might be laughing at *you*.'

'For goodness' sake,' says Haniya. 'You can't see what's right

229

in front of your nose. Didn't you learn your lesson with Suzette already? In Year Six?'

This hits the target as painfully as it was intended to.

Haniya is referring to the trip to an adventure centre in the final year of Leah's primary school, which Suzette also attended. Leah cried at the top of the abseiling tower and refused to do it, and Suzette mocked her for the rest of that week. Leah had told Haniya this in confidence and doesn't much appreciate it being thrown in her face now.

Haniya is still going on. 'Those people are not your friends. And they're certainly not mine! They didn't even invite me!'

'Only because they think you're stuck up!' says Leah, eyes blazing. 'And you know what? You are stuck up. All you ever do is study and you're no fun at all!' She regrets the words the instant they leave her lips and reaches towards her friend, who raises both hands as though warding her off.

'Fine,' says Haniya, voice wobbling a little. 'In that case I'll leave you to your new friends.' She turns and begins to march back in the direction they came from.

'Wait, Han!' says Leah, tears springing to her eyes as she tries to hurry after her retreating friend. Her toe catches a tree root and goes down, hard, crying out.

Haniya doesn't even stop to check she is okay.

'Haniya! Please don't leave me here! I'm scared on my own!'

And then Haniya actually begins to run. She is much slimmer and faster than podgy Leah, who is no good at any sports, even if she hadn't fallen and hurt herself. Haniya is on the athletics team at school and always does well in the cross-country championships they do in this park every year.

This is the thing that will stay in her mind for many years afterwards. Haniya left her there. Why will no one stand by Leah's side? Not her best friend. Not even her own mum.

She sucks at the bright sting on her hand and tastes blood, which makes more tears come.

Haniya has gone, back to the warm comfort of her home and her nice family.

Leah feels paralysed as she looks around. She could easily follow Haniya's lead and go home. Nan would want to know what had happened and be annoying about it but that wouldn't be so bad, would it? She might make her an instant hot chocolate and let them watch telly together.

But then Leah would go into school tomorrow and Suzette would say, 'What happened to you?' with disappointment and annoyance in her beautiful blue eyes, with those long lashes Leah would kill to have. And Leah would have to admit she got scared. Again.

They already take the piss out of her about how freaked out she is about this place but they don't understand the way she feels things differently to them. Tonight was meant to be about showing them she wasn't a stupid, scared little girl. She was like them.

Suzette says the spirit of Alice Goode roams here at night. Suzette knows loads about this stuff and has even talked about how she's tried a couple of spells. 'Only white magic though,' she said with a sniff, as if Leah thought she had been doing a bit of devil worshipping at weekends.

Don't think about devil worshipping. Or Alice Goode's wandering ghost, for that matter. Suze told her that Mr Reece told her his wife goes dancing in the woods at night because she's a pagan, which is so weird. She doesn't want to bump into her either. Or him, for that matter, the big creep. He's always looking at the girls and putting a hand on their shoulder or arm when he can.

An owl hoots a perfect *too-wit-too-woo* that almost sounds fake and for some reason this makes her want to laugh. No. She's not going to be mousey little Leah with her stupid swotty friend and the mum who doesn't want her. She's going to be like them tonight. Her real friends.

Leah trudges on to where they said they'd meet, by the bunker. Alex said he would bring vodka, which she has never had but she is going to try it tonight without Haniya's disapproving beak getting in the way of her having fun.

But for all her pretend bravado, her thoughts keep being tugged towards thoughts of Alice Goode and creepy things. She keeps glancing around, heart thumping practically in her throat, half expecting to see a thin-faced girl in an old-fashioned dress wringing her hands and wandering among the skeletal trees with her doll. Ready to claim her next soul.

Ever since they all learned about Alice Goode from Mr Reece, Leah hadn't been able to get it out of her head. She can't seem to stop picturing it all. The coffin lid slamming down and then earth being piled on top. All those stinking, plague-ridden bodies . . .

She's had nightmares about it. One of them involved that horrible doll thing at the visitor centre Suzette calls Scary Mary, because she reckons it looks like Mr Reece's wife.

But then of course she'd made the mistake of *saying* the doll gave her the creeps. Alex laughed at her and thought it was funny to lift it up and say 'your mother sucks cocks in hell' in a devil voice, which she thinks is from some horror film.

Leah is shivering hard from a combination of cold, shock at her friend's departure and thoughts of the story all swirling around inside her. She wishes she wasn't so pathetic, but tough like Suzette.

She's scared of so many things, from spiders to heights, but enclosed spaces are the worst of all. Nan says it's because she got stuck in a wardrobe when she was five and visiting some person Nan knew in the country. She'd been in what Nan called 'one of her sulks' that day; she still remembers it. But Nan had said her mum was coming to visit the day before and then her mum didn't bother to turn up – again. She was sad when they went on that visit to that stupid old woman's house and wanted to hide, that was all. But she hadn't expected to get locked in that horrible musty place with the old dead man's suits.

So, when Mr Reece started telling them the story of that poor girl who died in the plague and got buried alive, Leah had made a fool of herself and started *crying*. Ugh, what a pathetic thing to do. Everyone apart from Haniya had laughed at her, but Haniya hadn't defended her or anything. She never did. She was so bothered about looking after herself that she never put Leah first. The more Leah thinks about it, Haniya has never ever stood up for her, not once.

Mr Reece even thought it was funny and he was the grown up. He seemed to like telling them scary stories, especially when Suzette batted her eyelashes at him. She even started doing one more turn of her school skirt at the waist and that dirty old perv loved it. Then Mr Buckley saw and had a sharp word with her, and Mr Reece. Leah heard him saying something about how 'these youngsters love all the stories', but Mr Buckley said something about their age and being inappropriate.

He's nice, Mr Buckley . . . She tries not to think of him giving her a disappointed look now and forces herself to keep putting one foot in front of the other through the woods.

She brought a torch but somehow it would make things even creepier because she could imagine the light bouncing around and catching flashes of things in the trees.

Like faces. Or thin, scary girls.

Leah's teeth are chattering now. An overwhelming urge to be watching *Brookside* with Nan overcomes her. Why did she even do this?

It was definitely a mistake.

Then Leah can hear voices in the distance and relief spreads through her insides like a warm drink.

They're here, just like they promised they would be. Her real friends.

37

Rose and Adam survey Sandra Duffy's shattered back-door window for a moment, then Rose picks up a tarpaulin hanging limply over a rusting old barbecue. She wraps it around her arm before knocking away the jagged remnants of glass remaining in the window, reaching inside and finding the key in the lock. It's awkward to turn it at this angle but, finally she feels the click and is able to open the door and enter the kitchen.

They crunch across broken glass.

'I'll look upstairs and you check down here,' says Adam.

She checks out a door in the kitchen to what may be a cellar. Locked, and the key has been removed.

She bangs hard on the door. 'Hello? This is the police. Is anyone in there?'

Adam comes back into the kitchen. 'All clear upstairs,' he says. He gives the cellar door three hard thumps with the side of his fist, and they listen again.

'Was that something?' she says. 'Did you hear a knock? I don't know if I imagined it.'

'I'm not sure either,' says Adam. 'Stand back.' Rose does as asked. Adam shoulder charges the door with a grunt; once, twice, and then it flies open.

They peer inside to see a staircase leading down into something that is a cross between a cellar and a utility room. Rose fumbles for a light switch and finds one to her left. Light floods the space below them.

A fat metallic tumble dryer pipe snakes across the ceiling, which is low and made from basic beams and insulation. A washing machine and tumble dryer are in the far corner and an exercise bike is draped with what looks like a pair of dusty old curtains. Then she spots the table. It is covered in twigs, with scraps of cloth and balls of twine. She's so busy staring at this that she hasn't noticed something else in the room and it's only when Adam says, 'What the hell is *that*?' that she sees what he's looking at.

38

Sandra

The vet made me feel so guilty. I know I shouldn't have given poor Henry those tablets. I said it was an accident; that he ate them when I dropped them on the floor in error but she gave me a very suspicious look and a lecture about keeping medicines away from animals. They're going to make him eat some charcoal to be sick and she says she 'hopes' he will recover. He doesn't deserve this. But I needed him to stop clawing and whining at the cellar door. Maybe I should have asked someone to look after Henry. But who would I ask? And how would I explain it?

As I get back into the car, I think about what is happening back at home and it strengthens my resolve.

I wonder whether he is slipping away yet. If the panic has stopped and acceptance begun.

It was very difficult getting him into what will be his final resting place. Not that he deserves any rest. It was surprisingly easy getting Rohypnol off the dark Web but it was much stronger than I imagined it would be. I didn't expect him to completely collapse in the way he did. I thought there might be some level of cooperation involved. I suppose I pictured him being sleepy and floppy but able to move himself. Instead he was like a great big side of bacon I had to manoeuvre alone. It really wasn't easy.

He made a terrible fuss when he woke up and couldn't seem to work out where he was or why he was in there. Not that he stopped shouting long enough for me to get a word in edgeways. But when he did quieten down, I talked to him. Explained very carefully exactly why he was here. He did quite a lot of angry shouting and I thought for a while I hadn't made it strong enough and that he would get out. But finally he realised he couldn't do it and he started begging to be released.

But it was all water off a duck's back. I don't imagine he had much truck for begging when he did what he did.

In some ways I'm disappointed this couldn't happen in the proper location. But that would have been too difficult and frankly, I only have so many ideas. I was at a loss at first, then I realised the way forward and it felt just perfect.

It has to be special. Because he is the last one, you see. The worst, in some ways. Such a cocky little shit then and much the same when he turned up for his appointment with 'Jane' this morning in the park for a supposed personal training session.

As if I'd want a personal trainer! I get quite enough exercise walking Henry, thank you very much.

He didn't even make much effort to hide how little he wanted to be there. I was gratified to see that he had lost a bit of the lustre I've seen from watching him closely these past months. He looked tired. I know he came to the woods the other night because I've been tracking his movements via an AirTag that he doesn't even know is in his car. I don't know what he did and he won't tell me. Maybe he thinks it gives him some sort of power, which is a bit pathetic . . . but there you go. He hasn't got much left, has he?

I could have simply shot him, with the small hand gun I also got from knowing where to ask online. But shooting Brodie would have missed the entire point. I only got it as a backup plan in case I couldn't get him in there. I want him to experience the terror Leah felt that night, after they pushed her into that hole. He can probably feel the air running out, just as she thought was happening. It doesn't make any difference that she hadn't been buried alive. She believed she had, you see? She believed it.

His death will be relatively swift in comparison to hers. Leah's death took another seventeen years.

I picture my daughter that night, before the drugs made her face a skull, with lank ropes of hair and that tell-tale brightness in the eyes that the long-term addicted always have.

Back then she was all round cheeks and teeth. She looked so much younger than the rest of that group of nasty little bastards, from what I know of it. They made her think she was lucky, letting her join in for the first time at their campfire in the woods.

At first she had been enjoying herself. The vodka, mixed into the big bottle of cheap lemonade, barely tasted of anything at all, she said, and she was proud for being in control and not getting so drunk she did anything stupid.

I only heard all this so many years later, of course, right before the end.

Then Brodie, the piece of scum currently breathing his last in my cellar, persuaded her to take some magic mushrooms. She had been hesitant at first, having never done anything like that before, but Alex Weston had goaded her on, calling her a baby who shouldn't have been invited. He, at least, had been honest about his contempt. He didn't pretend to be her friend. Not like the others. Suzette Armstrong looked so disappointed when she wouldn't join in. But it was him, Ryan Brodie, who lifted her chin and looked into her eyes, then kissed her and told her to trust him. She'd never been kissed before and for it to be someone like him, who all the girls wanted and all the boys wanted to be, well . . .

Head spinning with happiness, Leah took the handful of dried, stinky plants and stuffed them into her mouth, almost gagging at the mulchy taste.

She's a bit hazy about what happened after that. But this is when Suzette pretended to get scared and say the spirit of Alice Goode was near. Suzette had been in a couple of school plays, Leah told me, and was convincing when she started shaking and crying. It brings me peace to know that Armstrong felt such fear when she saw what remained of my daughter in her final moments. The storm made it all perfect. Leah frightened her up the platform and I pushed her off. We're quite a team.

Anyway, it's unclear what happened next that night Leah ended up in that bunker. She started hallucinating that she was being buried alive like Alice Goode. It must have been terrible.

She could hear them laughing.

When they got her out and saw that she had wet herself in fear, it sobered them all up. She says she expected them to tell the whole school but maybe they were able to see that they had broken her.

Leah had always been a sensitive child. At least, that's what my mother said. I wouldn't know. I absented myself from her life as quickly as I could, because to me she was an encumbrance.

I was nineteen when I had her, and more immature than most. The only reason I didn't have an abortion, as everyone advised, was a rebellion of sorts. But there was also a terrible passivity to that whole time. As though I were insulated from everything and none of it felt like it was really happening to me. I wasn't especially nauseous so didn't go through any of the nastier side effects of pregnancy, which added to the unreality of it all. My periods had always been irregular and I didn't even know until I was five months gone. Mum noticed that I was sleeping even more than usual and that I had put weight on. She insisted I take a test, otherwise I may have remained in denial until my daughter was actually crowning and tearing me open.

By the time I reached eight months my mum insisted I see a therapist because I was so listless. All I wanted to do was watch telly or listen to music. I think I was in denial that there really would be a baby. The therapist was quite a nice woman and I wanted her to like me so I just said the things she wanted to hear until our sessions were over.

I wish I could thank my parents for everything they did for us in those early years. Dad had been very uncomfortable with it all when I was pregnant and I think that was partly because he knew Greg, the man who got me in that state. I don't really call him 'the father' because as my own dad showed me, that word has so much more attached to it. I had been working behind the bar at Dad's golf club and Greg was one of the regulars. He was a confident and friendly man in his forties who I suppose seemed like a bit of a silver fox to me then. Married, of course. I don't really know what I was thinking when I had sex with him. I don't know what I was thinking about a lot of stuff when I was young, to be honest. I think I'm a different person now, I really do.

Dad tried to hit him when he found out that he wanted nothing to do with the baby. I wasn't there but my friend at work reported it all back to me, a bit gleefully. Apparently, Greg stopped the punch before it ever landed and actually laughed in his face. I hate to think about that. My gentle dad, who had never been in a fight in his life, doing that for me and being humiliated. I wish he was here so I could say sorry. Mum too, for all the worry I caused her and all the care she gave my girl in those early years. But maybe it's best that they are both gone now. Dad, when Leah was tiny, and Mum a few years ago.

I never saw Greg again. He gave us a payout and we all had to sign something to say we had no further rights to contact him. He was no loss. Well, I say I never saw him again, but I looked him up on social media a couple of times. And when I say I looked him up, I may have organised a few surprises for him. I learned some skills that have come in really handy later.

But the fact remains that I abandoned Leah. Until I found her again, walking in the woods and feeling at my own lowest.

I sensed her presence and there she was, at the spot she could never really leave behind.

When Mum told me my daughter, at fourteen, was having some sort of crisis and wouldn't go to school, I should have come running. This guilt, rather than dealing with the individuals involved in the event, is what keeps me up at night. If only I had realised that this event was the thing on which my daughter's whole life would pivot.

She became depressed after that night in the woods and my mum wasn't really equipped to cope with any of it. I was in Southern Spain, working in a bar and having a lot of sex with an Australian man ten years my junior. Drinking. Smoking a lot of weed.

I didn't want to hear it. Didn't want to think I had a teenage daughter at all, let alone one who could barely get herself out of bed. She put on weight and did badly in her exams.

She was an embarrassment to me. That's the awful truth of the matter.

Now imagine the unbearable pain of carrying that around for the rest of your life; knowing that perhaps you, of everyone involved, let her down the worst of all.

It wasn't until near the end of her life that I found her again. The years of abuse had taken their toll by then but I tried to nurse her back to health. We had a few months together when we crammed in all the conversations we'd missed out on over the years. Including the one when she told me what happened to her that night when she was fourteen. I cried at the thought of how frightened she must have been. She ended up comforting *me*.

The loss and guilt when she died, so suddenly in the end, almost killed me. I thought she was getting strong again but she caught flu and in the end her heart just gave out.

It was one of the bleakest times of my life.

But then she came back to me. I never even believed in all that stuff before but it didn't matter now, because the essence of her was still here, with me, where she belongs.

And I realised I had a way of easing the guilt I felt. I had a way of making things up to her.

It's a silly thing to admit, but I enjoyed making the replica of that doll they stuffed in the bunker and that frightened her so much. I hadn't thought for a moment the original would ever come to light. The individual poppets were fun too. I have never been into arts and crafts but there was a satisfaction in shaping the natural world into something genuinely useful. When Leah was little, she once tried to get me to make paper chains with her and Mum. I said I was too busy. Memories like that are a knife to my guts. But I'm doing everything I can to atone. As a mother.

I bet Brodie almost passed out when he received the doll and the poem in the post. I am not intending him to be found, so I couldn't leave one with his body. There are floorboards in my cellar that can be removed. After it's over, I am going to put him in there and move out for a while until, well, until it's not unpleasant anymore.

You could say I have carried out the more practical elements of this enterprise but I couldn't have done it alone. The police have nothing on me; nothing concrete. And they could never guess that my darling girl is my accomplice in all this.

There's a thought nagging at the back of my mind now though; that she is slipping away from me. Sometimes I wonder if all my rage and guilt have somehow . . . created her? Maybe the person I see isn't really my Leah at all. Oh a psychiatrist would have a field day with me, I can tell you.

But I do have to face the difficult thought that, maybe after all this, I'm doing it for me.

It's far too late to stop now, though. There's only one more to go.

It's almost over.

39

'Is that a bloody *coffin?*'

It may not be the highly varnished, shiny-handled type you'd get from an undertakers, but the rectangular wooden box lying under the staircase can only have that purpose. Rose pictures Ryan Brodie lying in there, struggling to breathe. Maybe already dead.

She runs down the steps so fast she almost falls, jumping the last few and jarring her ankle.

'Ryan!' she yells. 'Ryan can you hear us?'

She bangs on the top of the coffin frantically but there is no response. The lid appears to have been nailed down; roughly, but comprehensively. It doesn't look as though there are any gaps for air to get through either.

'Jesus, he could be suffocating in there!'

Rose throws Adam an anguished look. He is halfway down the stairs, speaking rapidly into the phone.

' . . . yes, bring an ambulance. It may already be too late, so hurry!'

'We have to get it open!' Rose looks around frantically for some manner of implement she could use and spies a toolbox on a table that otherwise holds only folded laundry.

But Adam hasn't replied.

'Adam! Help me!' she cries, turning to look at her colleague.

243

The booming crack is so confusing, at first Rose can't take in what's happened.

Adam cries out and falls backwards, arms windmilling before landing hard in a crumpled heap at the bottom of the stairs. Sandra Duffy is at the top, holding a small gun.

Rose runs to Adam's side. He is conscious but glassy-eyed, and blood blooms and spreads across his shoulder. 'What the hell have you done?' she yells up at Duffy, who simply stares down at Adam, as though she too can't believe what has unfolded.

Rose looks from Adam to the coffin. Adam needs help. But Ryan might be minutes from suffocation.

Rushing to the coffin Rose lifts her foot halfway down and stomps hard on the wood, feeling resistance before it starts to crack open. She can't worry about injuring him. Her priority has to be getting air into his lungs before it's too late.

'Stop it!' screams Sandra.

But Rose doesn't stop. She pictures a bullet leaving the chamber behind her and burrowing into the flesh of her back, or entering her skull. She hunches her shoulders as if this will save her then gives one more stomp and the wood properly splinters. There's a faint moan inside the coffin.

He's alive.

40

Sandra

I never meant for this to happen.

The policewoman is standing very still, her hands raised and her pretty eyes boring into me. She seems like a nice young woman; serious, like she cares about her job. Her gaze keeps flicking in anguish to her partner, who has managed to roll himself over onto his stomach. I don't know what he's doing but I am confident he isn't armed. I don't feel in any danger from him.

I need my daughter, or what remains of her, to help me now. The essence that remained after her death and came back to me, when the guilt and pain became too much. The plan was all mine, but I needed her help; she was willing. I know she was willing. It can't be that my own rage created . . . all this. It can't be that.

'Leah!' I call out in desperation.

'Is she here now?' says the policewoman and I'm thrown by the fact that she isn't mocking me; it's almost like she understands. 'Does she help you to do these things, Sandra?'

I find myself giving a slight nod despite myself, being seen in this way after so long.

'I don't believe she would want you to go to prison for

killing a police officer, Sandra,' she says, only the slight quiver of her voice belying her direct gaze. 'My colleague Adam has daughters too – two of them – and he loves them very much. They're called Tandi and Kea. Do you want to take him away from them?'

I don't want to hear any of this. I know exactly what she's doing but it's too late now. A tiny thread was pulled all those years ago that became a tear that led to . . . this.

'Will you let me go to him, Sandra? Please?'

I can hear the faintest sound of sirens in the distance.

'Leah!' I shout, anguished, but she doesn't appear. 'Where are you? I need you to come to me!'

I picture myself being led away and imprisoned without saying goodbye. She won't come to me there. I need to see her one last time.

And there is only one place she might come back to me. Where I found her again. In the woods.

41

'Handcuff yourself,' says Sandra. 'I'm sure you know how.'

Rose stares at the other woman, unmoving. 'This is pointless, Sandra! Can't you hear the sirens? They're coming for you. You can make things better for yourself by cooperating now and—'

'Shut up,' says Sandra, dead-eyed. 'I said put your handcuffs on.' Then she yells, 'Do it!' and steps forward, striking Rose with the gun on her cheek, which blooms with pain.

Rose pulls handcuffs from her bag. Self-cuffing is tricky enough anyway and Rose's hands shake as she gets one wrist in, then has to balance against an old counter top to snap the loose bar into place. Her cheek throbs and her vision splinters as tears fill her eyes.

'Give me the key.' Rose hands the key to Sandra. 'Now come with me.' She has the gun trained on Rose and there is no trace of a shaking hand or apparent doubt about using it.

Rose throws an anguished look at Adam who seems to be breathing in short fast gulps and then at the coffin. Is she leaving both these men to die? But Sandra has the gun trained on her and Rose reminds herself that this is a woman who has taken part in the murders of three people. Even if she still doesn't understand exactly how.

'Please,' she says. 'Let me help him.'

'Walk!' screams Sandra, waving the gun around wildly.

'Okay, okay I'm going!' Rose stumbles up the stairs, awkward with her bound wrists and the throbbing pain in her face. Sandra is close behind her so the flimsy wooden steps vibrate.

Outside, Rose can hear the sirens getting closer. Thank God. But will they be in time?

The other houses in this quiet suburban neighbourhood seem to stare blankly back at them and Rose prays that no curtain twitcher comes out to see what is happening. Sandra looks as though she has nothing left to lose now and who knows how many people she will be prepared to take with her?

'Get in.' Sandra opens the driver's door of her car and cocks the gun towards the seat.

'Where are we going?' says Rose, trying to turn and see if help is arriving yet, while awkwardly manoeuvring into the seat.

Sandra ignores her.

The gun doesn't seem to move from its position, trained on Rose's head.

'I'm going to undo these. Don't get any ideas. Then I want you to start the engine.'

Sandra leans over and unlocks the handcuffs so quickly, there's no time for Rose to react. Looking into the rear-view mirror she can see an ambulance and maybe a police car at the far end of the road. If she can just delay long enough . . .

'Drive!' Sandra screams and presses the gun hard against Rose's temple. The cold metal seems to burn and she winces. 'I swear to God I'll do this if I have to.'

'Okay, okay!' Rose starts the engine. For a moment, she considers putting her foot down and heading towards the sirens but one look at Sandra's face is enough to put her off.

'And you'd better drive fast or I'm going to shoot you in the head and end this now. Head towards the woods. The Chaseside Lane entrance.'

Rose drives.

Other cars pass but no other motorist seems to pay attention to the drama going on inside this innocuous black Kia.

It only takes a few minutes to reach the little car park that is starting to become so familiar.

'Why are we here, Sandra?' she says as she cuts the engine and turns to the other woman. She tries to keep her voice calm and conversational, even though she is facing someone who could end her life in a second. 'What's it all about? Can you tell me?'

'You won't understand,' says Sandra. 'You couldn't possibly.'

'I might understand more than you think,' says Rose. 'How about if I told you that I have been haunted too? That someone is haunting me at the moment?'

Sandra stares scornfully for a couple of moments and then lets out a bitter laugh. 'That's the most pathetic attempt at humouring me ever,' she says. 'Did they teach you that at Hendon?'

'No, I—'

'Just get out of the car.'

Rose opens the passenger door, swiftly trying to calculate if there is any way she can duck down and run. But Sandra is too fast for her, fuelled by fury and desperation.

'Out and put your hands where I can see them.'

'It's okay, Sandra,' says Rose, getting out of the car and raising her hands. 'I'm doing what you ask. Look.'

'You probably know where we're going,' says Sandra, gesturing down the main track.

They start walking towards where the bunker is located, the ground boggy now from the recent rain. Rose feels her boots slip in the mud as she walks.

'I really do want to understand, Sandra,' she says. 'You've done all of this for good reasons. Even if I don't agree with them, I know they are genuine and deeply felt. And I wasn't talking rubbish before. I really do know what it's like to be haunted. It's lonely and frightening. Did Leah force you to do all this? All this killing?'

Sandra barks another laugh and swings the gun wildly, causing ice to flood Rose's veins.

'She didn't *make* me!' says Sandra. 'I did it all *for* her.'

'But why?' says Rose. 'What happened to your daughter, Sandra?'

As they reach the clearing before the bunker, a golden retriever seems to appear from nowhere, bouncing towards them. A young man wearing a beanie and big headphones is hurrying behind. Rose and Sandra freeze.

'I'll shoot him,' says Sandra in a low whisper. 'I mean it.' She puts the gun down at her side as the young man gets closer.

'Morning,' says Sandra. 'Nice dog.'

He can't hear, evidently, because he simply gives a vague smile and carries on after his dog. Rose breathes out with relief. Maybe Sandra doesn't want another death on her conscience? *Oh Adam . . . please be okay.*

They carry on walking, both breathing heavily and before long they reach the bunker.

'What happened here?' Rose repeats. 'Why don't you tell me, Sandra? Tell me what happened to Leah in this place?'

Sandra gives a huge sigh that seems to shudder through her whole body. But the gun still doesn't move from its position, trained on Rose.

'Those people,' she begins. 'You know the ones, you've worked it out, they put my daughter in there when she was fourteen and ruined her life.'

'What happened?' says Rose softly.

Sandra is staring down now and the gun has shifted position. Rose calculates whether she can knock it out of the other woman's hands when it jerks up again and wobbles, dangerously in front of her face.

'They gave her magic mushrooms and she tripped out of her skull thinking she was Alice Goode, the girl who supposedly got buried alive in the plague. Which, incidentally, I have always thought was a load of old bollocks. But it was a story that scared Leah half to death. She was a nervous child. So I'm told.'

'What was the doll all about?' says Rose. Sandra looks into her eyes. 'The guy thing? The one they called Scary Mary?'

'She didn't like it,' says Sandra. 'It always gave her the creeps. So they stuffed that in there with her, because,' she gives a desperate laugh that is more of a wail, 'because of course they did.'

'Look, Sandra,' says Rose as gently as she can. 'It was a bad thing they did, but they were only kids themselves. It was more than twenty years ago. Did they really deserve to die because of a childhood prank?'

'You don't understand!' says Sandra, taking two more steps towards her so Rose lifts her hands higher. Sandra pulls at her hair with her free hand, as though trying to distract herself from another pain. 'It was the turning point of her life, that night. No one talked about PTSD for things like this then! But that's what she had . . . crippling, life-ruining PTSD that sent her into the arms of whatever bad man or bad drug she could get until it killed her.' She stops, and now she is crying openly. 'But she really died that night, in there.' She points at the bunker with the gun and then sinks to her knees.

'Leah!' she screams. A crow takes flight from the surrounding trees, its panicked caw a desolate, lonely sound. 'I did it for you! I did it all for you!'

Rose forces herself to step closer and Sandra, shoulders heaving with tears now, lifts the gun to her own temple.

'No!' Rose cries.

At that moment a middle-aged man on a top-of-the-range mountain bike appears through the trees then comes to a skidding halt, his eyes wide and his mouth slightly open.

'Police!' yells Rose. 'Get away for your own safety. NOW!' The man turns the other way and, wobbling at first, attempts to flee.

Rose turns back to Sandra, palms raised and her voice more steady than it ought to be.

'It's just us, Sandra,' she says. 'Please lower that gun. Why don't you tell me how you did this because I can't work it out. Can you please do that? Explain?'

Sandra closes her eyes, still holding the gun to her head, her

251

shoulders slumping as though an unbearable weight is pressing down on her.

'We were a team,' she says in a whispery voice. 'I did all the stuff that needed to be done and she did what she could.'

'What *did* Leah do?'

Sandra wipes tears and snot from her face and looks up blearily at Rose.

'She beckoned Haniya out onto the lake,' she says, flat-voiced. 'And she scared Suzette up onto that platform. I did the rest.'

Rose feels as though gears are slotting into place in her mind now.

'And you did all the computer stuff?' she says. 'The real world things. But look, she doesn't want to do it anymore, does she, Sandra? Did she lose heart in what you are doing? Has she left you again?'

'Stop it!' Sandra screams and then with a sickening click, takes off the safety catch of the gun before placing it squarely at her own forehead.

Rose lurches forward but something is happening. Wind has started swirling around them, whipping the dry leaves up so they dance in the air and there's a sense, despite this intense movement, of utter stillness beyond where they stand. Rose's eyes begin to water almost painfully. She can't see properly and an intense nausea floods her stomach as though she is being flung around a fairground ride. It's hard to stay upright in the pummelling funnel of air moving around them.

Sandra lowers the gun.

Rose can see her mouth a question but a roaring sound fills the air and the trees above spin faster, as though they are on a revolving platform in the middle of these woods.

She tries to call out but can't catch her breath in this unnat-ural wind. Then she makes out a slim form standing in front of where Sandra now kneels. Sandra drops the gun and raises her arms as if to hug the figure, or whatever it is.

It feels like pushing against something elastic and weighted.

But Rose forces herself forward, tiny step after tiny step, wind shrieking so loud so it feels her eardrums will burst.

The figure bends over Sandra, who gazes up, tears streaming down her cheeks. Rose forces herself to touch the figure shimmering before her. A sensation of bitter cold spreads up her arm and her stomach turns over with the damp horror of it but then it is replaced by a desolate emptiness; a profound sadness deeper than any she has ever known. Rose's mind floods with all the things she has regretted in her own life: friends she has neglected, time wasted by living with ghosts instead of people who might love her. It's paralysing, this feeling, and for a terrifying moment she feels she might never escape; that she might be trapped forever in loss. Like these two women. But then she thinks about all the lives ruined by them, however good the reasons may have seemed for their actions. She can't let that happen. It goes to the core of who she is to stand up against it. She tries to shout 'No!' but it comes out slowed down and distorted. Still Rose she pushes further, inch by inch, until her hand closes around the real-world, cold metal of the gun.

A faster rush of swirling vertigo that makes her want to be sick. And then, there is only the woods; the ordinary place where people walk dogs and have picnics. But with Sandra curled into a foetal ball on the ground and Rose holding the weapon in her shaking hands.

Cries come from behind as the armed response unit finally arrives.

42

Pressing the buzzer, Rose tries to suppress the storm of butter-flies in her stomach.

The last time she saw Adam, it had been a fleeting visit to his hospital bed. He had been too groggy from the painkillers and anaesthetic to say much, and anyway, his two daughters were tight bookends, large-eyed with shock, grasping one of his hands each like they may never let go again.

The relief that he was okay, that he was *alive*, had almost overwhelmed Rose. This, coupled with the traumatic time she'd had, had effectively melted her professional shield. She'd been unable to stop tears from streaming down her cheeks after she had hurriedly delivered the fruit gift with a quick 'let's speak when you're back on your feet'.

She'd left it until he was home again before asking if he was up to a visitor.

The grey ticks on her message turned blue so quickly she half wondered if he had been poised to write to her. But no, she told herself sternly. The poor guy probably just happened to look at that moment. That's all.

She has had more stern words with herself on the way over about not being emotional when she sees him. She will be concerned, but cool and calm. That's absolutely what she will be.

When he opens the door though, his whole face lights up

at the sight of her and relief once again that he is alive, albeit with a strapped-up shoulder and a greyish tinge to his skin, is so powerful that for a second Rose can hardly speak.

'It's so good to see you!' he says. 'Come in, come in!' He doesn't seem to have noticed her silence and continues talking as he walks, a little slowly, into the flat. 'You need to save me from myself,' he says. 'I've already re-watched five episodes of *Breaking Bad* today and have a telly hangover.'

He turns to look at her and smiles. 'Sit, sit!' he says. 'Do you want a cup of coffee or anything?'

'No, no, you shouldn't be doing anything anyway,' Rose finally finds her voice and shoos him over to the sofa where he sits down carefully. 'I'm okay unless you want some?'

'Nah,' says Adam, shifting to change position a little. 'I'm sleeping badly enough as it is.'

'Sure you're up to a visitor?' Rose sits on the armchair opposite him.

'Definitely,' he says. 'It was good to be pushed into having a shower and tidying up this place a bit.'

There's a brief silence before they both speak at the same time.

'So how are you . . . ?' says Rose.

'Tell me all about . . . ?' says Adam.

They both laugh.

'You first,' says Adam.

'How are you feeling?'

'Ah this old thing,' he says, shrugging and then grimacing at the movement.

'Seriously though?' says Rose.

Adam pulls a face. 'I was actually lucky. You've probably heard already but there was a pile of painter's sheets where I fell. I sort of bunched them up and lay over them, holding them against the wound. Hurt like hell but it helped stem the blood loss.'

'Yeah,' says Rose softly. 'I heard. Good thinking on your part.'

'What about that?' Adam does a circular movement to indicate the bruise on Rose's cheek. 'Are you alright? She clocked you one, didn't she?'

'It's nothing,' she says. 'I wasn't the one who got bloody shot by that mad woman.'

'So come on then,' says Adam, sitting up a little. 'All I really know is that you were able to arrest her in the woods but I'm not clear on exactly how it happened.'

Rose blows air out and widens her eyes then carefully relays everything that happened after she left the house until Sandra was being led away, compliantly by then. She speaks for several minutes without interruption. Adam's eyes are on her the whole time. When she finishes, he lets out a low whistle.

'That is *strange*, man, even by the standards of our cases,' he says. 'What's your take on it all, then? What do you think was going on?'

Rose spends a moment framing what she has been thinking since it happened a few days ago. 'I still can't really get my head around it all,' she says. 'But the conclusion I've come to is that Sandra almost used the spirit of her dead daughter, or whatever that thing was, as a, I don't know, a weapon?'

Adam grimaces. 'Bloody hell,' he says. 'That's messed-up.'

'Yeah,' Rose shakes her head. 'So messed up. But from what she said in her statement after, she didn't have any regrets about any of this.' She pauses. 'As you say . . . it's a very strange one, even by UCIT standards.'

'One thing I was wondering,' says Adam, 'was whether she planted that porn on Reece's computer or not?'

Rose grimaces. 'Unclear,' she says. 'But there was a lot, going back years before that and almost as bad.'

'God,' says Adam. 'Good riddance to him then.'

'Yeah, quite.'

'What do you think about this as a theory,' he says thoughtfully, after a moment 'Maybe there was some kind of presence of her daughter that she managed to conjure up. But she

256

somehow kept it going through the force of her own guilt and rage or whatever?'

'Could be,' says Rose. 'But there was definitely a sense that Leah, what was left of her anyway, had stopped wanting to be involved. And she, it, whatever, stopped Sandra Duffy from blowing her brains out.'

She pauses. 'Anyway,' she continues, 'she confessed to the murder of Suzette Armstrong and Alex Weston, and the kidnapping and attempted murder of Ryan Brodie. We can only get her on the admissions of computer hacking for Haniya Shah, unfortunately.'

'What are we saying to Rami Shah?'

This hadn't been easy. As always with UCIT cases, there is an official version of events and another that is strictly confidential and seen by few eyes.

They weren't able to shed any further light on Haniya's death. It had been hard, telling him this. Rose relays this to Adam.

'And Brodie, he's recovering okay?' says Adam.

'Seems to be,' says Rose. 'He was about ten minutes from suffocating in there.'

'Shit.'

'Yeah,' says Rose. 'It must have been absolutely terrifying.'

'I suppose Duffy would say tripping off your head and being shoved into a bunker by your so-called friends would be terrifying too.'

'True,' says Rose. 'Luckily people aren't allowed to go around bringing down retribution on the heads of people who have done bad things, or where would we be?'

'Out of a job, for a start,' says Adam, with a smile.

'Speaking of which,' says Rose after a moment. 'How long are you going to be off?'

Adam's gaze slides away. 'I've got six months sick pay of course.' This is standard, if a police officer is seriously injured in the line of duty. 'But well,' he gestures at his damaged shoulder. 'All this . . . well it puts things into perspective a bit.

As you know, it isn't even the first time a suspect had a go at me.'

'I remember,' murmurs Rose, thinking of the stabbing when he worked in Vice.

'My girls . . . ' He doesn't continue for a moment or two, then swipes the heel of his hand over his eyes, which are suddenly glistening. 'They were too little to really understand what happened before. This time though . . . seeing their faces when they ran in after I came out of surgery. Kea kept saying, "Don't be a policeman anymore, Daddy, please."' Adam stops speaking and wipes his eyes harder. 'Sorry,' he says gruffly. 'It's like my emotions are all really close to the surface at the moment.'

'Don't be sorry,' she says, feeling something loosen inside at the sight of his tears. 'I can't even imagine how horrible it must have been for them. It was bad enough for me, I mean, us. At UCIT. All of us.'

Stop it, she thinks. Not now, but the tell-tale creep of heat starts at her throat and starts to work its way upwards anyway.

Adam looks at her and manages a watery smile. 'Thanks, that means a lot.' He reaches for a tissue from the box on the coffee table and blows his nose with a loud honk.

'Are you actually thinking about leaving the force?' Rose can hardly bear to hear the answer to this question.

Adam doesn't reply straight away. 'The thought of giving up that pension after all these years doesn't sound great,' he says. He sighs. 'I don't know, Rose. Maybe I just need a decent amount of time to recover. But I'm not sure I want to be in the frontline anymore, that's for sure.'

'Does that include UCIT?' Complex emotions churn in Rose's chest.

'Maybe it does,' he says. 'I don't know.'

'You take as long as you need. We would miss you, that's all.' Rose swallows. '*I* would miss you.'

There's a rushing in her ears and her cheeks blaze. The room feels claustrophobically hot. Rose is aware her feelings are daubed across her skin and she is helpless to do anything about it. It's pointless to pretend it hasn't suddenly got weird in here so she forces her gaze up to meet his eyes, which are soft on her.

'Rose . . . '

'Adam, about what . . . what happened before?'

Please don't make me elaborate further. Please know what I mean.

'It's okay,' he says quietly. 'I got that wrong and I've been kicking myself ever since. I really would rather do anything than make you feel uncomfortable, please believe me.'

'Look . . . ' she starts to say but he cuts her off.

'I mean, it's not like you didn't warn me off.'

'I did?' it comes out louder than she intended.

'You know, the night of Sam's party?' he says, looking down, clearly embarrassed now. 'You said the thing about work and relationships not mixing or something. How that was a terrible idea? I can't remember exactly, but along those lines. I should have taken it on board. I'm sorry I didn't.'

Rose can't think of a single word to say. They meet eyes. She can see that his chest is rising and falling faster than it should for a man recovering from being shot. But so is hers. She wants to tell him how she feels; that she has pictured them being together almost since they met. There are still so many obstacles, not least the fact that he has two daughters. But if he isn't working at UCIT anymore, maybe that makes things a little more straightforward?

'You've got it wrong,' she manages to croak.

Adam frowns for a second and then as understanding dawns, his eyes widen and something hopeful blooms in his expression. 'I have?'

'You have.' A tide of joy rises up inside and Rose can't stop the delighted giggle that escapes.

Adam starts to laugh too, looking a little confused. 'Er, how wrong?' he says.

'Very wrong,' her tone is low and she holds his gaze, allowing

259

all the desire she has been holding back for eighteen months to flood through her veins.

The air in the room is full of static and Rose can hardly breathe.

'Show me how wrong,' says Adam quietly.

Rose gets up and crosses the room to stand over him, aware of every centimetre of her own skin as he looks up at her. His gaze is intense. She kneels in front of him on the carpet and places her hands on the sides of his face before softly kissing him on the lips. He kisses her back, gently at first and then with more urgency. Rose leans in hungrily and then Adam breaks away, grimacing.

'Sorry, sorry, bullet wounds are such a buzz kill,' he says. 'It's not that I don't want to. I really do want to!'

She goes to move away but he takes hold of her hand. 'To be continued?'

'To be continued,' she says. They both start laughing, giddy with what just happened until Adam winces once again and presses a hand to his injured shoulder.

'Right,' says Rose. 'I'm going to leave now before I do you more of an injury.' There's so much to say right now. But it can wait. 'How about we resume this, er, conversation when you're stronger?' she says.

'I can't wait.' He grins up at her.

'Me neither.' Rose goes to pick up her handbag and Adam begins to struggle up from the sofa but she stops him with her palm outstretched.

'No, don't get up,' she says. 'I'll see myself out.'

'Come back soon, yeah?' he says, urgently. 'I mean it, Rose.'

'Try and stop me,' she says.

43

Back in her car, Rose can't seem to control the smile spreading across her face.

Her phone rings as she's putting on her seat belt. Glancing at it she sees NESS HOUSE as the contact and surprise catches in her chest.

'Hello?' she answers.

'Oh Rose, it's Ness here, Ness Rosetti . . . from Camberley Road?'

'Yes I know,' says Rose. She can't bring herself to be anything other than cool, despite her newly buoyant mood. This evidently comes across because there is a short pause before Ness continues.

'I feel very bad about letting you down before,' she says. 'Honestly had sleepless nights over it.'

Rose thinks of the grotty bedsit with its walls the colour of despair.

'Yeah, me too,' she says. No point in sugar-coating it.

'I quite understand,' says Ness. 'And also if you never want to talk to me again, but I wanted to ask if you had found anywhere else yet? I mean, I'm sure you have.'

Rose hesitates, pride stoppering her up inside. But what's the point, really? 'No,' she says, 'not yet.'

The sound of Ness letting out a big breath of air is amplified down the line.

'Well, in that case, the room is yours if you still want it.'

'What about your daughter?' Rose finishes the sentence inside her own head. What about your daughter swanning in and taking over anytime she wants?

'She's gone back to Canada,' says Ness. 'I think I handled it all badly and panicked because it was unlike her to come home like that. I should have told her that she had to take one of the other bedrooms and never let you down.'

'Look, Ness,' says Rose, running her hand through her hair with frustration, 'I don't have time to be messed about like this. How can I be sure you won't do something like that again?'

'Because I will send over a contract right now, if you'd like me to. And also, I promise. Ex-Girl Scout's honour.'

The warmth of Ness's personality, which drew Rose in so comprehensively before, begins to seep into her voice now and it's impossible not to feel herself softening.

'I mean it, Rose,' says Ness, more seriously. 'I think we really hit it off before and the very thought of having to advertise and have all sorts of Tom, Dick and Harriets traipsing in fills me with horror. Come on, what do you say?'

Rose stubs the cigarette out in the car ashtray. Maybe things can occasionally go right? Maybe there really is no catch this time?

Maybe even Rose Gifford sometimes catches a break.

'I say, when can I move in?'

But the pleasure of the kiss with Adam and her new home begin to dim overnight and all her other worries circle like buzzards over her head.

Her living situation, the disciplinary stuff and . . . what's happening in the morning.

She is going to have to sit across a table from Terrence Bigham and listen to him talking about things that are going to be very hard to hear.

44

'This is DC Rose Gifford at 11.53 on 28th November. Can you please state your name for the tape?'

'Terrence John Bigham'. The old man leans forward to speak into the recorder, a slight smile playing around his thin, damp-looking lips.

Rose is at a police station in Chingford, at the request of Bigham, who says it is geographically the nearest to where he will direct them after the interview.

That's all he'll say for now.

But their ultimate destination today is quite clearly Epping Forest. Rose is half relieved it isn't the woods at Elford Park, although at least then there would have been a certain neatness about it all. On the other hand, at this rate there won't be any green spaces left in London that she'll want to visit. She's certainly not going to be having picnics in the woods for some time, that's for sure.

She spent a lot of last night thinking about that dream; the one where she was digging in earth with her bare hands, looking for her mother's body. She had dismissed it after the debacle in the back garden of her childhood home. But maybe there really was something happening in her subconscious.

Or from elsewhere. A message?

Her stomach curls with a sudden hit of nausea and she takes a sip from her water glass, relieved her hand is perfectly steady.

'So Mr Bigham,' she says, 'can you also confirm that you've turned down the opportunity to have a lawyer present today?'

'That's right,' he says. 'No point in that now. This is just between me and you. Oh,' he looks up at the camera, whose eye is trained on them from the corner of the room, and grins. 'And them, of course.'

He's right, they aren't alone. There was no way this was going down with only him and Rose involved. The whole interview is being watched by a senior detective from Chingford's murder squad called DCI Mariam Butler and also Moony. The interview strategy has been carefully crafted between the three of them. But despite his protestations that this must be between him and Rose only, he seems to have accepted that other parties must be involved outside the room.

'Thank you,' says Rose. 'Now, Mr Bigham, we are here today because you claim to have information about two murders, is that right?'

'That's right.'

'Can you tell me the names of the two victims?'

Bigham looks at Rose, still with that half smile, as if assessing her.

'First I want it on the tape that I'll get what I want.'

This is all time wasting. There has been an inordinate amount of paperwork on all this.

'Fine,' says Rose. 'In return for this information, if it turns out to be correct and we do in fact find evidence to support what you say, then you will be transferred from Brixton to Gartree Prison. Okay?'

'All good,' says Bigham, placing both his hands palm down on the table. 'So the individuals concerned were called Ronnie Bentley and Kelly Gifford. I can't tell you one without the other.'

His eyes don't leave Rose's face as he says her mother's name. A cruel, cruel man, she thinks. But even to the last moment a part of her had hoped he might say something different. Kelly was alive, or Kelly died of natural causes.

But she keeps her expression neutral; tells herself she can do this. Has to do this.

'Starting with Ronnie Bentley,' she continues. 'Tell us the details surrounding that death please?'

Bigham sits back in his chair, as if he is about to tell an after-dinner story like some raconteur.

'Well, he was a Jamaican who started working for Mike as a club manager.'

Mike, is Michael Cassavettes, not only the kingpin of a massive criminal network in the nineties, but also the biggest supergrass the Met had ever seen. He even turned in his own wife in exchange for immunity.

'Go on.'

'The thing about Bentley was he started dipping his nib where it didn't belong, if you get my drift.'

'Please elaborate,' says Rose. 'What kind of places didn't it belong, specifically?'

Bigham sits back in the chair, one arm slung over the top.

'The thing you need to understand about Mike,' he says, 'is that there was only one person he was properly loyal to. One person in the whole world he'd do anything to protect and that was his son, Nico. Nico wasn't part of the family business. He had, shall we say, some issues.'

'What kind of issues?'

'I suppose you'd call them psychological issues these days.' He says this as if it's an entirely made-up concept. 'Tried to take his own life when he was barely a teenager. Then he got into drugs and alcohol. Was in and out of rehab for it. Mike was beside himself about that boy.' He has a wistful look in his eyes for a moment before continuing. 'Anyway, Nico met this girl in rehab. Nadia, her name was. She was a bit of a mess, that one.' He lets out a whistle and then laughs. 'But Nico was besotted with her.

It was all going well for him until one day he comes home and finds Ronnie Bentley and her at it like a pair of rabbits.'

'And what happened?'

'Nico beat him to death with a hammer.' This is said matter-of-factly. 'Right bloody mess, the like of which I never saw before or since, and I can tell you I saw some stuff in my time. The girl was covered in his blood, screaming. The room looked like an abattoir. It took quite some cleaning up.' He pauses. 'In more ways than one.'

'Where is Nico now?'

'Ah,' he says, 'Killed himself in the early noughties. Don't think he could live with what he'd done. He wasn't the same as his father.'

'And Nadia?'

'Mike paid her off,' he says to Rose's surprise. 'And we made sure we knew exactly where every one of her nearest and dearest lived, so she understood that this wasn't something to be spoken about.'

'How could you really trust an addict, though?' says Rose. It's almost impossible to believe Cassavettes wouldn't have got rid of her; a witness to what his son did.

'That's exactly what I said to Mike,' says Bigham with evident satisfaction, as if they were discussing something other than murder. 'But Nico was in such a state he couldn't do it to him.'

'So how exactly did you "clean it all up"?'

'We took Bentley to Epping and put him in the ground.'

'Can you remember exactly where?'

'Oh yeah, clear as day. There's a spot that's marked by an old horse trough in the middle of the forest and a clearing just near it. Handy spot. Can see it with my eyes closed.'

He pauses. 'And let's say it remained memorable for other reasons too.'

Rose doesn't break eye contact with him and waits.

Bigham sits back in the chair and crosses his arms. 'I'd like a short break.' He looks at Rose and then the camera eye on the wall. 'And then I'll tell you what happened to Kelly.'

266

45

'You doing okay?'

Rose is in the ladies toilets, looking into the mirror above the sink and trying to gather herself in with slow breaths when Moony comes in.

She nods.

'Are you sure?' says Moony. 'Because I can take over in a heartbeat.'

'No,' says Rose. 'He reiterated at the end of the session that he's only prepared to do this with me. There's no other way, much as I'd like to take you up on that.'

'Cruel piece of shit,' says Moony, with feeling.

'Why though?' says Rose, turning to her boss. 'What's the point of this? With me?'

Moony regards her carefully. 'I've met men like him before,' she says. 'Men who once commanded a great deal of respect and made things *happen*. People feared Bigham. He could get them to do exactly what he wanted. And for all these years he's been in prison, where, sure, he might have a bit of influence but he's still yesterday's man. He's old and he's sick. I think this is about control. About showing he can still be the big puppet master, making people dance to his tune.'

'Is that all it is?' Rose's voice has got harder. 'Are you sure

I'm not being encouraged to do this so you can catch a bigger fish?'

'What do you mean?' Moony frowns.

'Kevin Mortimer told me that there was someone in our ranks who answered to Cassavettes. I can't help wondering if I'm being used to try and reel him in further so he can tell us.'

Moony looks at Rose carefully for a few moments without speaking.

'I think you should just decide if you want to go back into that room, Rose,' she says. 'Because if you don't, no one is going to put pressure on you, I can promise you that.'

An answer of sorts.

Rose turns back to the mirror and places her hands on the sink, head bowed.

She thinks about Adele Gifford sitting in the armchair in that ratty old fur coat and about the night she clawed at the earth in the back garden while icy rain soaked her to the skin. Then she thinks about the photo of Orla and her mother, goofing about and being normal young women. Both dead now. She'll never be free if she doesn't find out what happened.

'I'm ready,' she says.

Back in the interview room, Rose senses that a little of Bigham's bravado has slipped. He shifts in his seat and coughs, wetly and for some time, before reaching for the glass of water on the table and drinking it down almost in one go. Evidently, the morning has taken it out of this old, sick man.

'Are you feeling up to continuing?' says Rose and Bigham nods.

'Yeah, I'm alright. Haven't got the stamina I once had, that's all.' He manages a lewd grin that turns Rose's stomach.

'So before we paused, you said you would tell us what happened to Kelly Gifford.'

Bigham looks at Rose for a few moments, half smiling.

'You're a tough one,' he says. 'Sure you're up to hearing this stuff about your own ma?'

Rose meets his eye levelly. 'I never knew Kelly Gifford, Mr Bigham,' she says. 'Why don't you tell us how *you* knew her first of all?'

Bigham shifts in his chair.

'Del, your nan, well me and her went way back,' he says. 'We used to hang out in the same gang as youngsters, like, and we always held a bit of a candle for each other. Went our separate ways as teenagers. She hooked up with Gary, your grandad, until he left her when Kelly was small.' He looks into the distance. 'Last I heard about him, he was living up north somewhere.'

Rose remembers Adele's bitter outpourings about the man who had left her to cope with a toddler on her own, and who never paid a penny in child support. He may be her only living relative, but she has no interest in tracking down some selfish bloke only to be disappointed by another member of her family.

'So we sort of got together again and had an on-off thing for years. I suggested her little enterprise to Mike for the business, like, and she worked for us in her own small way. But it was mainly because we had a connection.' He pauses. 'Kelly was a bit of a wild one from the start and Adele used to pull her hair out trying to keep track of what she was up to. Then she got up the duff.' He looks at Rose, and for the first time, the cruel lines of his face seem to soften. 'I don't know who your dad is and that's the truth. That thing I said before, that was just my little joke. No offence meant.'

'Fine.' Rose wipes her damp palms on her trousers under the desk but meets his gaze coolly.

'Carry on,' she says, determined to remain impassive, despite the fact that she would like to reach across the table and smack this nasty little man in the face. This is when, perhaps more than any other time in her career to date, she needs to bring it to the table. To be the cool professional that Rowland never believed she could be. Emotion can wait and until then, she will swallow it down and hold eye contact as long as she must.

'Anyway, Kelly was tight as anything with that Orla, the

one you showed me in the photo. But when she had you, Kelly changed. Calmed right down. Wasn't around much because she was trying to make money for you both. Did waitressing on cruise ships. Meantime, Orla started working for Mike.'

'Working for him how?' says Rose.

He gives a thin smile. 'In the clubs. You can see from that photo that she was a stunner. Lot of blokes like a redhead. Want to see if it's real, if you get my drift.'

Rose takes a slow sip of breath.

'And what happened to her?' she says after a moment.

'She couldn't handle the lifestyle,' he says. 'Became a bit of a mess. Anyway, when she died, Kelly went wild. Blamed me, blamed your nan. Came round shouting the odds one night. Said she was taking you and going straight to the police to tell them everything she knew.'

Bigham casts his eyes down towards the table.

'And so?' says Rose, her heart beginning to thrum faster. 'What happened next?'

Bigham runs a hand over his greasy bald head and makes a sound in his throat.

'It was just an accident,' he says. 'Adele never meant it to pan out like that.'

There's an annoying wait before they head out. Because Bigham is deemed to be a flight risk, even with his physical limitations, it has been decided air support is needed for the trip to Epping Forest. They are currently waiting to get authorisation for the police helicopter that will accompany their procession.

Rose stands outside the station, smoking another cigarette. She's lost count of how many she has had, and she's feeling sick now. It's freezing out here too, but she can't make small talk while they wait to go.

She tries to picture the scene, as described by Bigham.

Kelly had been angry and abusive, according to him, and this had sparked a rage in Adele, who screamed about her ingratitude for all the time looking after her child.

The fight had quickly become physical. The two women had grappled for a moment before Bigham had tried to intervene. Then, just as he had separated them, Kelly said she was going straight to the police station and Adele ran at her in fury, knocking her over so she smacked her head on the corner of the coffee table that Rose can picture so easily and which is in the lockup with her other belongings from the house. She'll burn it when she can. Although it's evidence now, isn't it?

Kelly died instantly.

'It was one of them things,' Bigham said with a shrug. 'No one meant it to play like that, like I said, least of all Del, who was in bits about it.'

'Why didn't you call the police?' said Rose. Her cheeks felt stiff.

Bigham had looked at her as if she was mad to suggest it.

'We thought it best to deal with it ourselves,' he said, in a patronising tone. 'Nice and tidy.'

It transpired that all this happened only two days after Bentley was put in the ground and so, for expediency's sake, it was decided by Bigham that Kelly could be 'laid to rest' in the same spot. The earth was still soft and freshly turned, so it was easier to simply lay the young woman's body on top of the other one, six feet down.

Like piling stacks of meat.

As he said, nice and tidy.

46

Rose is aware of every inch of her skin and the light seems hyperreal. The sky has a sickly whitish heaviness as though rain might be coming. Emotionally, she feels a strange numbness, as if this is any other day. Any other murder case.

They park a short distance from Chingford station in the small car park there. The two patrol cars, the van that carried Bigham, and Rose's own car immediately fill the space. Then they walk across the heathland, which is boggy in places from the rain. A single dog walker in the distance is watching them with interest. One of the uniforms has a murmured conversation with DCI Butler and then hurries over to tell the dog walker, presumably, to head in the other direction.

Bigham looks small and old, flanked on each side by uniforms who seem to swamp him, his hands in handcuffs. Although he is too old and sick to run, there has to be a chance that someone from his past might try to spring him. According to Moony, there are plenty of people too who may bear a historic grudge. For this reason there is one armed officer, as well as those monitoring from above. The rhythmic whoop-whoop of the blades of the helicopter seems to reverberate in Rose's insides, which feel tender, as though bruised.

Moony walks next to Rose as they enter the woods, cutting across at an angle pointed out by Bigham with a shaky finger.

There are still plenty of leaves clinging to the trees in this more sheltered forest but as they approach a clearing, the multicoloured leaves form a carpet, slippery with rain. There is an old tree that has roots stretching out above ground like gnarled old fingers and Bigham stops for a moment, looking around with a thoughtful expression.

'Nearly there now,' he says, sounding frail. He starts to cough.

'Are you alright?' says Rose. She is suddenly seized by the notion that Bigham may collapse and die here before this terrible business is concluded. The thought is too terrible and a mad urge to laugh washes over her.

Evidently unaware of the true nature of her concern, he gives her a grateful look. 'I'm alright, DC Gifford, thank you.' Rose looks away quickly to hide her disgust.

They walk on and as they enter another, smaller clearing just over a small brook, the sun seems to emerge from nowhere, bathing the ground in golden light.

If it weren't for the plethora of police officers, some of whom are carrying spades and evidence boxes, it would be a lovely place, Rose thinks.

Bigham closes his eyes and raises his face to the unexpected warmth like it's a benediction. The thudding of helicopter blades above is the only sound as they all watch him, waiting to see what he does next. He's taking his time; clearly in no hurry to go back into the stuffy air of the prison, and enjoying every moment of his final moments in nature.

An old stone water trough marks the spot it seems because he turns to look at Rose, his eyes completely blank and says, 'Here.'

Three uniformed officers start to dig.

Rose can feel Bigham's eyes on her but she fixes her gaze on the earth being removed and growing in a lumpy scar along the sides of the gradually deepening hole.

Then one of the officers, a man in his early twenties with a police baseball cap pulled over his brow gently taps the spade down in the spot he has just dug.

He raises a hand.

'Here!' he calls.

Time slows. The area must be secured and evidence be gathered with meticulous care.

Rose chafes her arms; despite the surprise gift of the sunshine, it's still chilly, although it may be partly the surreal horror of what is happening around her.

Kelly is down there, she thinks. My mother is in the ground.

But the words still feel abstract. It's all too far away to reach right now.

It's going to hit her, though, after this. She knows that.

The light is starting to fade as the suited-up officers gently remove what seems to be the last of the bones and place them onto sheets on the ground. The pathologist, a striking woman with a tight black bun at the base of her neck and large eyes, is called Afrouz Moradi. She nods at Rose and then gets on her haunches to look at the bones.

Bigham is back in the van, actually asleep at this final, crucial moment. Rose wants to shake him awake, batter him into understanding, so he can see the remains of two people he left to rot in the earth. But she decides she can't be bothered. Tiredness is pulling at all her limbs, and she half wishes she could lie down on the ground and sleep, like some twisted version of a babe in the wood.

Rose and Moony walk over and stare down at the brownish bones laid out neatly on the white cloth.

Rose is surprised how little she feels. It's like she is numb all over now this moment has arrived.

'Definitely looks like a mix of male and female bones,' says Moradi. 'We can start with the DNA database and then try dental records.'

Rose clears her throat; her voice suddenly thick. 'You'll find a DNA link for the female on the system,' she says. Moradi looks at her, eyes quick with intelligence and curiosity.

'Oh yes?'

'Yes,' says Rose. 'With me.'

Moradi looks at Rose, then at Moony, then back at Rose again. Rose hadn't been sure how much was known by the other officers she had been with today and now she has her answer.

'Okay then,' says Moradi quietly. 'Okay . . . '

They start to pack away.

If Rose is hoping for something – a glimpse of long dark hair through the trees, a soft whisper of breath at the back of her neck, or even just a sense of closure – she is to be disappointed.

There's nothing; only the percussion of the helicopter blades above and the harsh spotlights trained on the gaping hole in the forest floor as the muddy remains of two lives are loaded into the back of a police van and driven away to be processed.

47

Every time Rose looks at the bedside table, she gives the newly mounted photo a glance. It's the one of her and Kelly in the deckchair; Rose's little hands star-fished as if catching the sky and a sunny smile around the lips of her mother, stylish in a summer hat. The picture looks good in the pale wood frame she bought for it.

But there's an odd self-consciousness still, to having it up. Not being able to remember anything about this woman who gave her life seems cruel. It's incredible to her that she didn't spend more time imagining her when she was a child. But Adele had made her feel ashamed about wondering and any curiosity soon dried up. It became something else she pushed down to a deep place inside, stuffed away where it couldn't hurt.

It's going to take time to process it all.

She thought she was feeling nothing when she got back to the hostel last week, after the exhumation in the forest. But almost as soon as she walked through the doors into the nasty little room, pain and sadness had literally taken her out at the knees. She collapsed onto the rough carpet, her upper body over the bed, crying so hard and for so long it scared her. Rose couldn't remember ever crying like that before in her whole life.

At some point that evening she had driven to her old house and stood outside, staring at it like someone she might otherwise be sent to arrest. She could see lights behind the newer, nicer curtains and hoped there was a family in there, or a couple snuggling up in front of the telly. Or a young woman like her, tired after a difficult day at work, cosied up on the sofa and feeling thankful for her own little sanctuary.

After that, Rose had driven back to the hostel, only stopping to pick up two bottles of wine. She managed a bottle and a half before she threw up in the plastic sink in her bedroom and then fell asleep, face down on the bed.

It's fair to say it was a rough few days.

Scarlett is the one who suggested, when she rang to check up on Rose, that she hold a small memorial service for her mother at some point. She's still thinking about that. Her friend had stressed that this would be something normal and comforting now this painful story has been concluded.

Has it though? Rose sometimes wonders. But there have been no visitors yet of any kind, earthly or otherwise. It might not be possible to avoid in her working life, but if the dead could leave her alone when she isn't at work . . .

It doesn't seem an awful lot to ask.

She has spent a good deal of time wondering, though, why Kelly has never come back to her. Why was it Adele and Orla who came circling around to lead her to the truth?

Something hits her with a sudden clarity. Maybe it was a kindness. A mother who was no longer able to do anything for her child, and didn't want to be a source of fear.

Rose swallows. Not that this is the end of her worries; not by any means. Every time she thinks about the disciplinary case against her, she feels physically sick.

Still, maybe it's okay to try and relax for just a moment and appreciate that she has somewhere decent to live for the first time in her life. And although it is still early days with Adam, there may be wonderful things still to come.

She puts her hands behind her head and looks around at her new bedroom with a feeling of satisfaction. The curtains are closed and the two lamps in the room bathe the pale walls in a warm, cosy light. It has been surprisingly enjoyable decorating this room with small touches; a new throw in soft grey wool that she snuggles into in the evenings, a large black and white framed poster showing Piccadilly Circus in the 1920s that caught her eye in a shop, and a beautiful turquoise bowl on top of the chest of drawers where she keeps the small amount of jewellery she owns.

If it still feels a bit like playing house, she has decided this is simply a lack of practice at being somewhere nice and uncomplicated.

She hears her name being called from downstairs and smiles.

It has become a habit that she and Ness curl up in front of a cheesy reality television programme in the evening. They will always have something to drink. Sometimes a hot chocolate and sometimes a glass of red wine in one of Ness's voluminous glasses.

'Coming!' She uncurls from the bed and gets up, turning off the nearest lamp.

As she crosses the bedroom to turn off the other one, she suddenly stops.

A gentle warmth, barely there, as if a blanket of the lightest material imaginable was momentarily draped around her shoulders.

Rose looks around. She notices the old radiator, which seems to blast heat in unpredictable ways and at strange times. It was probably that.

But before she switches off the other lamp, she looks over at the photo again. And smiles.

Acknowledgements

One of the best parts of creating a story world is deciding exactly where things are going to happen. I knew I wanted very ancient woods in a particular location in London, but they didn't really exist exactly as I pictured them. The real-life place where I have spent many happy hours with family, friends, and dogs wasn't quite large enough or soaked in enough of its own folklore.

So, I decided to make up my own version. I called the area Elford Country Park. Eagle-eyed Londoners will know it is exactly where the real-life Trent Country Park is on the outskirts of the city. My version is much bigger and far creepier!

I have a huge number of people to thank for their help in writing this book.

It was a coincidence that I started writing a book about a climbing centre right before my youngest son, Harry Lownds, got a job working at one, but it was extremely handy. Thank you, Harry, for all the little nuggets of detail I needed for this story and also for – literally – showing me the ropes. ('The advanced level will be FINE,' he said. 'Not scary at ALL,' he said, as I gritted my teeth and swung terrifyingly between the highest trees in North London.)

I'm grateful to Angela Clarke for telling me about the horrors of flat hunting in London. (I'm glad you found somewhere lovely in the end, Ange!)

Liz George offered me great advice on landlord and tenant law and John Goss of 5, Essex Court was extremely helpful in talking me through how Rose's disciplinary nightmare might play out in real life. Huge thanks to both of you.

I couldn't have come up with the kind of real-world horrors that someone with high level tech knowledge can inflict on a victim without the help of David Kerrigan. (It's a good job he's such a nice person, that's all I can say . . .)

My good friend Xenia Pieri used her brilliant teacher brain to help me work out the logistics of the ill-fated Elford Park Outreach Project. Thank you, Xenia, and I'll see you in school!

Foodie genius Jennifer Schwartz helped someone who hasn't eaten meat since 1985 to come up with the meal Rose enjoys when she goes round to see Scarlett and Maz. (Shame Rose gets too drunk to remember it the next day.)

Neil Lancaster, ex policeman and now damned fine crime writer was a gem, yet again, in advising me on police matters. Couldn't have written this series without him.

Pete Lownds, you advise in a million different ways on every book, and you're my biggest supporter. It means the world.

Thanks to Phoebe Morgan, and also to Elizabeth Burrell and Susanna Peden at Harper Collins for all their work.

Finally, thanks to you, dear reader, for taking Rose and her unusual team into your hearts in the way you have. When you get in touch to tell me you've enjoyed these or my other books, it truly makes my day. Don't stop doing it! You can find me on social media or drop me a line at carolinegreenwriter@gmail.com.

Even in your dreams you're not safe...

The nightmare is only just beginning...

When DC Rose Gifford is called to investigate the death of a young woman suffocated in her bed, she can't shake the feeling that there's more to the crime than meets the eye.

It looks like a straightforward crime scene – but the police can't find the killer. Enter DS Moony – an eccentric older detective who runs UCIT, a secret department of the Met set up to solve supernatural crimes. Moony wants Rose to help her out – but Rose doesn't believe in any of that.

Does she?

As the killer prepares to strike again, Rose must pick a side – before a second woman dies.